LIGHT UNSHAKEN

UNVEILED SERIES
BOOK TWO

CRYSTAL WALTON

IMPACT EDITIONS LLC

Published by Impact Editions, LLC

This is a work of fiction. Names, characters, places, and incidents are a product of the author's imagination. Locales and public names are sometimes used for atmospheric purposes. Any resemblance to actual people, living or dead, or to businesses, companies, events, institutions, or locales is completely coincidental.

Book Layout ©2013 BookDesignTemplates.com

Cover Design © 2020 Blue Water Books

Author Photo by Charity Mack

Light Unshaken/Crystal Walton.

LCCN: 2015908105 (pbk) | ISBN 978-0-9862882-3-4 (pbk.) | ISBN 978-0-9862882-2-7 (eBook)

✵ Created with Vellum

FAMILIAR SHADOWS

ONE BEAT. Another. My pulse out thundered the sirens in the distance. Sidewalk dividers passed under my feet as quickly as my lungs rasped for air, but I couldn't slow.

Abby clung to my neck. "Jamal," she cried to the fourteen-year-old sprinting ahead of us on a race to his townhouse.

I cradled Abby's head against my shoulder and kept pushing. "It's going to be okay, hon." It had to be.

We rounded the corner onto Jamal's street. Bright flames raging against the summer sky jerked me to a stop. I held Abby tighter, tried to stay calm. A fog of charcoal smoke blurred the street like a distorted filter I could hardly see through. I glanced from one house to the next. Neighbors stood outside, staring at the fire, but no one moved. No one helped. Did they not care at all?

A flash of Jamal tunneling straight to his yard stole

my focus. I darted across the pavement. "Jamal, wait." I caught his arm. "You can't—"

"Reggie's in there."

The thought of his younger brother trapped inside turned my throat dry.

"I ain't losing him."

The intense love in his eyes gripped me in place. I clung to his sleeve, overwhelmed by the image of a fatherless son who'd chosen to love others the way a father should.

He tugged his shirt free. "I'm sorry." He backed up.

"Jamal!"

It'd taken less than a month of interning at the Portland Center for all the kids there to become a part of my heart. I couldn't lose any of them either. I spun toward the statues of people congregated on their driveways, desperate for someone to intervene. "Please," I begged.

Abby wrapped both legs around my waist and squeezed my neck tighter. "Miss E?"

I cupped the back of her head but couldn't find my voice. Waves of heat crashed against us. Sirens drew closer, my pulse louder. I tried to swallow, tried to utter anything more than the wordless prayer pouring out in tears.

A glimpse of my supervisor appeared through the haze of smoke. "Trey," I yelled.

He paused long enough for me to silently communicate that Jamal had gone inside, then hustled after him.

"Be caref—"

A shattering blast from the top of the house dropped us all to the ground. Glass and ash rained down from the busted window. Abby's scream rattled in my ears with my own heartbeat. It took five blinks before Trey came into focus again.

Our eyes locked, and once again I was staring into the fierce love of a father's heart. Less than a breath passed before he jetted inside.

Firefighters stormed the yard. Though the siren blared right in front of me now, I hardly heard it. Every noise seemed muffled until all three of them emerged through the billows of smoke. Another blast struck the air. Covered in soot, Trey ushered the boys off the porch into the grass. I transferred Abby to him, fell to my knees, and cast my arms around both boys' necks.

Time stalled again. It wasn't until I let go, and watched the brothers embrace, that my tears kicked inertia back into motion. Noise clamored from every direction. Footsteps tunneled all around us. We had to move.

Out on the street, Jamal still wouldn't let Reggie out of his arms. "I'm sorry."

I reached for his shoulder. "It's not your fault."

"Yeah, it is." He stared at the smoldering remnants of his home. "I couldn't do it."

I looked from Trey back at Jamal. "Do what?"

"The grant money you been trying to get..." He shook his head. "I wouldn't do you like that, Miss E. I

4 | CRYSTAL WALTON

wouldn't sabotage the center." His chin sank. "You guys and Reg... you's all I got."

I wasn't sure which broke my heart more. The fact that the kids knew the center was running out of funding, or that they felt as powerless to change it as I did.

"You let me worry about the grants, okay?"

His focus got lost in the smoke, as if he hadn't heard me. "I knew I'd pay for it."

"Pay for what?" I glanced at Trey again when Jamal didn't respond. "You're not making any sense."

Ash-tainted remorse looked up at Trey and me. "I'm sorry," he whispered.

"Sorry for—?"

An old Toyota sped up to the curb, an ambulance right behind it. "Jamal. Reggie." A middle-aged woman barreled through the crowd of bystanders and tugged both boys into a hug. "Are you okay?"

Jamal stared at a jagged piece of glass beside them. "We're fine, Aunt Sierra."

Aunt? Were they fatherless *and* motherless? My insides constricted even more.

Something switched in their aunt's demeanor. She took in the sight of their charred home, then stared Jamal down. "You do this? What've you gotten yourself into? You best start talking right now. You hear me?"

Jamal looked blindsided, and Trey had to grab my arm to keep me from intervening.

"He didn't do nothing." Reggie wheezed as he sat up. "It won't his fault. He was tryin' to protect the center."

"Reg," Jamal warned.

"The center?" Their aunt whipped a glare my way like she could smack answers out of me with nothing but her eyes.

I turned to Trey, still trying to make heads or tails of what was going on myself.

"They told him to leave the fan in the basement on, or —" Reggie coughed again.

Jamal grabbed his sleeve. "Enough, Reg."

"But—"

Two paramedics rolled a gurney up beside us and wasted no time getting Reggie situated to ride in the ambulance. Jamal and his aunt hastened to follow.

"Who's they?" I called out pointlessly. "What fan?"

Trey reached for my arm again.

I pulled it back. "We have to find out…"

Without the need for words, he nodded for me to let it go.

My arms fell to my sides as flashing lights pulled away from a street left doused in confusion. "I don't understand." I didn't fully expect Trey to hear me, but I wasn't surprised when a comforting hand rested on my shoulder.

"They're okay," he said calmly. "That's what matters."

A hundred questions racing through my mind wanted to argue, but I knew he was right.

Another car pulled up to the curb—this time, one I knew by heart. "Riley?"

My fiancé jogged around his front bumper and

closed me in his arms before I got another word out. The weight of all that had just transpired plunged me deeper into an embrace that made everything feel safe again.

"I got here as soon as I could."

At the sound of his voice, it finally registered that he shouldn't have been there at all. I leaned back. "Why aren't you still at work? Your shift isn't over until seven."

From the look on his face, I might as well have asked him why the sky turned dark at night. "Em, I'd drop anything to be where you need me. You know that."

When I'd texted him from the center, I hadn't intended for him to dash across town. But now that he was here, the realization of how much I truly did need him right then drew me back into the comfort of knowing he'd always be there for me. "Thank you," I whispered.

A ring from Trey's cell phone drew Riley and I around. I could tell from the look on his face that it was either his wife or his lawyer. His shoulders sagged as he ignored the call.

Frankly, I couldn't blame him. It burned me to watch him have to deal with the battle of a divorce on top of having to fight for the center to stay open. I still didn't understand how his wife could choose her career over him.

"You guys go on. I'll make sure Abby gets home." Trey shifted her to his opposite hip, where she clung to his side equally as tight.

The trauma in her blue eyes brought the disillusionment in Jamal's rushing back to mind.

Trey must've read the question in mine. "I'll text you as soon as I hear something." He nodded toward the car. "Go on and get some rest."

He and Riley exchanged a glance, and I doubted there was any point resisting.

"The minute you hear—"

"I promise."

I exhaled slowly as Riley's arm circled around me. The rational side of me knew there was nothing else I could do right then anyway. Still, it was hard to leave.

Once in the car, my body sank into the seat under the weight of the day. Yet something about having Riley beside me kept me above the surface. His fingers stayed laced with mine the entire way home. I ran my thumb along his, grateful he knew when I needed his presence more than words. By the time we passed the Reed College entrance sign, my shoulders had fully relaxed.

He parked in front of my building, kissed the backs of my fingers, then met me on the curb. Leaning against the side of his Civic, he drew me to him and rested his chin over my head. "Jamal and Reggie are going to be okay," he said softly. "And so will the center."

I latched on to his reassurance. "I know." It would all be okay. If I'd learned anything from staying at Reed and interning all summer, it was that Trey's hope and vision for the center could pull us through anything. I only hoped my help would make a difference too.

"You need me to stay?"

This time *I* was the one giving *him* the no-brainer look. His mouth quirked, and I couldn't help smiling. Whether it made sense in the moment or not, the contentment I'd given in to since he'd proposed eclipsed everything else.

His cell rang, but he didn't take his eyes off me.

"You gonna get that?"

With one hand behind my ear and the other sliding to the small of my back, Riley curled me toward him again. "Wasn't planning on it."

His hair fell around his face in perfect disarray as he leaned in. My fingers ran through it and down to his neck. Staying caught up in moments like these all summer had made every unanswered question feel a world away.

Reminders of his pending record deal cut into the thought like an unexpected dance partner twirling in out of nowhere. It nearly knocked me backward with an upsurge of unknowns flooding my mind again.

"Hey." Riley tipped my chin. "You okay?"

Familiar shadows closed in. A chill broke through August's heat and shook down my body with ripples of something that'd been gone for months. Fear. I couldn't place its source, only that it didn't belong.

What was going on with me? Brushing it off, I fiddled with the hem of his shirt. "Yeah, sorry. It's nothing. I think I'm still a little shaken up from the fire, is all."

His fingers grazed my earlobe on their way into my

hair. After all this time, his touch shouldn't have been able to undo me still. But there I was, gripping his sleeve for balance.

His thumb brushed over my cheek. Before he could say anything, Trevor's Outlander pulled up to the curb, followed by A. J.'s Acura. Were they just now getting back from Cannon Beach? Talk about one long day trip.

I looked around my gang of friends congregated on the sidewalk, relieved none of them knew about the fire. I didn't want to have to get into it right then.

My roommate's yawn broke the silence. Slanted at a forty-five-degree angle, Jaycee balanced herself against Trevor's shoulder. "Coffee's calling."

I pitched a brow at her. "You didn't stop for some on the way home?"

She swayed an empty to-go cup at me. "You can never have enough coffee."

Trevor chucked a balled-up beach towel at A. J. "Beat you to Paradox."

"You wish." A. J. toweled his wet hair and rubbed out the sand left from a game of beach volleyball, if I had to guess.

Ashlea pressed her fair-skinned arm against his tanned one, practically begging to be noticed. Poor girl. He didn't make his feelings for her very easy to read.

Ignoring the guys' playful digs, Riley kept his focus on me. "How about a night in our favorite getaway spot?"

"Mm." I could almost feel the peace of the sports field settling over me.

A. J.'s keys clanked against each other. He opened his car door, shot Trevor a chin flick, and climbed in without a word.

Ashlea's icy look might as well have stabbed me on her way off to her own apartment. Riley, on the other hand, didn't even acknowledge A. J.'s cool departure. He'd probably gotten used to it, as I should've by now. But when did a rift with one of your closest friends ever become normal?

Maybe I needed a night under the stars with Riley more than I thought. "Sounds perfect."

"Uh-uh." Jaycee squeezed her way between us. "You promised, Em."

Riley looked from her to me. "Promised what?"

"She promised to help me pick out bridesmaid dresses." Jaycee twirled a strand of her auburn bob into a pin curl. "Well, we won't actually go shopping until after winter break, since spring styles won't be out until then, but we're gonna dream shop in magazines tonight. Get a head start on ideas." She fluttered her fingertips together.

Why stop at Paradox? The prospect of wedding planning obviously passed for a sufficient adrenaline booster. "Save me," I mouthed to Riley from behind her.

Laughing, he tugged his cell phone from his pocket. One glance at the screen, and his gaze seemed to take him somewhere else.

I whirled my hair up into a ponytail. "Who called?"

He looked up from his cell. "My agent."

"Did he leave a message?" The question came out softer than I'd intended it to.

"He'll probably call back." Riley pocketed his phone and returned his attention to us. "So, wedding magazines and bridesmaid dresses, huh?" He rubbed his jaw with his knuckles. "Sounds like fun."

"The best. But, sorry, girls only."

His grin tipped to the left. "I owe Jake a run anyway."

Traitor.

"Good call, bro. Trust me." Trevor hauled his shoeless fiancée over his shoulder before she could react and jogged up to our apartment building. One quick peck, and he was off to the campus café to get her another coffee.

I glared at Riley. "Thanks for coming to my rescue."

"C'mon, it won't be that bad. What's enduring a few frilly magazines compared to sharing in your best friend's excitement? It'll be fun," he said in a near-exact Trevor-tone.

"Yeah, well, if I go missing, it's because I'm mummified in a roll of tulle somewhere."

"Way to be a trooper." He always knew when to flash that darn smile I was so insanely in love with. At the stoop, he caught me up in a tender kiss, the sobriety from earlier moments returning. "I can still stay if you want me to." He curled a stray strand of hair around my ear. "Or come back."

If he kept kissing me like that, he'd be lucky if I let him leave at all.

I glanced up at my apartment window and tamped down my knee-jerk response. "If Jaycee has anything to do with it, I won't have time to dwell on anything else. I'll be fine." I faced him again and lifted on my toes. "I wouldn't mind one more kiss though. You know, for good measure."

"Mm." Riley inched in. "Maybe we should make it two."

Or three. As it was, it took me five solid minutes just to let go of his shirt.

His lips hovered above mine. "Call you later?"

I nodded, somehow finding the conviction to reach for the doorknob. "Pray for me," I teased.

His laugh followed him down the walkway to his Civic. I inhaled as I faced the door. Truth be told, I would've taken about any distraction tonight—tulle involved or otherwise.

A text notification dinged in the stairwell.

The hospital cleared Reggie for release. They're staying with a friend of their aunt's. Everything is fine. Sleep well.

Relief swept in at knowing the boys were okay, but sleep was still up for debate. Once in our apartment, I dropped into a kitchen chair, towed one leg up onto the cushion, and snagged an apple from the wire fruit bowl. Whatever Jamal hadn't wanted Reggie to tell us was still nagging at me.

"If you spin that apple one more time, the polish on

that sucker is gonna make Mr. Clean jealous." Jaycee brandished her best I-caught-you teacher-look at me from the couch.

I tossed the fruit back into the bowl. She'd kill me later for not filling her in on everything right away, but I still wasn't up for it. "Sorry," I said instead. "Lost in thought."

"Mm-hmm." She slid down the microfiber slipcover onto the floor. "Luckily for you, I have the perfect remedy." She dragged two backpacks from underneath the couch and dumped at least twenty wedding magazines onto the carpet.

I pinched my lips together. "Been stocking up?"

"Just a tad." She pushed a quarter of the pile my way and draped a magazine with fuchsia headlines across her lap.

"Jae, your wedding isn't until June." I glanced up from a glossy page to meet the stare of an exasperated bride-to-be.

"I've been dreaming about getting married since I was eight years old. I think ten months is close enough for me to start planning." She fanned through the pages. "Look at how many options there are. It's going to take that long just to narrow down the possibilities."

I didn't mean to snort.

Jaycee shook her head, clearly equating my noninterest in wedding planning with some kind of treason against the bonds of womanhood. "You're telling me you haven't dreamed about your wedding since you were a kid?"

I flipped over another page plagued with gaudy dresses. "Not really. I mean, other than—"

Riley's signature ringtone blared from my pocket. Lifting the phone to my ear, I motioned to Jae to give me a second. "Hey, babe."

"Em, you're not going to believe this."

Between his speed talking and level of animation, I missed half of what he said other than something about his agent finally getting ahold of him.

I hopped up and moved over to the window. "Wait, wait, slow down. He said what?"

Riley might as well have been standing on the other side of an open-ended tunnel. The entire room shook with the echo of three single words that were about to change everything.

2

CONVERGENCE

I WANTED TO ANSWER—TRIED to answer—but those three words crowded out every other sound.

Nashville. Moving. Soon.

Recording an album was what he'd been waiting for. What *we'd* been waiting for. I knew this was coming. I'd prepped for spending time apart, but I'd expected that to mean a commute. A few weeks there, a few home. But moving?

"W... when?"

Riley's pause throbbed from the other end of the line.

"The twenty-fourth," he said slowly.

The carpet freed my feet. I whipped around the partition wall into the kitchen. Reaching for the calendar on the fridge, I knocked off the magnetized penholder beside it. Dozens of pens rolled across the linoleum as I scanned the dates for the only one that mattered. *Friday?*

"Em, talk to me."

"So soon?"

He let out a breath. "I know."

The room fell silent. Each tick coming from the wall clock struck my ribs like some kind of internal countdown.

An engine cranked in the background. "I'll be over in five minutes."

He hung up, and my arm slid to my side. I drifted to the nearest chair in the living room.

Jaycee tossed the magazine off her lap. "What's wrong? What'd he say?"

Without facing her, I clasped the edge of the cushion on either side of my legs. "He's leaving."

Old fears cropped up without warning or mercy. I choked them back, hating that they were robbing me of how happy I was for him.

A knock on the door came much sooner than it should have. I didn't want to know how many traffic laws Riley had broken in order to get to my apartment that fast.

He met my eyes from across the room the moment Jaycee let him in. Worry stormed the look of excitement he had every right to have. "I'm sorry. You already have enough to process tonight. I should've waited to tell you in person tomorrow."

His unwarranted apology doubled the guilt needling into my side.

Knelt in front of me, he rubbed my thigh. "Listen, nothing's set yet. I can stay—"

"Absolutely not." I started for the door. "You've worked too hard for this. You can't forfeit your dream now."

"It's only a secondary dream," he said, as though reiterating a fact I shouldn't have had to question.

I froze with my hand on the doorknob. Not a single shade of uncertainty tainted his voice. No hint of hesitancy. All I'd have to do was ask, and he would stay. The words fought the frail barrier keeping them buried in my throat.

After seeing Trey's wife hold on to regret for thirty years, I wasn't about to let Riley marry me wondering, *what if?*

I balled my sleeves under my fingers and waited to look up until hard lines of resolution regained their hold. "You're not sacrificing this opportunity. It's too important. You have to go." I opened the door. "Besides, I'm coming with you."

Jaycee's comment to Riley trailed into the stairwell, "Should've seen that one coming."

The door swung open again. "Em, wait. You can't drop everything and move to Nashville with me. You have to finish your internship. Your senior year."

I stopped a few steps up from the foyer, hand clenched around the rail. "Secondary dreams, Riley. Works both ways. I'm not going to bail on you."

"Bail on me?" A muffled laugh echoed his flip-flops as he jogged down the stairs.

"What's so funny?"

"You're very cute when you're being completely irrational." His grin never played fair.

I nudged him backward, but he caught my hand and brought me close. "Even cuter when you're trying not to smile." His thumb brushed over the corner of my mouth.

I strove to hold my lips in place. Useless.

His hand slid to the nape of my neck, and my worries slid down the staircase. For the longest moment, he held my gaze without saying anything at all. He didn't have to. The depth in his eyes already told me he knew why I was afraid of being apart.

Something twitched inside me. I didn't stop to think. I pulled him to me, knotted my fingers through his hair, and kissed him with feelings I'd never have words for.

No air. No space. Only longing.

He responded, pressing in. The keys clipped to his belt loop clinked against the cement wall behind us. His hands trailed down my sides to my waist. I shifted, ready for him to switch places and take the lead, but he lifted me back instead. "Emma," he rasped. "How strong do you think I am?"

Far stronger than I was, apparently.

He pushed off the wall and jogged down the last few steps. At the foot of the stairs, he stopped and rubbed his neck. The door opened in front of him, and Trevor breezed past us on his way up to the second floor with coffee in tow.

I slipped outside before the door closed again. Under the glow of the streetlight, I drank in the night's cool air.

Riley reached my side.

"I'm sorry." I blew out a breath. "I don't know why I'm reacting like this. None of this is as easy for me."

"Easy? Are you kidding? Em, I never stop dreaming of when I won't have to tear myself away from you at the end of the night when I'm dying to stay." He raised both hands to shield the curtains of hair falling into my face. "I'm committed to sharing my life with you. Every part. Even the waiting."

His response couldn't have been a clearer depiction of the kind of love I wanted to give him in return. Patient, unselfish, strong enough to bear all things.

"I know a lot's gonna change." He brought my hand to his chest. "But not this." He cupped his fingers over mine. "Nothing's ever going to change this."

Unable to speak, I held on. To him. To us. To everything I'd learned to trust.

My lashes swept toward him, silently asking for another draw from his reservoir of grace.

He kissed the crown of my head. "C'mon, take a walk with me."

Thoughts of being apart eased further away with each stride across the campus. At the edge of the sports field, Riley slid me a lopsided grin.

I eyed him back. "I know that face. What are you up to?"

He swayed his head from side to side. "Nothing. Just this." He hoisted me over his shoulder and jogged to the middle of the field.

The view above us stole my focus the minute we toppled onto the grass. There was nothing like lying there under our own private planetarium listening to nearby maples and red cedars waving in the breeze. I took it all in. Just as he'd planned, no doubt. He always knew exactly what I needed. Even my questions and concerns about Jamal subsided under the peace this part of the campus always washed over me.

Riley stretched his hands behind his head and sighed with an audible reverence. It was hard to blame him. I curled into the crook of his arm and settled into one of the few places where life made sense.

Minutes drifted into the sound of crickets singing along with the wind. Riley joined them, humming a perfect soundtrack to a perfect setting. It still amazed me how effortless the beauty of music was for him.

He drew figure eights over my arm with his fingertip. "What if they don't like my music?" he whispered.

Where'd that come from? "They gave you a record deal. I'm pretty sure they think you're amazing."

"Not my label. The public. Having to measure up to other artists they love..." He released a labored exhale. "I don't know. I was excited about it all at first, but now that it's sinking in, I'm not sure I'm ready for this." He peered at the dark sky. "What if I'm making a mistake?"

He couldn't be serious. Fans were going to adore his music as much as I already did. No question. Was he honestly doubting that?

My own doubt from earlier crashed into the uncertainty pulling at his voice, and I hated my initial reaction even more. He'd always been the steadfast one. The rock to steady me when I felt shaken. Even now, I knew he was still trying to be, but it was my turn to be strong for him.

I propped myself up to face him. "You're not making a mistake. This is what you were made for. You're going to thrive in every part of your career." There wasn't a question in my mind about that. "I shouldn't have freaked out when you first told me."

He smiled softly. "I would've done the same. I don't want to leave any more than you want me to."

"But that's just it." I sat all the way up. "I *do* want you to go. I've *always* wanted this for you. And I want to support you in every way I can, even from back here." Swallowing, I plucked a blade of grass from beside us and twisted it around my ring finger. "I'm not the same girl I used to be."

My eyes found his again, and I prayed he could see every ounce of faith I held in him. "I'm not going to let fear stand between us and all we've fought for. Not again. It's going to be perfect, Riley. I promise."

He looked at me so long without a sound, I wasn't sure he was going to say anything at all. Slowly, he brushed my hair from my face and left his thumb over my temple. "I love you, Emma," he whispered. He brought his lips to my forehead. "More than you know."

Not more than I loved him. I nestled against him, realizing then just how brave he needed me to be. I looked up at the stars and breathed in. "Would you come by tomorrow before work? I need to redo today. Do things right and—"

"Tomorrow, Em." He pulled me closer.

I closed my eyes and held on a little while longer to the very thing I'd have to let go of. Being brave could wait for tomorrow.

3

REDO

THE MORNING SUN kissed the treetops and warmed my cheeks through the living room window. A new day. A new chance to be strong and support Riley's dreams, no matter where they led him.

The rumble of the teapot boiling butted into a thought I didn't want to chase. Hopping on one foot instead, I slipped on my other fuzzy sock and rounded the partition. If anything could gird me with strength, surely it was chai.

While my tea bag steeped, I grabbed a frying pan from the drawer under the oven and accidentally clanked it into the pot next to it. The sound bounced off the kitchen walls all the way down the hall like it was following some sort of sonar radar to the last place I wanted it to go.

I held the pan to my stomach and bit my lip.

A loud *thud* answered the awaited silence. A minute later, a tousled replica of my best friend emerged from our bedroom. Jaycee squinted at me through half-opened lashes.

My shoulders nearly touched my ears. "Sorry."

Her arms stretched with a yawn. "I needed to get up anyway." She stumbled into the kitchen on autopilot and snagged a mug almost the same size as the coffeepot. "Trev should be here by eight. He made me clear my whole day for him. He's up to something."

We exchanged a foreboding look.

"That reminds me." Jaycee swirled creamer into her coffee. "I can't take you to the center today, but Trev promised me he'd have something worked out."

No telling what that meant.

She leaned against the counter and breathed in the hazelnut-scented steam from her mug. Her eyes immediately fluttered open, awake and alert.

I scanned the label on the coffee can. "Sure this isn't laced with something else?"

A don't-ask-don't-tell grin snuck around her mug.

"Oh." Pushing off the counter, she held her mug away and wiped a streak of coffee from her chin. "Shoot, I forgot to tell you. Trev heard from his advisor yesterday about that internship he wanted. Guess someone ended up backing out last minute, so Professor Jenkins got him in."

"That's awesome."

"Yeah. Except that means he can't do the coaching gig you asked him about." Jaycee scrunched her lips to the side. "Sorry. I know you were counting on him."

"It's fine. His internship's important. Seriously, don't worry about it. I'll come up with someone else." Someone like...? The one person who'd be perfect for the job was barely talking to me.

A gentle knock at the door rippled into the room.

"That's my cue." Jaycee pivoted on her bare foot and made a beeline to the shower.

With my hand on the knob, I straightened my shoulders.

Riley whisked me into his arms before the door had a chance to swing shut behind him. "Good morning."

He wasn't going to make being strong very easy on me.

I unwound his arms and eased out of danger territory. "I was just making us some breakfast."

"Really?" His voice slanted with his brows.

"I even made coffee."

"Now I know it's serious. Did you have Jaycee taste test it first?"

"Very funny."

He followed me into the kitchen. "Breakfast... My own barista... What's the occasion?"

"I heard you have some news we should be celebrating."

His smile fell. "Emma."

Hands on my hips, I fixed a glare on him. "This is my redo, remember?" I tugged a band off my wrist and swept my hair up into a loose ponytail. "Okay, I admit I'm the world's worst actress. Just humor me, all right?"

I pored over the stovetop, as though the pan of eggs would provide some kind of golden armor I needed to make it through this. "So, you heard from your agent?"

"You don't have to—"

Bits of eggs flung onto the linoleum as I spun around.

He laughed. "I'm not sure that flustered look will ever be less adorable."

"Ahem." I shook the spatula at him. "Your agent?"

He gave me a short yes-ma'am nod and took a seat at the table. "Brett called after my run with Jake yesterday. Said Momentum Records had a change in schedule, and they want me to come out to Nashville Friday." Riley kneaded his shoulder blade like he was still convincing himself it was all real.

I ducked into the fridge in search of the shredded potatoes. "Have you called your parents? I bet they're beside themselves." I pushed a gallon of milk to one side and a carton of orange juice to the other. Swishing liquid filled in for Riley's reply. I peered over the door to where he was picking at a scratch in the tabletop.

"It's complicated."

"What's complicated about it?" The refrigerator door closed, potatoes still inside. "This is a dream come true for you. Your parents will be thrilled."

"You don't know my dad." He scooted his chair in and leaned on his elbows. A second later, he dropped his arms on the table. "We don't have to talk about them right now."

"Yes, we do."

The look on his face disagreed. Fine. I didn't want to waste what time we had left together arguing.

The air conditioning kicked on, and the question I couldn't put off nearly froze dead in my throat.

I swiped the cup of coffee I'd made for him, downed it fast enough to make Jaycee proud, and clanked the mug on the counter like a drained shot glass. I wasn't sure which was harder to swallow—black coffee or the prospect of being without Riley. I breathed in and forced the words out.

"Did Brett mention how long you'd be gone?"

Another lengthy pause expanded between us. Too long.

Riley's chair legs screeched against the floor. His hands, warm and tender, found my shoulders. "I didn't expect this to happen so quickly." He turned me around. "I was hoping I wouldn't have to move out there until after you graduated and we wouldn't have to be apart."

"I know." I fashioned a nearly passable smile on my face. "But sometimes our plans change for the better, even if we can't see how at first. Right?"

Could he tell I was trying to convince myself more than him? Inhaling, I rested a hand on his shirt. "I have to believe we can do this and that we'll be stronger for it."

Grinning, he interlaced his fingers around my back. "My valiant fiancée."

"I don't know about that. I just want to be as brave as you make me feel when you look at me."

With that very reflection in his eyes, he drew me closer. "You already are."

Enclosed in arms of promise, I yielded to hope. Yet as quickly as the serenity came, it retreated behind the question still persisting in the forefront. "How long, Riley?"

His chin drifted to his collar. "At least a semester."

At least?

"I'm not sure it'll take that long to record the album, but they want me to spend some time in the industry. Get acquainted. Work on some new music."

I tried to channel Jaycee's usual optimism. "It'll fly by. We'll both be busy. Your days will be packed, and I'll have school, my internship. We'll hardly notice how quickly time passes. And we'll talk every day, right?"

He smiled the way he always did when I rambled. Before his mouth moved, his eyes spoke the words we'd exchanged countless times before. "You're braver than you think you are."

"So are you." I stretched on my tiptoes to kiss him. "It's going to be amazing. I know it. And four months apart is nothing, really."

He cocked a brow.

"Okay," I admitted. "Maybe not *nothing*." As it was, the clock was already smirking at me, like it couldn't wait to tag along the next few days as an uninvited third wheel.

The corner of Riley's mouth tugged sideways.

I swatted him with the dish towel. "Hush."

"I didn't say a word."

Neither had I, but sometimes I swore he could hear my babbling thoughts.

Still grinning, he pulled a tiny piece of egg out of my hair. "How about we don't focus on anything else except right now? We'll worry about Friday when it comes."

"Deal." That was one bargain I could easily accept.

At least, it was until the clock took another stab at me after breakfast. I knew we couldn't drop all of our responsibilities to spend every minute together before he had to leave. Still, part of me wished we could.

I slid our plates into the dishwater, gripped the counter, and strong-armed thoughts of Friday out of my mind.

Riley ran his hands along my arms from behind me. "Thanks for breakfast. You know, I could get used to waking up to breakfast with you every morning."

I turned around. "Oh, really?"

He brought my wrist to his mouth. "Mm-hmm."

"You're trying to distract me, aren't you?"

"That depends." He edged closer, his lips right above mine. "Is it working?"

"Maybe."

The front door blew open. Riley and I turned in time to see Trevor flying into the room like Kramer sliding through Seinfeld's front door. I laughed until I noticed someone follow him in—someone who hadn't stepped foot in my apartment since the end of last semester.

4

REMINISCENT

"Em, I need to steal Jae this afternoon, but don't worry." Trevor winked and patted A. J.'s shoulder. "Bowers is gonna give you a ride instead."

A. J., me... alone?

Evidently, I wasn't the only one who thought this was a bad idea. A. J. stood at the living room window with his back facing the rest of us, clearly dreading the prospect of going anywhere with me.

My heart winced. How had we gotten here? We were supposed to stay friends. He'd promised.

Riley cleared his throat and drew my focus back to the rest of the room.

Truth was, after the way A. J. had barely spoken to me the last few months, I had no reason to expect that to change now. I turned and kept things light instead. "All right, Trev, how much did you have to bribe him to drive me?"

Trevor's full patronizing tenor kicked in. "Just 'cause he's getting to see the UFC fight this Saturday on me doesn't mean he wouldn't have driven you pro bono." He jabbed A. J.'s arm. "Right, bro?"

A. J. turned, a statue coming to life. "Of course." His hollow tone betrayed the soft look in his eyes.

Riley's hand tightened around mine. Unlike Ashlea, who seemed unconvinced A. J. had let go of his feelings for me, Riley had been gracious toward him this whole time. He'd never once shown a hint of jealousy or concern.

Until right then.

"Why don't you let me call work real quick?" Riley pulled out his cell. "Give me a minute to let them know I'll be in late, and I can drive you."

"It's just a car ride." A. J. trucked past us into the stairwell. "You coming?"

Just a car ride. One he obviously wanted to get over with. Other than a possible speeding ticket, Riley had nothing to worry about.

"It's fine," I whispered before kissing him goodbye. "I'll see you tonight?"

He kissed me once more. "Seven o'clock sharp."

I stretched out my arm as far as it would go before releasing his hand. If I could've found a way to stretch out our time together, too, I would have.

Once outside, I stole a moment alone in the sunshine to recharge my faith. If I could handle Riley leaving, surely I could endure a single ride with A. J.

Our silent walk to the parking lot begged to differ. Apparently, my need for extra strength today wasn't over. The sun-coated paint on A. J.'s black Acura ZDX emitted heat waves into the air like some kind of invisible force warning me to enter at my own risk.

I sank onto the hot leather seat. The scene seemed oddly reminiscent of the last time we were in this same car, heading up to the same city. Except that everything had changed since then—including A. J.

My mind sprinted to catch up with the pavement passing outside my window. I'd hurt him last year. And if this summer was any indication, he hadn't let that go. Maybe it was selfish to hope he ever would. But if nothing else, at least we could make the car ride bearable.

"So, when are we having that rematch on the basketball court?" I asked with as much lightheartedness as I could assemble.

A. J.'s mouth tipped into a reactive grin. "Whenever you're ready to lose."

Should've known competitiveness would be the hole in his armor. "Ha. Don't hold your breath. I've been watching the kids play at the center. I've learned a few moves that'll make you dizzy."

"Psh, you wish."

Laughter seeped out before I could stop it. I missed our teasing.

"Thanks, by the way, for driving me." I slipped a ten-dollar bill into the cup holder.

A burst in acceleration sent the back of my head colliding with the headrest. A. J. eased off the gas pedal, but an edge clung to his voice. "What's that?"

"Gas money."

"No way." He yanked the bill from the cup holder and tossed it in my lap. "You can barely afford your rent."

"Portland isn't exactly a drive around the block. I don't want to take advantage of your generosity." Couldn't he at least glance in my direction to see my sincerity?

"It's no big deal. Don't worry about it." He wrenched the gearshift into the wrong slot, his voice gruffer than the confused engine.

Two could play the stubborn game. I wadded the money into a ball and flicked it at him. "I'm not taking it back."

Huffing under his breath, he swerved while fumbling around the floorboard in search of the bill.

The beginning of an impish smile crept up the side of his cheek a minute later. "I'll tell you what. You beat me at basketball, and I'll let you pay me for the gas."

"You're really that sure of yourself, aren't you?"

A. J. slid his sunglasses down his nose and stared at me as if I'd asked a no-brainer. "I'll even give you a ten-point lead."

"Wow, I see that head of yours hasn't gotten any smaller. Still holding out for that J. Crew model career?"

For one brief, candid moment, A. J. laughed with me, and things felt as they'd always been.

Almost.

An unexplained sense of gravity returned to his voice. "Consider the gas a donation to the center. What you're doing there is really great."

A pang of insufficiency twisted into my side. Last spring, I'd been so certain that switching internships was part of God's plan for me. That I was there for a reason. Lately, that reason felt more like failure than anything. It struck me any time I remembered the look in Jamal's eyes, like he'd let us down somehow instead of the other way around.

I released my tangled seat belt. "Sometimes I wonder about that. I'm trying to help Trey out where I can with the business part, but I feel like it's not enough. Like I could be doing more for them."

"I doubt he sees it that way."

Picturing Trey's contagious smile made it hard to disagree. "He has a special way of looking at most things." It was one of the many reasons I admired him so much... and the same reason he could drive me crazy.

"If we can keep the center open, he's thinking of offering weekend classes to the community. Wants me to teach on finance. I've been piecing together some lesson plans from my coursework, but I'm really nervous. Tutoring the kids isn't the same as teaching a real class, especially for people who have so much more life experience than me."

When I finally stopped to take a breath, I had trouble finding one. A. J. used to be so easy to talk to. It was hard to remember we weren't as close now. I tucked my hands under my legs. "Sorry. Didn't mean to unload on you."

He lifted the bill of his hat, then tugged it back down. "Don't underestimate yourself, Emma." Without turning to face me, he placed the crumpled-up ten-dollar bill in my hand. "The center's lucky to have you."

Same as they'd be lucky to have him if he'd consider the coaching position. I leaned into my door panel and stared at the exit signs passing by, knowing it wouldn't be fair of me to ask him.

An uncomfortable silence returned, but maybe that was the way it was supposed to be.

A. J. parked across from the center's meager building but didn't shift his focus from the windshield. "You want me to walk you to the door?"

I followed his line of sight to a cluster of guys on the street corner. "The door's twenty feet away. I'll be fine." I climbed out of the car.

"Don't be so gullible you forget where you are."

A city bus turned off a side street and chugged past us. I lifted my shirt over my nose as a trail of exhaust rustled a plastic bag wedged inside a trash can a few stops ahead.

Okay, maybe the center wasn't in the nicest of areas. Still, I'd never felt unsafe here. At least, not until last night.

I willed away thoughts of the fire. I'd be fine. It was broad daylight, for Pete's sake.

A guttural laugh from the corner drew my glance

over the hood of the car toward three guys staring in our direction. The way the one in the middle smirked at me sent a chill down my spine with enough force to reconsider A. J.'s offer.

I hunched over the open window instead. "Thanks again for the lift. I really appreciate it."

"No problem." A. J.'s gaze finally flicked to me. Yet even hidden behind his sunglasses, the hollow look in his eyes was too painful to miss. I almost preferred he didn't look at me at all than to look straight through me.

Elbows clasped, I backed away from the car. "See you later." I skirted around the side of the building, away from the palpable glare coming from the corner.

A. J.'s tires didn't screech away until I'd had ample time to make it safely inside. Figured. It was his nature to protect, despite whatever else he might've felt toward me. If only that made the rift between us hurt less.

"'Sup, Miss E?" Four of the center's regular kids strode down the walkway toward the side door. "Was that guy in the car out front messin' with you?" Brandon asked. "'Cause I can take him." He tossed a basketball in the air, caught it, and flexed his bicep. "I been working out."

His little eleven-year-old self couldn't have gotten any cuter. The thought of our kids running into whoever those guys were turned my blood hot. I didn't know what they were selling, or what game they were hustling, but they were messing with the wrong place.

I looked behind me, looped an arm around Brandon's

shoulders, and prodded him down the walkway. "Thanks for looking out, but I think I've got it covered."

"A'ight, but you let me know. I watch out for my girl."

He strutted inside with his friends snickering behind us.

At the door to the classroom, I caught his basketball midair. "How's that book report coming?"

Brandon swayed in place. "Aw, Miss E, you can't be calling me out like that. I got a reputation to manage."

He held out his hands for his ball, and I placed a notebook in them instead. "How about a reputation for passing school?"

He flipped up the bill of his hat. "That ain't gonna win me the ladies."

Like a big brother, Trey pulled him into a headlock and lugged him into the classroom. "It might win you that one." He winked in my direction.

"If my heart weren't already taken," I said with a wave of my engagement ring.

The door closed a trail of grumbles and laughs behind it.

I toyed with my ring. Alone, thoughts from the morning rushed in again. Between worrying about having only two nights left with Riley and gnawing over questions about the fire, Brandon was probably closer to finishing his book report than I was to concentrating on anything else today.

My focus drifted to the basement door and to what Reggie had said about the fan.

Trey snuck out of the classroom to grab his mug from his desk.

"Hey." I hopped up and met him by the door before I lost the chance. "Did you hear any more from Jamal's aunt?"

"They're all doing fine." He tucked a pen inside his pocket. "The boys are gonna be moving in with their grandparents for now."

"Nearby?"

"Boise."

Idaho? "So far away?"

Trey smiled tenderly. "It's probably best for them right now."

If there was any consolation, I took comfort in that.

"What about the house?"

"From what I understand, they were able to save the first floor. Sierra plans to rebuild the second story." He took a sip of coffee. "Thank goodness for insurance."

When my eyes flickered to the basement door again, Trey set a hand to my arm. "I checked," he said, without my needing to ask. "The fan was off. I brought it up to the office to be safe."

I followed his nod toward an outdated box fan in the corner of the room. Mindlessly chewing the corner of my thumb, I stared at the dusty blades. "Do you really think someone wanted to burn down the center?" If so, why'd they ask Jamal to do it? And why not torch the place instead of waiting for a fan's old motor to ignite?

A heavy exhale drew my eyes back up to Trey's. "I

think some people in this neighborhood would rather us not be here."

"But why?" Couldn't they see we were there to help?

"Some people fear love."

I stared at him. "That doesn't make sense."

"It does to someone who's never encountered grace." He patted my arm when my blank stare didn't budge. "That doesn't mean we stop giving it." Leaving his Gandalf-like wisdom for me to chew on, Trey reached for the doorknob, nodded once more, then dipped back into the classroom.

Alone again, images of Jamal's neighbors, who stood by without helping, collided with the image of Trey's selfless love rushing him into open flames. I'd always known there were few people like him in the world. I just never thought there'd be people conspiring against him and all he stood for.

Conviction rose inside me. I might not be as strong as he was, but the center was a part of me now too—a part I'd fight for. I cast one last glance at the fan, rolled my chair up to my desk, and rifled through a stack of overdue bills cluttering my inbox.

An envelope slipped out. The sender hadn't bothered to fill in the return address, but the Palmer Foundation was the only benefactor from the last batch of grant requests I hadn't heard back from yet.

Please be good news.

I scanned the first two sentences of the form letter and dropped it. After seeing the word *unfortunately* on fifteen other rejection notices, I didn't need to read any farther, but a comment toward the bottom of the page caught my eye.

Not enough activities? Seriously? We weren't the YMCA. Tutoring should be more than enough to warrant financial assistance. And it wasn't as if we weren't trying to get a sports program going. If they'd make an investment in us, maybe we could actually hire the kind of staff they seemed to expect us to have. I shoved the letter into my side drawer with the others and slumped in my chair.

There had to be somebody out there willing to help us. I pinned my bangs back with a paperclip, unburied my grant notes, and Googled the second to last organization left on my list. I transferred their information into my letter template and breathed a prayer while the decrepit printer spit out the page a row at a time. *Give us a chance. Please.* The center was all some of these kids had.

Movement flickered outside the window. The guys from the corner slinked around the building opposite ours, but not before the apparent ringleader flaunted a dark look my way.

A tinge of apprehension stirred up memories of my former internship supervisor almost forcing himself on me last year in Xander's parking lot. Maybe it was a good thing A. J. drove me in today instead of Riley. He didn't need any reason to worry about me while he was gone.

Drawing my shoulders back, I returned to my post and tackled the pile of paperwork closest to me.

Daylight made a steady descent down the side of the building as the afternoon crept toward the end of my shift. The closer it neared, the more intently I checked the clock.

"If you keep tapping that pen on your desk, you're gonna drill a hole through it," Trey said from the back door, where the kids were outside playing a pickup game of basketball.

"Sorry." I dropped the pen.

"Got a hot date tonight?"

I threw him a sassy look. "Always."

"Mm-hmm." He crossed the room and sat at his desk. "I don't think staring out that window is gonna make him get here any faster."

"Tell me about it." I spun the pen in half turns. "Sorry to be so distracted today. Yesterday was a lot, then I found out Riley's leaving on Friday. And to be honest, it's sort of torturous to be at work right now. Not that you're not great company, but you know."

Trey's gray-peppered eyebrows reached above the top of his square glasses. "Mm-hmm," he grunted again. "Is my man going home for a week or something?"

"I wish. No, he's moving to Nashville."

"Nashville?" Trey's chair sprang forward. "The record deal finally came through? Aw, sweet, this is the break he's been waiting for, right?"

The mess of computer cords kept my gaze locked beneath my desk. "Yeah."

"Don't sound too enthused or anything."

"No, no, I'm excited for him," I backpedaled. "Just not looking forward to being apart for so long."

I squelched my nonsensical emotions. But when my eyes scanned over my desk calendar, a date caught me in the gut. The twenty-ninth. My parents' anniversary. At least, it would have been… if he were still here.

Gnawing on my thumb again, I looked across the room. My heart sank in response to the weathered lines that had deepened along Trey's forehead since his wife filed for a divorce. My eyes drifted back to the calendar, and something in me couldn't stop the question from rising.

"Trey? I know it's none of my business, but has Laila ever said why she's doing this? Surely whatever perks her new employer's offering her in Seattle can't be worth more than your marriage." I picked at a chip in the laminate desk. "Couples live in separate states all the time. I mean, I know it's not ideal, but they commute. Make it work." Didn't they?

Trey looked at a picture frame on his desk with sullen eyes. "Her dream's there."

"What about the center? I thought you two shared this dream here." My shoulders slumped a little farther with each grasp in the dark. "You have thirty years together. You've been through so much." She couldn't be throwing it all away now, especially when he needed her more than ever.

He moved the frame back. "It's not that simple."

"But shouldn't it be? You both promised for better or worse, and..." I clamped a vise over my splintered attempt at making sense of her choice. Trey's broken heart didn't need my rationale. It needed my compassion.

"I'm so sorry, Trey. I didn't mean to come off sounding like I was judging you or—"

He lifted a hand. When he rose from his worn chair, I wanted to slither down in mine. Yet instead of reprimand, nothing but grace led him over to my desk. Still without words, he motioned me up and into a side hug. "Some marriages make it, Emma."

His ability to understand the unspoken reached straight through doors I'd kept closed all summer. My gaze rebounded from him to the date of my parents' anniversary and triggered a hurt rooted deep inside me. Not everyone got to choose whether their marriages lasted.

"Riley's not Laila," he whispered.

But Seattle wasn't Nashville. This would be different from when Riley lived there before. This time, he'd be living the dream he was destined for—a dream that could take him anywhere.

"Just keep learning to love him, and you'll get through this."

"But what if...?" My assurance trembled against questions that had no place in my heart anymore. I shouldn't have been thinking any of this. Swallowing, I tamped it all down.

In the quiet, a peace calmed my spirit, and I clung to it with all I had.

"You worry too much, kid." Trey patted me on the back. "Riley's smart enough not to go looking for a hamburger when he has a steak waiting for him at home."

I stepped back and blinked at him. "Did you really just quote Paul Newman right now?" Surely, he hadn't.

"Not precisely." His laughter mushroomed. "If it'll make you feel better, I can have a little guy-to-guy chat with him before he goes."

I blinked again. "You wouldn't."

His grin disagreed.

"Trey." Riley didn't need any hamburger talks, and he certainly didn't need to think I was still wavering about his leaving. It was bad enough I'd panicked when he'd first told me.

Trey's burly laugh vibrated across the compact room. "You sure?" He pointed past me to the window overlooking the main street. "'Cause now might be the perfect time."

One glance out the window, and I flew through the door to meet Riley before Trey could corner him inside.

5

ONE CONDITION

RILEY'S GRIN toppled sideways as he strolled up the narrow walkway. "You guys have surveillance cameras out front?"

I stashed my hands in my pockets and dragged my sneaker over a dandelion poking through the sidewalk divider. "I might've sort of been on the lookout for you for the last half hour."

"Then I guess I better make sure the wait was worth it."

His eyes found my lips. Even a foot away, my pulse accelerated, already sensing his touch. He kissed me as though he'd been staring out his own window all day too.

He leaned back. "Did I pass?"

"My Jell-O legs aren't answer enough for you?"

"Just checking." His smile might as well have been

another kiss. He reached for the doorknob. "Let me stop in to see Trey before we go."

I pulled him in the opposite direction. "Trey's busy, and we want to beat rush hour traffic."

"At seven o'clock?"

Okay, bad excuse.

He opened the door. "It'll just take a sec."

I shuffled in behind him and shot Trey a look of warning.

"Riley, my man." He winked at me while giving Riley one of those half-hug-half-handshake guy hellos. "Congratulations. Heard you got a sweet deal in Nashville." He boxed the air and nudged him in the shoulder. "Big dog now, eh?"

Riley rubbed his jaw. "Yeah, guess I got pretty lucky."

Luck had nothing to do with it. Would he ever recognize his own talent? I threaded my fingers through his, praying he'd sense my reassurance.

He looked from me to Trey. "Listen, I wanted to ask if you'd mind keeping an eye out for Emma while I'm gone. I'll be away for a few months. Might be gone until January."

So, that's what this is about.

Trey sat on the edge of his desk. "Don't worry, bro. I got your back." He leaned forward and lowered his voice. "But I gotta be honest. Your girl's kinda stubborn."

Riley laughed. "So I've noticed. Which is why it'll give me some peace of mind if you could see her in and out when she's here."

I butted between them. "I hate to break up the little bromance you've got going on here, but you guys realize it's rude to refer to me in the third person when I'm standing in the same room as you, right?"

The desk shook with Trey's laughter. "Like I said."

Riley curled me to his side. "I really appreciate it. Means the world."

"You got it." He fake-punched Riley's arm again. "Hey, live it up in Nashville for me, huh?"

"I'll see what I can do."

The skin on my arm burned against Riley's cool fingers on the walk to his Civic.

"Don't be mad," he said, already knowing. "I'm not saying you need a babysitter, but after the fire…" His voice softened. "I just need to know you'll be safe." He lowered his face beneath mine when I didn't respond. "Would a peace offering help?"

With one look, his eyes drained every bit of fight from me. He set an MP3 player in my hand and folded his fingers over mine. "A little music to listen to while I'm away."

I flaunted a replica of his usual grin. "You mean I won't have to wait to buy the album?"

He scratched his cheek with his key. "That sounds weird, doesn't it?"

"Not to me. I always knew you would do it."

His brow furrowed.

"What?"

"It doesn't seem right. You not being there with me. None of this would be happening if it weren't for you."

"There you go, giving me too much credit again." I inched closer before he could argue. "You'll just have to relay every detail, play-by-play, over the phone."

"Every day." His grin gradually waned. A resurgence of his earlier concern deepened as he took both my hands in his. "Promise me, Em. Promise me you'll be careful while you're here."

I didn't want him to be fretting over this when we were nearing the end of another day. Keeping things light instead, I brandished the lawyer-look we always teased each other with. "On one condition."

He dished it right back. "Which is?"

"You have to promise to test out your new music with me before you record it."

Riley cocked his head to the side and squinted. "Deal. But only if you give me an honest critique."

"Always."

Even as I said it, a question needled into my promise. Would listening to his music over the phone change the way it sounded?

He toyed with his keys, sobering yet again. "I'm gonna leave my car for you to drive."

I scooted backward. "Riley, I—"

"I'm not taking it all the way out to Nashville." He pushed off the fender. "If you have a car, I won't feel like I'm abandoning you as much. And at least you'll be able to get around without needing A. J.'s eager assistance."

Seriously? That's *what he's worried about?* "Okay, first of all, you're not abandoning me. And second of all, you don't need to worry about A. J. Trust me. He isn't eager to give me a ride or be around me, period." His guarded eyes from the morning had made that clear enough. "It's like it pains him to look at me or something."

"Because he's trying not to feel anything for you. I've been there, remember? Not an easy task."

A. J. was probably doing what he felt he needed to. I just hated that it had to be this way.

Riley shook his head. "I should probably cut the guy some slack for hanging out with us still. I wouldn't have been nearly as noble."

"Then it's a good thing you'll never have to find out." I curled into his side and into one promise that would never be hard to keep. Riley was, and always would be, the sole possessor of my heart.

He couldn't honestly be questioning that. My stomach tensed. Unless I'd given him a reason to. Was that why he'd kissed me the way he had when he picked me up today?

My mind raced for a way to reverse all my actions since he'd told me he was leaving—the right thing to say, do—some way to replace all our doubts with faith.

"Just keep learning to love him."

Trey's words washed over me with the sunset. I tucked my shoulder under Riley's and let everything else fade except how easy the beauty of a sky transitioning from day to night could make love feel. "Can we stay right here?"

He clicked his key fob. "I have a better idea."

6

UNRAVELED

I DON'T KNOW what time Riley had walked me home from the sports field last night. Only that it had been too soon.

It never failed to amaze me how unfair time could be. It could jet away from you in a heartbeat when you begged it to slow and could stall endlessly when you pleaded with it to pass. I wasn't unfamiliar with the tension in that dichotomy. It had been clenching my heart all week. But today, even my muscles seemed to be hunkered down in some kind of defense mode needed to make it through tonight.

Strong, remember?

I shook out my arms, turned up the volume on my MP3 player, and pushed harder on the elliptical. My legs circled in a fury, but my mind was somewhere else. Somewhere that, for the moment, belonged only to me. With my eyes closed and headphones on, I drifted into

Riley's songs and the reminder that his music was worth any sacrifice.

"Excuse me. May I ask what you're listening to?"

I looked up toward a witty version of my favorite half-smile. Sometimes, he made forgetting everything else so effortless.

Riley leaned against the front of the machine. "I couldn't help noticing you're enjoying your music."

I tugged my earbuds free. "Oh, it's this great new artist," I played along. "Maybe you've heard of him. Riley Preston?"

He rubbed his chin with the back of his hand. "He's pretty good, huh?"

"Mm." I slanted a brow. "Not bad on the eyes either."

"Is that right?"

"Mm-hmm. But..." I scanned from side to side and lowered my voice to a whisper. "I hear he's engaged." I clicked my tongue. "Lucky girl."

"I hear he's the lucky one." He slipped his hands into his pockets and raised his shoulders. "Listen, I know I might be way out of my league, but maybe we can go out on a date some time."

I hopped off the elliptical. "How about tonight?"

He returned my sassy grin. "You read my mind."

It was a good thing he couldn't read mine, or he'd know what a hot mess I still was just thinking about tonight.

Maybe I wasn't the only one. The playfulness in his

eyes faded as he tucked a strand of hair back into my ponytail.

A prominent drop in my stomach followed his touch. I didn't think I'd ever taken my time with him for granted. But now that it was our last night together, I wasn't so sure. I studied his face, trying to capture a pristine copy in my memory. My stomach sank a second time. What if he was capturing memories of his own? I looked down at my sweat-dampened shirt. "Um, do you mind if I shower first?"

"I actually have to drop something off in the mail, so I'll meet you back at your place." He kissed my cheek and headed in the opposite direction toward the campus center.

I jogged to my apartment and got ready in a whirlwind. Too bad a shower couldn't have removed my tension as easily as it had the residue from my workout.

Hold it together. For him. You can do this.

My internal pep talk held up on the drive to his apartment and kept me from caving when Riley's chocolate Lab let out a series of welcome-home barks from the window. It even carried me through an hour of packing... until I reached a stack of sheet music.

I fanned through the pages. Some had so many eraser marks, the paper had almost worn through. Others had lyrics crossed out and new lines written above them. All Riley's songs. All a part of him from a chapter in our lives I wasn't ready to close.

I looked around the small space that'd been his home

for the last four years. Even though most of his things were staying, the apartment felt hollow now, barren.

Jake belly-crawled his way out of a hiding spot between the couch and a pile of clutter. He set his chin over the box and looked up at me with empathetic eyes.

I scratched his ears. "I know the feeling, buddy."

Across the room, Riley sat back on his heels and lifted a flap on another box. "I'm gonna move all these into the study so they're out of Jackson's way. I want him to be able to put out his own things. Make the place his own while he's subleasing for me."

"That's great." I held on to the sheet music without looking up.

Evidently, I didn't have to. My voice must've given me away. Already beside me, Riley dipped his head below mine. "You okay?"

I wanted to tell him about everything—my talk with Trey, the weight of his divorce, the pain of my parents' anniversary, even the nagging fears about Nashville. But I couldn't. I couldn't deepen the concern shadowing his eyes with the concern clouding mine. He needed me to be brave, not broken. "I'm fine," I said. "Just tired, I guess. Hungry."

A timer beeped from the kitchen and led him up off the floor. "Then it's a good thing dinner's ready."

Somehow, we'd made it through the last half hour evading the savory scents of the pot roast filling the apartment. Distraction at its best. But once at the kitchen table across from Riley, time stilled again. No more outlet. The unrest churning inside me had no escape except through my rambling lips. Riley's amused grin hung on to every nonstop word spewing out.

"I gotta hand it to Trev," I mumbled between bites. "The boy's earning some serious pre-wedding bonus points for whisking Jae away to work on their vows."

I swirled a carrot in the juices left on my empty plate and rubbed my feet on Jake's back beneath my chair. My talented cook studied my every move, as though savoring me more than the home-cooked meal we'd shared. What was he thinking about? I pulled my hair over my shoulder and twisted it into a tight swirl that unraveled the second I let go.

He walked around the table, his gaze never leaving mine, and extended a hand in front of my seat. "Dance with me."

I bumped my fork off the table. "What? Here?" A glance at my shoeless feet and dusty jeans trailed over to the collection of boxes around the perimeter of the living room.

Riley's smile left no room for resistance. Despite my lack of confidence in dancing, I slipped my hand into his and followed him onto our cluttered dance floor.

He closed me in his arms and in the sound of his voice as soft hums merged into lyrics. "Come find me. Under a cloudless sky, I'm waiting for you here. Dance with me, where the grass and trees absorb every last fear."

He laced his fingers through mine. "Hold me close.

Let every whim and every sorrow drift into the night holding back tomorrow. Right here now, let's fall in love underneath the stars. Dance until daylight chases away the dark."

The longer he sang, the harder I prayed the sky we'd fallen in love under would extend all the way to Nashville. I shoved back the tears rising at the thought.

We slowed until our feet barely grazed the carpet. Riley rested the side of his face to mine. "This is what I'll be thinking about when we're on the phone. How you feel in my arms right now." His gentle laughter shook against my chest. "The way you cling to me so you won't fall."

He kept me close when I tried to prove him wrong. "Not a chance," he whispered.

I balled his henley in my fingers. Amidst an undertow of unanswered questions, this much I was sure of—the love I shared with Riley had forever ruined my heart for anything less. He might've been leaving his apartment, but not his home. He'd given his heart to me, and it was the only home I needed. It would be enough.

The clock ticked against my certainty. I pointed to his bedroom, trying to stall. "We still have to go through your dresser, right?"

"It's late, Em. I should get you back. Five o'clock is going to come sooner than you think."

The tension of time pulled my muscles taut again. Riley had stayed with me until I'd fallen asleep most every night this summer. Now, I would've given anything to stay awake with him until morning.

He drew me to him again. This close, all he'd have to do was say one word, and the veneer of composure I'd feigned all evening would crack.

"We're going to be okay."

The whisper of assurance I'd learned to trust echoed Riley's promise. "I know," I whispered back. But somehow, we still had to make it through saying goodbye.

Neither of us spoke on the way home. Despite having driven the same route from his place to the campus countless times, knowing this would be the last time brought the unknown crashing into the familiar.

His Civic idled alongside the curb. My fingers whitened around my door handle. "Stay." I forced back the million exclamation points punctuating the simple word.

Riley ran his hand along the bottom of the steering wheel, taking too long to respond. He swallowed. "Not tonight." The streetlight caught a look in his eyes that almost singlehandedly dismantled my resolve not to cry in front of him. "It'd be too hard." His fingers skimmed my cheek and disappeared into my hair. "For both of us."

I scrambled for something to say—anything.

He brushed his thumb to my lips with a caress as tender as the kiss that followed. Fear fed into longing. His touch a tonic, I drank deeply. Each heart flutter. Each sensation. He withdrew slightly and then kissed me once more, making it clear why tonight would be too much, even for him.

He rested his forehead to mine. "I love you, Emma."

With his face in my hands, I drew from the last recesses of courage I had left. "I love you too." I crawled out of the car, steeled myself before turning around, and leaned through the passenger window.

He stretched across the seat. "See you in the morning."

"Bright and early." I held my weak smile in place until the glow from the streetlight fell behind me. I pushed up the walkway, through the glass door, and up the stairs.

My keys trembled in the lock. The tremor followed me inside and backed me against the cool door. And there, hidden in the shadows of my apartment, I gave in to the tears that now came without restraint.

7

UNGUARDED

A TWENTY-MINUTE DRIVE with Riley to the airport drop-off curb wasn't long enough. He curled my fingers around the keys he placed in my hand and smiled softly before opening his door.

I circled to the back of the car and laughed the second I reached the trunk. The bags he'd packed to move all the way across the country for four months were the same amount Jaycee would've packed for a four-day weekend getaway.

He set a large duffle bag on the curb, propped his guitar case against the bumper, and tossed a carry-on bag over his shoulder.

His friend Jackson parked behind us and pulled Jake's kennel off the bed of his Tundra. "Should I take him up to the check-in?"

Riley nodded. "Thanks, man. Be there in a minute."

I rocked on my heels. "Sure you don't want me to come in with you?"

"Only if you want the entire airport to see me cry."

I shoved back his teasing grin. "Cute."

A pensive look gradually replaced his laughter. Keeping his eyes on mine, he kissed my fingertips and lowered them to his chest. "You hold my heart, Em. Promise me you'll always trust this. No matter what." The urgency in his voice rivaled the jets' engines in the background.

"Always."

He dropped his bag to the ground and cupped the back of my neck. It didn't matter that his fingers had touched the skin behind my ear a hundred times, it still left me unhinged. But it was the promise in his eyes that anchored me most.

An unguarded kiss deepened and then slowed. Leaving his thumb grazing my cheek, he leaned back. "I love you."

I gripped his sleeve. "I love you too."

Following one last kiss to my forehead, he shouldered his bags, breathed in, and finally turned to the airport.

A chill that didn't belong in summertime filled my empty arms as the distance stretched between us. He disappeared behind the mirrored door, and something inside me closed.

"It's going to be okay," I whispered to myself.

I climbed into Riley's car, clenched the keys he'd

given me, and faced the rearview mirror. "How about you start with making it through today?"

***

WITH A LITTLE COAXING, time graciously agreed to pass until the night ushered in a wave of restlessness. Fourteen hours of staying preoccupied between work and classes had apparently drained the power of distraction dry. The familiar felt stilted, my routine out of sync.

The movie Trevor and Jaycee were watching in the living room hadn't kept my attention. Studying hadn't helped. And my now-rearranged dresser drawers were all but laughing at me. Could I blame them?

I crashed headfirst onto my bed. Halfway into smacking some sense into my head with my pillow, my phone rang. For a second, everything else stopped. I bolted from my prostrate position and floundered through the yards of blankets in search of my cell. A dozen highlighters rolled off the mattress onto the floor.

"Hey," I breathed into the phone now attached to my ear.

"It's kinda late to be working out."

"No, I was... um... trying to get to the phone." I wrenched a textbook out from under my back and sank my forehead into my hand. Nothing beat sounding like a pathetic teenage girlfriend.

Unlike Trevor would've, Riley skipped over the opportunity to tease me. "I'm sorry I'm just now calling.

I sort of hit the ground running as soon as I got off the plane. They don't waste any time getting you acclimated, which is great. Don't get me wrong. Just a bit over-whelming."

He had to be tired, yet his animated tone eclipsed the exhaustion I expected to hear.

"Oh and get this. Brett called during my layover in Chicago. Told me he found a girl interested in being my manager. When I got to the studio today, she was already there waiting to meet me. Can you believe that? She said she knew potential when she heard it." A self-conscious laugh merged into an exhale.

"Of course she did. Just like every other raving fan will."

"So you keep saying."

We'd save that argument for another time. "Okay, so where's my play-by-play?"

Barely taking a breath, he filled me in on the studio, the people he'd met so far, and how demanding his schedule was going to be.

"I had no idea how much was involved in recording an album," he went on. "I'm starting to wonder if we're going to be able to pull this off in only four months."

The statement caught me in the gut. Neither of us had money to fly and see each other if this ran longer. He couldn't be talking about an extension already.

Riley must've missed my reaction. Either that or was trying to divert it. "They have me staying in a one-bedroom condo less than a mile from the studio. There's a park right across the street from the neighborhood. Jake's gonna love the trail around the lake."

"Sounds perfect."

"Almost. Wouldn't mind having this girl I'm in love with here with me."

I slipped one leg out from under the other. "Then who'd take care of your car?"

He laughed. "You kidding me? I'd have that thing impounded in a second in a tradeoff for you."

Unsolicited emotion trekked up my throat. I shoved it down and straightened my blankets. "Tell me about the music industry."

"Oh, man. I'm stoked about that part the most. I couldn't have asked for a more networked manager. She knows everyone. Has connections I couldn't dream of making on my own. And she already has amazing ideas for the album."

"That's really great. I'm so happy for you." I genuinely was. The reservation weaseling itself through my rib cage had no right to be there.

"I'm sorry," he said out of nowhere.

"For what?"

"For how hard this is."

I hugged my leg to my chest. "I'm fine."

He paused, and I could almost see his eyes lifting to mine. "Em, I know your voice better than my own."

And my heart. Even when I tried to hide it.

"It's killing me not being there right now, but we can

make it through this." An audible smile filled his voice. "My valiant fiancée, remember?"

"So you keep saying."

His laugh cuddled me in place of his arms. "Are you in bed right now?"

"Yeah."

"Good. Close your eyes."

I sat up. "Why?"

"Just close your eyes," he nudged again.

My lashes fell in submission.

"Picture us on the sports field. No one else is around. It's only us, the empty field, stars above us. You there?"

I sank into the mattress with memories blanketed around me. "Yes."

"Dance with me," he whispered.

Drawing on our last night together, I danced in a world where music hung between us instead of miles. Minutes waned as he sang, but I hung on.

"I should let you get some sleep," he said.

"No, don't go yet." Even if it didn't mean the same thing as when he was here physically, I needed him to stay.

The streetlight outside my bedroom window buzzed in the silence. "Riley?"

"I'm here," he said softly.

I rolled onto my side and ran my fingers down the moonlight draped across the bed. "Will you keep singing for me?"

Another pause. "Always."

He must've put me on speakerphone. His guitar's soft cadence strummed into my bedroom with the song he sang for me the night he proposed. "Whose eyes are these, searching helplessly for joy? Eyes that stir a forgotten desire and unveil a hidden void?

"How do they awaken things, things I thought I'd lost? And revive my fragile hope in a love worth the cost?

"Why is it a mystery to me? Why does it have to be? I wonder if she sees what I see—this hidden treasure, whose eyes unveil me. If she could only see what I see."

One with the music, his voice led me into a dream where I never had to let it go.

8

PRECAUTIONARY

I CHECKED my cell while pushing open the door to the campus center. Three-thirty on the dot. Props to Professor Clarke for actually letting our business statistics class out on time this week. I wasn't up for spending another Wednesday drive into Portland, trying to dodge a speeding ticket. Even though Trey gave me grace, I preferred not to rush.

At the row of mailboxes, I did a double take inside my mail slot and caught my name written in Riley's handwriting on a folded piece of paper, taped shut.

So, this was what he'd dropped off in the mail the night before he left. Figures he knew it'd take me almost three weeks to check my mail. I pored over the short letter, devouring every word until my eyes latched onto one sentence that stood out from the others.

Remember, you're braver than you think you are.

Shaking my head, I smiled. *Think so, huh?* I held the

letter beside my best "brave" face, snapped a picture with my cell, and pulled up Instagram.

A photo on Riley's account stopped me short. An unfairly sexy blonde had her arm around his neck, a champagne glass in one hand and what looked like some kind of contract in the other. *Who—?*

"Emma," someone called from down the hallway.

I stuffed my phone in my pocket, along with my unanswered question, and turned toward the familiar voice.

A. J. stopped a few feet away at an invisible boundary line and stared at the wall of mailboxes, as if inspecting some unknown building code.

If whatever he'd caught up with me to say was going to be as uncomfortable as he appeared, I wasn't sure I wanted to know.

My clasp tightened around Riley's note. Maybe osmosis would spark the bravery he seemed to think I had.

A. J. shifted his book bag strap up to the top of his shoulder. "Trev told me about the coaching position you guys have open at the center. I met with Dean Sullivan about it. Since it'd be working with kids and sports, he said it could pass as a practicum."

My keys hit the tiles. I scrambled to swipe them from the floor without making my reaction any more obvious.

Right. At least he ignored it.

He took off his Trailblazers ball cap, forked his fingers through his hair, and slid the hat back on. "I thought I could at least go up one afternoon and check it out. It's not like I'd have to make a commitment today or anything, right?"

"Yeah," I finally said once my brain caught up to the conversation. "You can come out and spend some time with the kids. No strings attached. I promise you won't be disappointed. You'll end up receiving way more than you give." That truth hit me square in the chest the second it left my mouth. "It's not really something I can explain."

"I think I know what you mean." A. J. picked at a chip of flaking paint on the wall beside him. "Since I'm done with classes for the day, I was thinking maybe this afternoon would be a good time to go."

If his fingers weren't boring a hole into the mailboxes, his eyes certainly were. Was he waiting for my permission? Even after the summer, I wasn't used to seeing him this way. Hesitant. Unsure. It didn't fit the A. J. I knew.

I fiddled with my keys. "Um, today would be great. I'll call Trey and let him know you'll be by at some point. I'd offer you a ride, but Wednesdays are the nights I work till nine. Doubt you'd want to stick around that late."

"Yeah, yeah, no problem. I'll just, uh, see you later, then." He shuffled backward without glancing at me for longer than a second or two at a time. A short distance away, he turned and jogged through the crowd toward the gym.

Had anyone else noticed how awkward that was? See,

this was why I hadn't asked him about the position to begin with. He'd make the perfect coach. The kids would adore him. And a sports program might up the chances of us getting funding. But what if the strain between us was too much?

I held on to Riley's note and his belief in me. Guess we were about to find out how brave I really was. That reminded me... I shot him a quick text on my way outside.

It wasn't that long of a walk back to my apartment. Still, I'd checked my phone for a reply five times before reaching my door. Where was he? And was that his manager in the picture with him?

I jerked the thought to a halt before it ran off down a rabbit hole. The last thing Riley needed was for me to be acting like some clingy high school senior worried about her boyfriend who'd gone off to college without her. He was busy, probably needing space with everything being new.

Okay, so after three weeks, maybe it wasn't still *new* new, but I refused to be *that* girl. Tucking my phone in my pocket, I toed off my shoes by the heels.

Jaycee sprinted down the hall, muttering to herself the way she did when she was on a mission. I followed her into our room. A sweater sailed from the closet and landed on the corner of her mattress beside an overflowing suitcase.

"Jae? What's going on?"

She peeked out from behind the closet door. "Oh,

sorry. I'm not ignoring you. Just trying to make sure I don't forget anything." She pushed her hair off her face and left her hand on her forehead. "If I get stuck in rush hour traffic, I'm gonna kill Professor Greaves for keeping us late today."

Apparently, I wasn't the only one with professor problems.

"I thought you weren't going home until Friday?"

Jaycee rolled up a pair of jeans and stuffed them inside the perimeter of her bag. "My dad called. Said Mom's been sick for the last week. I thought I better go home a few days early to help get everything ready for Saturday."

She held a black cocktail dress in front of her to examine it with her fashion meter, no doubt. "Sweet Sixteen parties are kind of a big deal at my house. I know it's killing my mom not to be at her best."

"Well, don't stress. You're the queen of planning parties. Everything will turn out perfectly. Mandy's gonna love it."

She stopped midstream in one of her trips between her dresser and suitcase with a pair of sparkly heels dangling from her fingers. Her restless expression yielded to a smile. "Thanks."

I flopped onto my bed while she assembled sets of earrings and necklaces to go with each of her outfits. "Is Trevor going with you?"

"He's coming down after class on Friday. So, he'll make the party at least." She jumped on top of her suitcase to force it to close. "You sure you'll be okay while I'm gone?"

"What will I do without my mom-away-from-home?"

She tossed her pillow at me.

"I'll be fine, Jae. I have three classes plus my internship. Think I should be able to keep myself busy."

A *ding* lit up my cell with Riley's delayed text.

Booked all day. Will call at nine.

I folded the pillow under my arms. Sometimes staying busy didn't help.

With her hands hovering over her bags, Jaycee gave her packing job one last assessment. "You should invite Becky and Ashlea over one night if you get bored."

We looked at each other for a split second before busting out laughing.

"Okay, maybe not Ashlea," she said. "But seriously, call me if you need anything. We won't be that far away."

"Stop worrying."

"Says the girl who waited two days to tell me she was in a fire."

"I wasn't *in* the fire."

Her cocked brow dared me to get into semantics with her.

That was one fight I knew better than to start. "I know where you're coming from, but it's been quiet at the center. Promise. The only thing you need to be worrying about is having a great time with your family." I set the pillow aside and met her by her dresser. "Give your parents hugs for me and tell that baby sister of yours to stop growing up so fast."

"Right?" She slid her arm through her toiletry bag straps. "We're getting old, Em. It's sad but true."

Laughing, I lugged her bulging suitcase down the stairwell. Each drop onto the next stair thudded louder than the last. The thing weighed a ton. "You sure you're coming back?"

"If I weren't, you'd be carrying a lot more than one suitcase right now."

We reached the curb the same time as Trevor.

"You gonna be okay with your partner in crime missing?" He toyed with the top corner of Jaycee's jeans. "There's no permanent damage, right? I mean, it had to be painful separating two people attached at the hip."

Our synchronized eye rolling perpetuated his amusement.

"You know, Trev, I had the strangest notion the other day that maybe by senior year that joke would get old."

His mischievous grin ruled out that possibility. "You could use a little humor in your life."

I replicated his grin. "That *is* why I keep you around."

Ignoring my sarcasm, he whisked Jaycee into his arms. "I'm good for a few things."

Oh, brother. Jaycee giggled, and I took my cue. I could only handle seeing so much affection before I had to excuse myself from the premises.

"Have a great time. Drive safely." I waved goodbye and headed back up the walkway to our apartment.

"Oh, Em," she called. "I left you something in the bathroom. A little precautionary measure. You know, to keep you focused."

No telling what that meant. Did I want to know?

Curiosity got the best of me. With only a few minutes before I had to leave, I stopped in the bathroom. A train of colored sticky notes lined the right-hand edge of the mirror, one underneath the other. *YOUR DAILY PEP TALK*, the first one read in all caps, followed by smaller print underneath it.

Read out loud:

I am courageous.

I am not alone.

I am loved.

I will make it through.

Leave it to Jaycee to make me laugh while getting teary-eyed at the same time. Precautionary measures? I shook my head but couldn't blame her for being on guard after my brief exile into depression last year.

Following her instructions, I repeated each declaration out loud on my drive in to work. As ridiculous as I probably looked and sounded, professing the words made them a little easier to believe. At least, until the black Acura parked outside the center stoked a reminder of another fire waiting for me. I'd invited A. J. into the only thing besides Riley that held my heart.

9

ECLIPSED

I GLANCED up from my desk toward the sunset sneaking through the office's front window. The same cluster of guys A. J. and I'd seen weeks ago guarded the street corner across from the center like a pack of dogs defending their territory. The tallest one stared right at me. His expression tore through the window and held my lungs in a vise grip against my chair.

"Emma."

My knees clanked into the bottom of my drawer. Biting back the pain, I turned as Trey unhooked his jacket from the coat stand in the entryway.

"I'm really sorry I have to dip out early. More paperwork to sign." He kept his tone light, but the burden of his divorce wore through.

My heart ached for him. I tucked the voicemail messages I'd written down earlier under my keyboard. He didn't need to deal with bill collectors right now.

"As much as my attorney's charging by the hour, you'd think he could get it all done in one shot." Trey pressed down his coat collar. "You know the difference between a lawyer and a mosquito?"

"Same thing as the last five times you told this joke?"

He laughed his husky laugh. "Still true. I'm tellin' ya, they'll suck the life out of you." He jostled his keys from his pocket. "You sure you're good with closing up? I know I told Riley I'd look out—"

"I'm good, Trey. I promise." I stole another glance behind me toward the window. No sign of the earlier loiterers. Nothing but a few pieces of loose trash blowing down the vacant street.

I ruffled through a pile of outstanding bills on my desk. "I have this last stack of invoices to key, and then I'll be heading out myself."

A. J. stood on the outskirts of the room near the back door with his focus glued to his Nikes.

Trey looked from him to me and cleared his throat. I hadn't expected A. J. to stay this long. I wasn't about to ask him to stay after everyone else left.

Trey must've sensed my hesitation and evidently had no qualms speaking up for me. "A. J., you mind sticking around until she locks up?"

He raised his head like a toy soldier coming to life from a wooden pose. "I'm happy to stay and walk you to your car, Emma."

I saw his lips move. Knew it was A. J.'s voice, but it

sounded wrong. Too formal. Too obligatory. For his sake, I wanted to pretend I'd be fine on my own. Even more, I wished Riley were here instead.

A. J. blinked away from the death stare Trey had homed in on him. "I should probably stick around anyway. Clean up the court a little. Prep for next week."

"All right, then." Trey tucked on his leather Newsboy cap. "Time for me to hit the road before my lawyer finds another way to prey on my wallet." Feigning a look of horror, he hummed the *Jaws* theme on his way out.

If he could keep things light with what he was going through, so could I.

Smiling, I rested my arms over the papers on my desk and faced A. J. "Thanks for staying. And for coming today. Taking time out to ball with the kids meant a lot to them."

They already adored him. I saw it as soon as I got in —a huddle of boys soaking up his pointers as if he'd been handing out twenty-dollar bills. One glimpse of their connection was enough to confirm he belonged here. My heart swelled with hope—for them, for the center.

"It was fun." Though honest, A. J.'s short-lived smile couldn't overthrow the detached look in his eyes. He shuffled in place, hands in his pockets, visible tension plaguing him now that we were together. Alone. Again.

He stopped over the threshold leading to the basketball court. "I'll be out back. Holler when you're ready to go."

Even if we couldn't be as close as we were before, I'd hoped working together might at least bring the camaraderie back and lessen the heated tension.

The door shut behind him with the obvious answer.

Stillness settled across all four corners of the office. It seemed darker than it had a minute ago. I turned on my desk lamp, restricted my vision to the 3x2 foot space on my desk, and focused on why I was there.

Sometime between finishing one stack of bills and preparing another one for tomorrow, the night had absorbed the last slivers of daylight. I stretched my neck from side to side. It had to be close to when Riley said he'd call. I checked the clock. *Five after nine?*

I clicked on my cell. The screen stayed black. I clicked it again. Nothing. *You've got to be kidding me.* I scoured through my desk drawers for a charger. Of course not. Just perfect.

Purse in hand, I pushed up from my desk. It had been hard enough getting used to talking with Riley less frequently than I'd expected we'd be able to. I wasn't about to miss the one time we got to connect each night.

I stopped long enough to peek out the back door. No sight of A. J. "I'm running to my car for a sec," I called anyway.

A muffled, "okay," trailed back, probably from inside the utility closet.

I made my way to the exit and down the dark walkway. Up ahead, a coarse rustling noise followed the shadow of something flickering in the streetlight. A pang of caution stopped me short. I clinched my purse strap. Waited. When nothing but my ridiculously erratic breathing filled the silence, I crept around the building into a gust of wind.

Something flew straight at me. My heart leapt far enough up my throat to block my scream from escaping. Arms flailing, I fended off the object until it fell to the ground, defeated. I shoved my mangled hair out of the way and stared my menacing enemy head-on.

A foil hamburger wrapper. Wow. I really needed to pull it together. Another burst of wind swept the piece of trash down the street, taking my unwarranted fear with it. I climbed into Riley's car, grabbed the charger from the glove box, and slipped it into my purse while hustling back.

If I didn't get to talk to him until tomorrow because of this, I'd—

The pavement gripped my shoes halfway across the street. Two faces emerged from the shadows. Their perversely intoxicated expressions sent an instant and paralyzing fear up my body.

No breath.

No sound.

The tallest guy advanced with a look taunting me to try to outrun him. A stocky one flanked his left side at a lag.

My pulse out rang the crude banter rebounding from guy to guy closing in on me. Riley's keys dug into my palm with the pain of his absence. I stumbled backward with nowhere to run, no way to steady my heart rate.

"A. J.," I yelled.

My heels scraped into the brick wall, the rising fog trapping me in place. I couldn't wait for A. J. My mind raced. I had to do something—anything.

The guy closest to me made the first move.

Adrenaline surged. I stomped the assailant's foot, twisted his arm, and maneuvered out of his hold. I kneed the second one in the groin and sprang for Riley's car.

Someone yanked me backward like I was a doll. My purse slammed onto the concrete as I crashed into the wall.

The tall one straightened, still wheezing from my knee's impact. Slow, dark strides trampled over my hope of escaping. Right in front of me, he smiled. Cigarette-tainted breath poured into my face and onto the ring of sweat soaking the top of my shirt.

"A. J.," I screamed again.

A hand covered my mouth and shoved the back of my head harder into the bricks.

"T, let's bail," a third kid called from a significant distance behind the other two.

The apparent leader jetted around. "Go up to Twenty-Third Street and make sure we don't get no unexpected guests." His voice held authority. The kind I doubted anyone in his crew would test.

Staring at me, the kid didn't move at first. The look

on his face blended into the darkness stretching behind him. My eyes screamed for him to intervene.

"Dee!" the leader shouted this time.

The kid flinched. Without a word, he jogged backward, turned, and ran in the opposite direction—away from the center and away from his chance to help me.

The leader grabbed my chin and forced me to look at him. The intent in his gaze seeped through my clothes and crawled over my skin. One flex of power, and he could rob Riley and me of everything we'd been saving for each other.

Tears burned.

God, please.

His dark eyes smoldered above a sinister smirk. Glancing at his friend, he ran his finger under my necklace. "Looks like señorita gots more than one pearl to give us."

I spit in his face with all the vehemence I had in me. Seething, he wiped his cheek with his sleeve. I tried to break free, but he blocked my arms. The corner of his ring cut into my chin and ignited another scream for help. He pounded my whole body into the wall again. I reached for the back of my head. The scene swirled. Coarse bricks scraped through my shirt as I slid down the building.

Consciousness drifted. A third figure emerged. Had that kid come back? Muffled voices trailed the hazy shapes scuffling around me. A wounded yelp followed a sharp *snap*. Someone dropped to the ground. Movements blurred. A second person fell a foot away.

In the darkness, it turned quiet. Too quiet.

Just as someone knelt in front of me, everything went black.

10

BROKEN

MY BODY, limp and weighted, hung above someone's footsteps. Tops of buildings swayed from side to side next to the clouds. A wave of nausea pulled my eyes shut again. I tightened my clasp around my carrier's shirt, no strength to resist.

He lowered me into a car and leaned over to fasten my seat belt.

I pulled him close enough for his face to come into focus. "A. J." Relief swelled. My fingers slid from his cheek down his cotton shirt.

His chest rose and fell above a pounding heart. He lifted my hands from his body and set them in my lap. "You're safe now. Try to be still. I'm getting you out of here." Though his words soothed, his voice pulsed with adrenaline.

The driver's door opened and closed. He shifted the

car into gear and gunned it down the abandoned street. An interstate sign passed above us as he pulled out his cell.

"Who are you calling?"

"911—"

"No." I tugged his arm and swatted his cell to the floorboard.

"What are you doing?"

"Don't. Please." My body shook with my voice. "We can't." My eyelids fell again to shut out the blurred trees passing along the edge of the highway.

The car swerved into the right lane. "I'm taking you to the hospital."

I shook my head. "No. Just… just take me home." I set a hand on his arm. "Please."

He let out a hoarse exhale. His blinker snapped on, throttle picking up. He reached for his cell again.

"A. J.—"

"I'm calling Trey. Somebody needs to go lock up the center." He must've read the look of concern on my face. "Don't worry. Those guys are long gone by now."

Please be right. I settled back into my seat. My eyes stayed shut until the car stopped moving. In front of my apartment, he unbuckled my seat belt and helped me out of the car.

I stumbled to my feet. "I can make it to the door."

He caught my elbow when I slanted to one side. "Don't be so stubborn. If you won't let me take you to a doctor, at least let me carry you inside."

The distance from the curb to the door stretched farther than it should have. I nodded.

He lifted me in both arms into a source of safety I craved more than I realized. Warm and comforting, his muscles contracted under my back and legs each time he mounted another stair.

In my room, he drew back my covers and laid me on the mattress. Everything about him exuded strength. No wonder he didn't have any problem taking down those two guys.

Had he been hurt at all? Before he could straighten, I grabbed his hand. He winced softly. "A. J., your knuckles."

"It's nothing." He slipped his fingers out of mine and gently dabbed a tissue to my chin.

Evidently, he wasn't the only one who'd been running on adrenaline. Now that it was beginning to drain, pain spiked in its place. I steadied his hand, pulled the bloody tissue away, and cupped the base of my neck.

His brow furrowed. "I'll be right back."

A minute later, he returned with a glass of water and a couple of pills. "Here."

"Thanks." I sat up to swallow the pain meds. A rush of lightheadedness passed but didn't block out flashes of the night replaying through my mind. I started to get out of bed. "My phone."

A. J. eased me back down. "I got it." He retrieved it from my purse and slipped it onto the charger next to my bed. Shaking his head, he swept a strand of knotted hair off my face. "Try to rest."

He'd almost reached the bedroom door when I sat up again. "Wait," I called. "Thank you. For not leaving me at the office alone tonight. I don't know what would've happened..." I shuddered at the possibility.

He kept his back toward me and his hand over the light switch. Looking over his shoulder, A. J. smiled softly, then turned off the light.

The weight of my eyelids took over. For the second time that night, everything went black.

THE MORNING BROUGHT a barrage of aching reminders of a night I wanted to forget. Fatigue plagued my shoulders. Trying to sit up sent me right back down. Vague dreams of A. J. taking care of me gradually faded behind the light coming through the window. I squinted at my clock. *11:00?*

I threw back my covers and pulled my cell off the charger. No missed calls. Only a text from after midnight.

Sorry, Em. Last-minute rehearsal ran longer than I thought. Don't want to wake you. Will call in the A.M.

Residual body aches didn't compare to the pain of missing Riley. My thumb hovered over the Instagram app. Something in me hesitated, but the need to see his face ultimately overpowered any reservation about what else I might see.

He'd posted five new pictures, all from the recording studio, where the people huddled around him looked like old friends instead of new acquaintances—including a manager hanging by his side like she was afraid to lose him as much as I was beginning to be.

I winced, more from the runaway thought than the dull ache spreading up my neck. Either way, another dose of pain meds definitely wasn't a bad idea.

I grabbed my water, forced my legs over the side of the bed, and steadied myself against the chair until my vision caught up with my movement. I traipsed toward the kitchen, groping the wall as a buffer until my feet skidded to a stop in front of the living room.

A. J. had stayed the night?

Fragments from what I thought had been a dream became clear now. He'd checked in on me each hour, probably worried I had a concussion.

A lump mounted in my throat.

Stretched out on the couch, his strength and stoicism lay transformed into a scene of serenity—one I didn't want to disturb. Dust particles floated in rays of sunlight streaming through the blinds like laser beams to tiptoe over without triggering an alarm.

I knelt beside him and studied his face. Thankfully, it didn't appear he'd been injured in the fight other than the scrapes on his knuckles. The stubble on his cheeks had surpassed a five o-clock shadow hours ago, but he'd lost his usual tension lines. If I woke him, they'd return the moment he realized he was still here, alone with me.

Unless something had changed. I'd caught a glimpse of my old friend in my room last night. Maybe I hadn't lost him completely.

I rested my fingertips to his face. "A. J.," I whispered.

He darted straight into the air and scanned the perimeter of the room, as if a drill sergeant had awoken him in the middle of the night. It only took one look at his face to see boot camp would've been his preference. His cheeks matched the color of the much-too-short maroon blanket he'd pulled off the top of the couch last night.

He scratched the back of his hair. "I meant to slip out before you woke up."

I tottered to my feet and shuffled into the chair behind me. "Thanks for staying. That was really sweet of you."

He tossed the throw pillows into their designated positions in either corner of the couch. "How are you feeling?"

I cradled the bottom of my head. "Nothing taking Advil for a few days won't fix."

"Good, good," he said while striding toward the front door. He stopped, already on the other side of the entry-way, and looked behind him. His eyes met mine. For the briefest moment, they were as genuine as they'd been last night. "We should file a police report."

I met him at the door. "I'm not going to jeopardize our chance of getting funding. That's probably exactly what those punks want. You've seen them on that street corner. Like they've been staking it out or something." I tucked one arm under the other. "I don't know what their personal vendetta is, but we can't let them win."

A tendon in his neck twitched. "This isn't a game."

"I know—"

"Do you?" His jaw pulled tight.

I blanched at his tone. Couldn't he see I was trying to do the right thing for the center? We couldn't afford any bad press right now.

Face softening, he started toward me but backed up instead. "I'm sorry. I gotta go." He hustled down the staircase and through the exit without another word. The draft soaring in his absence stole my rationale for expecting anything more.

I locked up, sank into the corner of the couch, and balled one of the accent pillows in my lap. He'd only stayed because he was that kind of guy. I shouldn't have thought we were friends again just because—

My cell rang into the stillness.

"Good morning," Riley said. "How's my dance partner doing?"

His sweet voice washed over me. "Better now." If I closed my eyes, I could nearly feel the security of his arms.

"Me too. Hearing your voice... Man, I miss you, Em. Jake and I are about to pull a *Ferris Bueller's Day Off* stunt. I'm telling you, he snaps at my fingers if I even mention seeing you without him. I'm gonna have to get a tighter leash before January comes around. No way that dog's getting kisses before I do."

Our laughter triggered tears too close to the surface.

"Hey, you all right?"

Flashes from last night stormed in and ignited a storm of its own inside me. I wanted to tell him what had happened. I wanted him right here to hold me while I cried until I'd drained every last fear from my heart. But if I let him hear how shaken I was, concern—or worse, guilt—would drive him back home. I wouldn't risk that. I wanted to love him, not worry him.

"I just miss you is all. How are things there?" I quickly added to hide the sound of my voice cracking.

"Amazing. I don't know how I didn't fall in love with Nashville the last time I lived here. You can hear live music from almost anywhere. The city holds this constant energy. Not sure how to explain it. It makes me feel… *alive*. You know what I mean?"

"Your voice kinda gives me a clue."

"Sorry. It's obnoxious, isn't it?"

I drew swirls over the microfiber cushion with my finger. "No more than Trevor's."

"Ooh, now I know it's bad. I'll try to tone it down. It's sort of hard to do here. Everything's so… vibrant, I guess is the right word."

"Better than being in Portland?"

His pause ached. "Just different."

I squeezed the throw pillow and clenched back the irrational response fighting to uproot my faith. Riley came to life behind the microphone. I saw it in his pictures. He was meant to be there. And I was genuinely happy for him.

"Told you you'd thrive in every part of your career." I lifted my glass of water to my forehead. "How's the album coming?"

"I can't wait for you to hear it. The quality is so much better than that demo I made. Jess and I've been working nonstop to make sure we get a few great singles out of it."

"Jess?"

"My manager. I told you about her, remember?"

I downed the rest of my water and managed a garbled, "Mm-hmm."

"It's a good thing one of us knows the ins and outs of the industry. I'd be lost without her. Half the time, I feel like I'm barely keeping up with it all. No wonder there's a coffee shop at every intersection. Jaycee'd be in heaven." He laughed, sounding like he'd already hit up five shops before he called. "Though, she might've met her match. Jess drinks the stuff around the clock. Black. I don't know how she stomachs it."

She probably didn't, if the size of her waist in the pictures was any indication.

"If I have to keep up this crazy schedule too much

longer, I might end up drinking mine black too." A note of exhaustion seeped through his animation. "I'm sorry I couldn't call last night. Nick pulled a last-minute rehearsal. We were there half the night. I keep telling myself all the pressure will be worth it." Another sigh. "Wish you could be here, Em."

But I wasn't there.

I didn't respond. Couldn't. If I opened my mouth, I'd shatter the flimsy blockade shielding him from the geyser of emotions building since last night.

Not that staying quiet helped. My lingering pause sent a proverbial red flag soaring through the phone line.

"What is it?" he said. "What's wrong?"

Everything. "Nothing." The angst from what happened probably had me overly worked up. "I'm just dealing with some stress from work."

"Do you need me to come back—?"

"No." Even if he thought giving up this opportunity wouldn't be that much of a sacrifice now, he'd end up regretting it down the road.

"Break's over, Preston," someone in the background called.

"Just a sec," he said away from the phone. "Sorry, Emma. I gotta get back to rehearsal. We'll talk more later, 'kay?" He paused again. And this time, I felt the gravity of his feelings through every breath. "I love you."

"I love you too." I willed away my tears. "Always."

I pulled my legs up and wrapped my arms around them. With A. J. gone and Riley's voice no longer nearby, the emptiness in the apartment closed in. I hugged my legs tighter and grasped for the courage the darkened street corner had stolen last night. Because whether or not I wanted to face it, the fight before me wasn't anywhere close to being over.

11

UNSTABLE

I THOUGHT LYING low for a week would help. Thought the distraction of classes might overshadow the images clawing into my thoughts every time I closed my eyes. But the second I pulled into the parking spot across from the center, dark memories seeped into the car and held me against my seat the way that guy had held me against the bricks.

I gripped the wheel and prayed until the flashes faded. My fingers unclenched a breath at a time. Resolve replaced fear as I straightened the single pearl along the necklace Dad gave me. I'd kept my promise to him. Found myself, a sense of calling. And my internship was tied to it all. I wouldn't let my attackers undermine that promise. Staying away from the center for a while sufficed as a compromise after Trey had carped about my decision not to file a police report, but a week was long enough.

Breathing in, I lifted my chin and opened the door.

Trey peered up from a filing cabinet when I stepped into the office. "Welcome back."

"Thanks." At my desk, I dropped my purse in my drawer and appraised the piles overtaking my workstation. "Did you survive without me?"

A. J. passed through the office on his way to the basketball court with a kid hanging from each arm. "Like you have to ask."

Trey's throaty laugh seconded A. J.'s response.

Grinning at the pair of them, I thumbed through my inbox. "Any word from my last grant request?" The flaps of a tri-folded letter lifted open from underneath a stack of bills. I scanned the first two sentences for the foreboding, *unfortunately,* but it wasn't there. My heart jumped. "Trey, I can't believe this. They're interested."

"Were."

I looked up at him. "What?"

"They *were* interested. Even came by earlier in the week. I thought all was a go, but it seems an anonymous call convinced them otherwise." He eased the classroom door closed.

Anonymous? My hand fell to my lap. "What'd they say?"

Trey slumped on the corner of his desk with the same heaviness pressing me deeper into my chair. "That there'd been a rape on the premises."

Heat climbed my face. "What?" Those guys who attacked me were behind this, weren't they? But why?

And how in the world did they know who we were contacting?

"If our staff can't assure their own safety, how can we provide a stabilizing environment for the kids?" He folded his arms. "It's a compelling argument."

Blood hammered in my ears. "It's manipulation. Not to mention a lie."

"Doesn't matter. The damage is already done."

I crumpled the letter into a ball. "I can't believe I've been lying low for nothing. These guys have some balls. And does the foundation live in a bubble? Obviously, there's going to be danger and instability. That's why we're here. To help. Do they think you picked this neighborhood for the view?"

Trey crossed the room and set a calming hand on my tense shoulder.

My chest deflated into the back of the chair. "They didn't even give us a chance to explain what really happened."

"Which is why we probably wouldn't have wanted to partner with them anyway."

I studied his honest eyes. "Do you ever lose hope?"

He craned his neck back with a chuckle. "Not if I can help it." He squeezed my shoulder. "It's all about keeping perspective."

"I'll be sure to try that."

His laughter followed him into the classroom.

I didn't care who those creeps thought they were. This wasn't over. I lugged my notepad out from my drawer and keyed the last organization from my grant list into Google. The Success Foundation. Right here in Portland. Surely, they'd understand.

After the printer inked the page with my plea to invest in the center's mission, I set the envelope in the outgoing mailbox and exhaled a prayer. *Please be the one.*

After spending almost an hour clearing a path to the bottom of my desk, I stretched my chair's tilt mechanism to the max. An echo of A. J.'s banter with the boys out back joined the laughter Trey was instigating in the other room. In the middle of the two, I took in the sounds that made this home for all of us. We were going to be okay. We had to be.

I stopped inside the doorway to the classroom on my way to file a stack of paperwork. The kids' energy pushed the room's borders as effortlessly as they pushed the borders around my heart. Leaning into the jamb, I shook my head and grinned. *Perspective.*

Laughs and hollers erupted from a group of boys at a middle table. A single face ushered into focus. The innocent smiles in the classroom clashed against the image of the sinister ones that had branded me with wordless taunts.

The papers in my hand hit the floor and sprawled across the tiles. In one paralyzing sweep, fear ripped through the hope that my nightmares were over.

Heat flooded my cheeks with the memory of the attacker's hot breath on my face. I cupped the base of my head. The imprint of the brick's abrasive texture crawled over my skin as if it were happening all over again.

The room slanted. What was he doing here? Did they send him to make sure I kept my mouth shut? To find an inside way to finish what they started? Is that how they were finding out who our grant contacts were?

I clutched the trim to keep my balance. Something urged me not to stare, but I couldn't look away.

Centered in a group of kids his age, the guy who left me in his friends' hands that night laughed and joked as any normal high schooler would.

He shucked off a black jacket and spun the flattened bill of a bright red ball cap to the side of his head. While one of his friends dropped a beat, he drummed a pair of pencils over a notebook. And I simply stared. Not at a hardened assailant. At a regular teenager.

He glanced up from the table. His chair dropped to all four legs. He looked away, his olive cheeks turning a shade darker than his hat. Yet even in such a short connection, he couldn't hide the shame harbored inside eyes too young to carry it.

The pull of two irreconcilable images gripped my heart in a game of tug-of-war I didn't want to play. I had to get out of there.

The door clipped my shoulder on my rush into the hallway. Bracing the water fountain with one hand, I dabbed cool water on my face with the other. *Breathe.* But the trauma from that night kept twisting inside me —the anger, the fear. It backed me into the wall. *Brave?*

My cell trembled in my hand. If I could just hear his voice, maybe I'd believe it.

"Riley Preston. Leave a message."

I ended the call before it beeped, hating that he was so far away, so unreachable.

His ringtone jarred the silence. I immediately swiped the screen. "Riley."

Blaring music assaulted my eardrum.

"Em?" he hollered. "I'm at a concert. Too loud in here. Can I call you later?"

An inward wince wrung all sound from my voice.

"Emma? You all right?"

Was I?

"Hold on," he yelled. "Let me go outside."

"No, it's fine." My heart followed my foot down the wall to the floor. "Everything's fine. We'll talk later."

"You sure?" he yelled once more.

I swallowed. "Yes, later." Always later. I hung up. The stress of everything going on weighed my phone to my side.

Someone approached from the opposite corner. I flinched again. The same alarm from seeing him in the classroom fueled the heat already spreading through my body.

He raised his palms. "It's not what you think." His accent lined up with the Puerto Rican flag tattooed on his left shoulder. He eased closer.

My pulse thundered. I backed away, but he kept approaching.

"T went too far. I'm not like... I just wanna—"

I turned to run and stumbled straight into A. J.

He steadied me by my wrists, moved me behind him, and pinned the kid against the wall with a forearm to his throat. "If you *ever* so much as *think* about touching her..."

The corners of the kid's eyes sagged the same way they had the night I first saw him.

I grabbed A. J.'s heaving shoulders without understanding why. "Stop."

A. J. slackened his hold, but an undeniable warning radiated in the movement.

The kid hunched over his knees until he regained his air supply. Straightening, he flicked a terse nod at A. J., like he respected his reaction.

Trey appeared at the other end of the hall. "Dee."

The kid looked between all three of us, then pounded through the side exit with his head down.

"Dee?" Trey called after him again, but he didn't slow.

The door swung behind him and caught a spray can that had fallen out of his backpack onto the threshold. Clashing metals clanked into each other. The *bang* shuddered down the hall with waves of a question that wouldn't let me go.

What was he doing here?

REWRITTEN

I BOLTED STRAIGHT UP in bed. Damp sheets fell to my lap. Another nightmare—same as the last two nights after running into Dee in that hallway.

Vivid memories of the attack clung to the shadows in my room and stole the ease of falling asleep that I had found in Riley's arms all summer long.

A month apart confirmed days would move forward, with or without my heart. I'd learned that much last year. But now, even dreams lost the solace they used to provide.

My cell's blue notification light blinked against the white ceiling. I tucked the phone under my pillow to block the glow. Not sure why I bothered. Jaycee had probably grown accustomed to seeing it as much as I had begun to.

Most mornings now greeted me the same way: my phone by my side, waiting to relay another of Riley's apologetic messages for calling after I'd already gone to sleep. I'd tried to play it cool when our talks had gradually dwindled to once a day. But missing his calls altogether now was beginning to take its toll. I bundled my blankets and strained to find a hint of his faded scent left on them.

Jaycee reached across her nightstand and tapped her halogen lamp to life. "Don't worry, you guys will figure it out."

"Not if his schedule has anything to do with it." How was he keeping up with these insane hours?

Jaycee slipped her feet out of the covers and untwisted an eye mask from her hair. "It's just gonna take a little time. Long distance relationships are hard."

People shouldn't be able to wake up coherent enough to rattle off adages.

"Thanks for pointing that out." I trudged to my dresser.

My phone buzzed. Jaycee pinched back a loaded comment and flitted out of the room to give me some privacy.

"You'll never guess who I met with," Riley said the second I answered. He waited, suspense mounting. "Tim McGraw! Can you believe it?"

"That's awesome." I slid into my desk chair and curled the corners of my textbook pages back and forth.

"I'm sorry I couldn't take your call last night. Jess managed to get me an interview with Tim, and I only had a half hour to drain him of all his advice for a new artist."

Giddiness would've overpowered his voice if shards of exhaustion weren't splintering through. "This is crazy, right? Sometimes, I'll be at the studio and think, this can't be real. This can't really be happening."

"It's not crazy. I told you you'd thrive there." Of course things would work out for him. He was where he belonged. I hadn't stopped believing that. But while his future was coming together perfectly, mine felt like it was coming apart.

I immediately wanted to kick the thought and all my unwarranted doubts right out of the room. I shouldn't have been wavering over any of this.

"Em?"

"Hmm?"

"I asked how work was going."

I shifted in my seat. It killed me not to be able to talk to him about what was going on. It was hard enough trying to keep it on the down low from people I barely knew. Hiding it from my fiancé was pure torture.

"Oh, sorry." I fought to refocus. "We're still in the red, but I'm hoping we have a potential grant lead." As long as those creeps didn't find a way to sabotage this one too.

"If you and Trey have anything to do with it, it'll work out."

His words weaved a knot in my throat. I couldn't fail these kids.

"Listen, I gotta run. Jess just pulled up. We have a breakfast date."

My heel slipped off the seat. "A date?"

"With some bigwigs. Business stuff."

Stuff that was bonding them. The knot expanded down my chest.

"You okay?"

"Yeah." Where was my voice? I clamped a hand over my knee to stop my foot from tapping a hole in the carpet. Useless. I pushed off the chair and paced instead. "It's just... how closely do you and Jess work together exactly?"

In spite of my gritted teeth attempting to hold it back, the question sputtered out with all the immature implications tangled around it.

"Emma." Audible disappointment raked over the sound of my name. "Do you honestly think Jessica—or anyone else for that matter—could hold a candle next to you?"

A candle only burned for so long.

Unrelenting, the voice of doubt I'd banished last year sent old insecurities branching through me like a ruthless weed. Questions flared. A barrage of noise flooded my heart. Wave after wave beat against the quiet whisper in my spirit.

Enough!

Someone slammed on a car horn in the background. Riley heaved a sigh. "I have to go."

And I had to stay. Fight or no fight, there was no

changing the distance between us. "I love you," I said anyway.

"I love you too, Em." He paused again, and I could almost hear his silent prayer. "Please don't ever doubt that."

I clung to his promise. I trusted him. It wasn't that. God had brought us together. I was sure of it. Same as I was sure He was working out the dreams He'd placed in each of our hearts. But what if those dreams caused Riley to outgrow his old life? Maybe I should've laid down my own. Gone with him instead of staying and interning here. Had I made the wrong choice?

The kids' faces swelled to mind in the middle of a war I didn't understand. No, it was the right decision to stay for them. But what did that mean for Riley and me? Our dreams were supposed to knit us together, not separate us.

Pacing didn't silence the questions. I stopped in the middle of the room. My lashes fell. *Father, where are You in all of this?*

Instead of answers, I heard the whisper of a song. One of my dad's. No lyrics, only a melody—achingly beautiful chords capable of stretching into the parts of my heart nothing else could reach.

Tears rose. I grabbed the lonely guitar stashed in the corner of the room and sat on my bed. I wanted to play Dad's song. Wanted to remember, to feel it again, but I couldn't. Couldn't play. Couldn't connect. My guitar used to bring me comfort. Now, it felt out of place no matter how I positioned it across my lap.

A soft patter on the window multiplied into a steady flow of raindrops tap-dancing down the pane. I stared at the reflection trapped in the glass. The same emptiness from last year bordered dangerously close to reclaiming a hold over my eyes. Why was I failing again? I'd changed. Grown. I should've been stronger than this.

I returned my guitar to the corner, hid my weakness behind it, and resorted to the unemotional companion of studying instead. *Focus.*

The bedroom door creaked open. "Enough with the books," Jaycee said on her way in. "It's Friday." She peeked at the time. "Okay, I guess you can study a little longer, but we're going out tonight." She raised a hand to cut off my scripted objection. "No buts."

At this point, I was game for anything that would keep me from falling apart at the seams. I left the frayed mess of runaway emotions on my desk and clambered up from my chair. "Where are we going?"

"Nuts and Jolts."

The place Riley and I first met. Fabulous.

She fanned through the hangers in her closet. "A night out with your friends is exactly what you need." She tied a glittery scarf over her plain jean jacket and turned with a brown ankle boot in either hand. "It'll be fun."

Fun. I mulled over the word and waited for it to settle

into a place of familiarity. As long as I was with my friends, I could have fun. Even at Nuts and Jolts, right?

As usual, Jaycee seemed to interpret my expression. She crossed the room, wrapped her arms around me from behind, and sank her chin onto my shoulder. "No one expected this to be easy for either of you." The compassionate eyes looking at me in the mirror didn't hold a hint of chastisement. "Just don't lose sight of the things you know to be true."

I stared past her, temporarily transported to the front of the airport. "That's what Riley told me the day he left. Made me promise to trust his love no matter what. I never thought that'd be a hard promise to keep." I pulled a cream sweater over my head and tried to tame my hair and my voice, but the question rattling my faith still came out in a hoarse whisper. "What if he doesn't come back, Jae?"

She rubbed my arm. "I know things have changed, but not the ones that matter."

What if you're wrong?

13

OPEN ARMS

A BASELINE of chatter rumbled over the floorboards and echoed off the café's cobblestone walls. The spotlight that had first introduced me to Riley now hollowed the empty stage. I stared at it anyway. Remembering, missing.

I wound my tea bag string around my mug handle a third time.

Jaycee angled toward me, away from the rest of our friends. "You all right?"

My tea bag string unraveled. "Fine."

Her question jarred me back to our table where our friends sat, each with a spark of life I was missing out on.

Trevor slapped five wooden tiles onto the Scrabble board covering most of the tabletop. "Fifteen points, baby." He threw his hands up in a gangster pose. "Booyah."

Jaycee chucked a balled-up napkin at him. Becky

giggled. But I couldn't latch on to their energy. Their conversation dissolved into background noise as the vacant wooden stage swept into view again from the corner of the room.

Images of Riley with his guitar and microphone flashed in and out like a candle flickering in the wind. The raw ache in my chest from all that'd been going on blared above the memory of his music.

A shriek exploded in front of me. "Ah! Trevor!" Becky lunged from the table to dodge the stream of water gushing over the side.

Trevor snagged every napkin within reach and compressed them over the expanding pool. "Sorry, Beck," he said between chuckles. "Little too much caffeine in that last espresso. Didn't mean to bump the table."

Jaycee raised her empty mug to shield her laughter. Following her lead, I reached for my own laugh suppressor but stopped midstream when A. J. caught my gaze.

All humor drained with the rest of Becky's drink as a scrutinizing stare trapped me in a moment of connection I couldn't explain or escape.

With one labored blink, a careful display of indifference overtook his eyes again. He diverted his attention to Becky and the commotion still bouncing around us.

No one else seemed to have noticed, but I saw it. Felt it. And worse, I didn't know what else to do except pretend I hadn't.

The drone of my friends' conversation lulled me back to my thoughts until a series of screeching chair legs cued me it was time to leave.

The day's earlier drizzling had progressed into steady beads of oversized raindrops. Everyone congregated in a huddle at the door. Trevor hooked an arm around Jaycee's waist and made a run for it to the car. Squeals followed Becky and Ashlea's trail. I lagged behind, not giving the rain the satisfaction of penetrating beyond the surface.

"Well, this seems oddly familiar." A. J. strode up alongside me with his hands in his pockets and eyes sharper than the ragged gravel under our feet.

"Blank stare, shoulders hunched, detached from the world. You should really stop letting him do this to you. It's not healthy." The edge that'd stormed the look he shot me across the table seared into the bite of his sarcasm now.

Rain beat onto my hot cheeks. "Riley isn't *doing* anything to me." If I'd asked him to stay, he would have.

"Right," he said. "You just think depression's an admirable trademark. Is that it?"

I swallowed the sting. "I don't expect you to understand."

A. J. caught my elbow and drew us both to a standstill in the middle of the parking lot. "And why is that? 'Cause I'm not capable of the kind of love you two share?"

"You know that's not what—"

"Forget it." He let go of my arm and blew past me. Gravel churned against the silence.

Something unspoken suspended him in place several feet away. "I'm more compassionate than you think." He turned. "I know where this path leads you, Em. I watched you walk down it before, remember?" An undertone of sadness tugged at the frustration darkening his face. "Not this time."

Each stride away from me pushed the impact of his words deeper into my heart.

It wasn't only about Riley leaving. The attack, Dee, the grant rejections, this constant tension between A. J. and me. It was too much. Couldn't he see that?

My chest heaved with everything I wanted to say. I didn't care if everyone was staring at me, or that it was pouring down rain. Nothing mattered except someone who was supposed to be my friend stalking off.

Jagged tears burned hot in my throat. "You want to walk away? You want to avoid me? Fine. As if that would be any different from the entire summer."

If anger was what it took to break through his shield of apathy, then let him be angry. Let him be furious. At least that was something real.

He advanced straight toward me.

Fight draining, my voice depleted to a hoarse whisper by the time he reached me. "You promised, A. J. You promised we'd still be friends." Rain dripped from my hair and blended into tears I didn't bother to wipe away.

Less than a foot across from me, he hesitated for the

slightest moment and then drew me close. Despite my resistance, he held on until I gave in and clung to his shoulders.

"I'm trying," he whispered.

Minutes passed to the sound of raindrops playing percussion against the hoods of the cars around us.

Our friends must've left in Trevor's Outlander. When I finally withdrew from A. J.'s arms, we were the only ones left in the parking lot.

The reality of what had just taken place set in. Perfect. I'd let A. J., of all people, witness my meltdown.

He pitched a tent with his hands above his head, a slow grin hiking to the left. "Mind if we get out of this rain now, or were you intentionally going for the wet cat look?"

If he were anyone else, it wouldn't have made sense for a single comment to override everything leading up to it. Yet one teasing remark, and all slivers of self-consciousness vanished under the ease of a friendship I'd thought I'd lost for good.

"We wouldn't want to mess up your hair or anything." I flicked the top of the perfectly molded sculpture. "Wow. Go a little overboard with the hair gel this morning?"

"Hey, hey, hey." He ducked out from under my reach and patted his hair to assess the damage. "It takes a lot of hard work to compete with the Goblin King."

My grin turned into outright laughter. "Only you

would bust out a *Labyrinth* joke while we're standing in the rain, after I just bawled my eyes out."

With a smile that felt real for the first time in months, A. J. drooped his arm over my shoulders and steered me toward his car through an obstacle course of puddles. "Hey, I can't help it if you have a thing for David Bowie."

The pellets of rain torpedoing down stole my chance to make some clever comeback. I dove into his car's cozy leather seat the second he hit the unlock button.

He cranked up the heat to full blast to dry us off. As much as I'd teased him for being a college student with an Acura ZDX, this was one time I was thankful his parents could afford luxury. God bless the inventor of seat warmers.

We were a good ten minutes into the drive before he turned off the heat. Without the noise, soft music from the stereo became audible. *Open Arms?*

I looked from the player to A. J. and tipped the psychedelic colored CD cover out from behind the cup holders. "Since when did you start listening to Journey?"

He snatched the case and tossed it back into its secluded compartment. "Since when did you start nosing around people's stuff?"

"Touchy." I held my hands high in the air.

He turned up the volume to drown out my laughter, which only made it worse. He scrambled to turn off the stereo altogether. "Okay, okay. Keep laughing, and I might toss you back out in the rain. You're getting my leather seat soaked."

I threatened to wring out my shirt right there.

He rolled up the window. "Easy, Rosy."

As soon as he'd said the nickname he'd given me last year, our laughter tapered off into a silence that seemed louder than any previous noise.

He lined up my car door with the walkway in front of my apartment a few minutes later. Slouching in his seat, he dragged his hand over various points on the steering wheel. "I started listening to Journey at the end of last year," he said out of nowhere. He kept his voice soft and his eyes on the windshield. "Guess it reminded me of you."

I toyed with the knob on the vent while my thoughts followed the wipers' back and forth motion. There'd been plenty of times this summer when I'd retreated to memories of the way things used to be between us. I never imagined A. J. would have done the same. If he missed our friendship, too, where did that leave us now?

14

BUOYANCY

WHATEVER HELD Jaycee silently amused the next morning clearly had nothing to do with the magazine she was pretending to read or the chocolate Pop-Tart she was devouring a piece at a time.

I let go of the kitchen table. My chair dropped onto all four legs, but the sharp noise didn't garner so much as an upward glance from Miss Unreadable or shake the overzealous grin she'd been sporting all morning. I drew an invisible circle on the table with the bottom of my mug while silently trying to lure it out of her.

So much for Trevor's theory on us being clairvoyant. Giving up, I chugged my tea and grabbed the nearest reading material within reach. Big mistake. Stuck with *Bridal Guide* in my lap, I tried not to regurgitate my breakfast onto the airbrushed models' fuchsia bouquets.

"So…" The word arced with a note of intrigue.

I looked up at the first excuse to sever contact with the ghastly magazine. "So, what?"

"So, last night? Complete meltdown, duking it out with A. J., crying in the rain... Ring a bell?"

"You guys saw that?" *Figures.* I combed my fingers through my air-dried hair. "It was bad, wasn't it?"

No telling what everyone must've thought about the scene A. J. and I'd made.

Jaycee's scrunched expression said enough. "Maybe a tad on the dramatic side."

We cracked up at the same time. Jaycee flung her hand over her mouth, but it was too late. Coffee seeped all the way down her chin.

I took in my best friend through a misty blend of gratefulness and humility. "Thanks for dragging me out last night. You were right. I needed it." More than I'd realized.

She towed her legs into the chair, seemingly uneager to voice the infamous I-told-you-so speech I was entitled to hear.

My back sank against the chair's wooden slats. "I knew this time apart from Riley was going to be tough, but sometimes I feel like I'm drowning." A wave of frustration nearly pulled me under all by itself. I flicked the corner of the placemat. "It's ridiculous."

"Figuring out a committed relationship isn't ridiculous. It's hard."

"I have a ring on my finger, Jae. A ring! What's to figure out? He made me a promise. I made one back. It shouldn't be hard." None of it should be. Wasn't that the entire point of what we'd already been through? God had healed so many broken places in both of us last year. He'd fought for us. If our relationship was part of His plan for our lives, it shouldn't still feel like a battle.

"Em, just because something's blessed doesn't mean it's easy."

Doubt hammered against my heart. And in the hairline cracks it created, shame for allowing fear to break me all over again festered.

"What if I can't do this?" I whispered.

Her eyes smiled with compassion. "Then you lean on friends who remind you that you can."

Gratefulness swelled again as I dabbed away my tears. "I'd never make it without you guys. You know that, right?"

Grin reemerging, she wiped a streak of coffee off her mug. "Sounds like A. J. was the real life jacket last night."

She really was never going to let me live down that embarrassment, was she? "Maybe, but you've rescued me from rock bottom plenty of times. I don't know how you do it."

"Girl, I've been taking diving lessons since the day I first met you."

I snagged the cushion from the next chair over and threatened to swat her with it.

Laughing, she latched onto the table to keep from toppling over. "So, does this mean you guys are friends again?"

"Yeah," I said slowly. "Yeah, I think it does. Well, sort of." I stared absently at the magazine cover. "I still sense there's something left unspoken. Sometimes when he looks at me, it's like I can feel this silent pain in his eyes. I don't know how to explain it."

"You need to be careful, Em."

"Jae, it's not like—"

"Shoot." She sprang out of her seat and glared at the clock, as if it'd committed some monstrous betrayal. "Is that clock right? Shoot! Shoot! Shoot!" Her voice squealed in escalating octaves. "Professor Greaves is gonna kill me. I was supposed to meet him in the ETC at ten-thirty to set up for a presentation."

She made it to the bedroom and back before I had time to set my dishes in the sink. I tossed her a banana when she reached the door. "Something to supplement that imposter breakfast combo you had going on earlier."

"Thanks for looking out." Jaycee slipped the banana into her purse and winked. "We'll finish talking later."

"After work."

"Be careful," she called behind her.

A breeze from the stairwell coursed into the apartment and settled over my shoulders. Yet rather than stifle, the silence following me down the hall felt surprisingly like a friend—one I'd missed.

I wasn't naive enough to think things were back to normal between A. J. and me. If I were honest, they'd never be exactly as they'd been, but something broke last night. I sensed it.

At the bathroom sink, I dropped my pressed powder, flexed my hands against the counter, and stared in the mirror. My chin still bore the mark left by that thug's ring, but the dark circles under my eyes were gone. No imprint of restlessness to hide.

How could one good night's sleep reverse the effects of countless nightmares? The meltdown with A. J. must've had more impact than I thought. I felt lighter. Freer than I had in weeks.

Jaycee's sticky note train waved at me from under the ceiling vent. "I am courageous. I am not alone. I am loved. I will make it through." Maybe I would. Even if I wasn't fully whole yet, life seemed a little less broken today.

A sense of assurance stayed with me all the way into downtown Portland until I parked Riley's Civic in my usual spot. Fresh graffiti defacing the bricks on the front of the building stared back at me.

The agitation in my stomach grew into a slow boil. *Dee.* I yanked open the door and barreled across the street. He wasn't getting away with this.

I blew into the office. Brandon's head popped up from Trey's chair.

"Where's Trey?"

Brandon lowered his feet from the desk. "Just missed him. He got a call, then hustled out. Said somethin' about final signings."

The divorce. I couldn't think about that right now. At least it'd finally be over.

Basketball dribbles rang from out back. Still fuming, I stormed through the screen door and scanned the court. Dee sat on a bench with headphones on, looking like he was at home. Like he was one of us.

"You."

Dee tugged his earbuds free. His confused gaze bounced from me to the rest of the kids on the court staring at us.

I towered above him. "What are you really doing here? You think this is some kind of game? That you can just stroll up in here and vandalize the place?"

He tottered to his feet. "What?"

"The graffiti. I saw the spray paint fall out of your bag the other day." Did he think I was stupid?

His brow creased. "I don't got nothin' to do with that."

"Like you didn't have anything to do with those guys who attacked me?" Something clicked. "Or the fire? Is that why you're here? To finish off what they'd tried to get Jamal to do for them?" *Cowards.*

Dee didn't lift his eyes from the backpack at his feet.

My chest burned. "What are you hiding?"

"I ain't hidin' nothing."

"Then open your bag."

He backed up. "No."

A. J. intercepted me before I could snatch it from the ground. "Em, calm down."

I tried to push around him, but he led me into the

office, away from the uncertain glances flitting around the court.

He tossed Darius a basketball. "Get a scrimmage going. Vests are in that tote. You know the drill."

The noise on the court resumed its regular flow but didn't shut out the drumming in my ears.

"Why are you letting him stay?"

A. J. leaned against my desk. "It's not my call."

"Yeah, well, Trey's compassion might've overruled his judgment this time." Were we honestly supposed to believe Dee up and left his gang to come here for tutoring?

Unbidden, the fatherly look on Trey's face from that day in the hall rushed to mind and bled into the blind-sided look on Dee's face from a minute ago—both clashing with the questions knotting inside me.

I stopped pacing. "What's he really doing here, A. J.?"

"Making a mistake," Dee said from the back door.

The vulnerability in his voice turned my throat raw.

Without giving us a chance to respond, he shouldered his book bag and hurried to leave.

Trey collided with him through the front door. "Whoa, slow down." He held him by the shoulders and looked at me for an explanation.

Between the hurt in Dee's eyes and the question in Trey's, mine were about to reveal how overwhelmed I was. Conflicting feelings backed me through the screen door onto the basketball court.

Thankfully, the beginning of a game kept the kids'

attention diverted from me. I hurried into the utility closet to keep it that way. The tension followed me in, rebounded off the tiny space, and balled up inside my chest.

I needed to move. Needed to do something—anything other than stand still. I rifled through the shelves in search of a bucket and something to scrub the wall with.

A shadow stretched in from the doorway. I looked behind me. "I'm fine, A. J."

"I know." He strolled in and tinkered with the clutter on the shelves. "Just thought you might want some help. You know, with being fine."

His dimples fought to garner a smile from me.

"Thanks, but I'm good." I stopped at the spigot to fill the bucket, then waddled toward the front of the building while trying not to douse my pants.

Bolded streaks of black spray paint caught the sun's glare and laughed at the sight of my little scrub brush. I set the bucket at my feet and rolled up my wet shirt cuffs anyway.

A glimpse of a wooden ladder peeked out from the side of the building, followed by A. J. rounding the corner. Apparently, "I'm good" hadn't translated.

"What are you doing?"

He eased the ladder off his shoulder and propped it against the wall beside me. After dusting off his hands, he shimmied a large sponge out of his back pocket. "Oh, just releasing some energy. You?"

A grin broke through. I dipped my fingers in the bucket and flicked water at him. "I can do this myself, you know."

He steadied the bucket with one hand, soaked his sponge with the other, and met my eyes. "You're not alone, Emma."

His sincerity almost unleashed the tears I'd stifled in the office earlier. I faced the bricks and dragged my brush over the part of the graffiti I could reach from the ground.

One wall at a time.

He worked beside me, no need for words. Clouds drifted in. Minutes drained with the murky water running down the sidewalk. But no amount of scrubbing blotted the vulnerable look in Dee's eyes from my mind. Was I wrong about him?

With my fingertips like prunes and nails darkened around the edges, I pushed back my hair with my sleeve.

A quick glance caught A. J. wiping a paint-tinted smear of sweat across his brow. He was sowing as much into the center as I was. Same as Trey.

"I'm sorry," I said slowly. "For acting like I'm alone in all this."

"That's a lot to load on your shoulders." He wrung out his sponge.

"I know." I slumped against the wall. "Guess I'm used to doing things that way."

"Makes it hard to pretend to be fine all the time."

A laugh snuck through my tight lips. "You didn't buy

that, huh?" At least he hadn't pushed. "Thanks." I dragged the tip of my Converse sneaker over the pavement. "It's nice to have someone who understands."

"Any time." His soft voice followed his chin to his shirt.

At some point while we scrubbed, the sky had turned gray. I closed my arms over my body to block a damp breeze blowing in.

A text notification dinged into the silence—a message from Riley.

Been running around all day. Will you be up after 11?

I thumbed a quick reply, pocketed my phone, and kicked off the wall.

A. J. folded the ladder. "Things that bad?"

Of course he'd notice. "Just hard." I dumped the rest of the water down the storm drain.

"Nashville not turning out the way he planned?"

I tossed the brush into the empty bucket. "No, it's great. You should hear him. He's alive there. Energized. And he should be. It's like he was meant to live there."

A. J. hooked an arm through the ladder rings. Rather than press, he simply waited.

I stared at the water stains spreading up my pant legs. "I'm just not sure how to compete with that world."

"I thought it was a world he wanted to share with you."

"It's easier to share it with his model lookalike manager." I cringed at the petty words as soon as they spewed out on their own.

A. J. shifted the ladder and his tone. "I doubt Riley's stupid enough to give up what he has."

I twisted my necklace and looked from the pearl from Dad to the sapphire from Riley—both given to me with promises I could trust. But what if time changed things?

I released my necklace and a long breath. "I keep wondering if I should've gone with him."

A. J. shrugged. "Part of your heart's here."

His eyes held mine. Heat pricked the tops of my cheeks. He didn't think...

Smile to the side, he nodded at the building. "The center."

Right.

A steady drizzle speckled my forehead and cooled my skin.

A. J. faced the sky. "Guess that's our cue."

A black and tan SUV rolled up to the curb. Some guy dressed to the hilt strutted out and jogged down the side of the building with a briefcase over his head. He probably didn't even see us standing there. A. J. and I exchanged a glance and hurried behind him.

Shaking off the rain, we filed into the office in time to see the businessman extend a hand toward Trey. "Jim Brake from the Success Foundation. I believe we spoke on the phone."

What? Why hadn't Trey told me he'd heard back from them?

"Trey Williams." He returned the guy's handshake

and tipped his head at me. "And this is Emma Matthews. She sent in the proposal."

I scrambled to dry my wrinkly fingertips. A. J. eased beside me and snuck the bucket out of view.

"Thank you," I mouthed to him right before Mr. Brake turned to face me.

"Of course. Miss Matthews."

I shook his hand. "Nice to meet you."

"Hope you don't mind me popping in. We like to do things in person." Mr. Brake set his briefcase on the nearest chair, wiped the water off, and snapped open the brackets.

Pulling out a folder, he straightened. "Here we are." He handed Trey some kind of packet. "It's only a provisional endorsement at this point. We'd like to monitor the center for a while before committing."

Hadn't the notes I included in my grant proposal convinced them they wouldn't find a better investment?

Trey angled his glasses to read the document.

Mr. Brake waved a hand over the top page. "It gets a little heady. Legal jargon." He peered across the office. "How about you show me around first?"

Expressionless, Trey didn't miss a beat. "Why don't we start in the classroom? Maybe the rain will taper off in a while, and A. J. can show you out back."

"Perfect." Mr. Brake grabbed his briefcase.

Trey motioned for me to follow. Somehow, he had managed to transform the earlier group of rowdy teenagers into a composed classroom of students attending to their assignments.

From the front of the room, my gaze braced over Dee again. Trey must've convinced him to stay. At his seat, he alternated between the eraser and sharpened side of his pencil as many times as he alternated looking out the window and poring over the paper on his desk.

The second he caught me staring, the enjoyment on his face recoiled behind the same unsearchable expression he held that night on the street corner.

Trey nudged me forward. "Emma, why don't you help Dee with the essay he's writing?"

I knew that tone. He was up to something. And with Mr. Brake there, I couldn't turn him down. I fabricated a compliant smile and headed toward the last person in the room I wanted to approach.

Dee must've seconded my apprehension. Squirming in his chair, he jammed a paper into his textbook, shielded his eyes with his hand, and didn't look up even after I reached his side.

I peered back at Trey. Following a quick nod at me, he turned to talk to Mr. Brake.

I faced Dee again and cleared my throat. "Mind if I take a look at your essay?"

Not a single movement. For a minute, he looked dead set on refusing but then flicked the paper at me.

I did a double take at the heading across the handwritten page. "'An Endless Night.' What class is this for?"

Dee sent a sharp glance around the room from one

desk to the next. Tugging the bill of his cap down, he sank in his seat and mumbled, "Creative Writing."

"Creative Writing?" I had to have misheard him.

"It was either that or band," he said, as if he'd chosen the lesser of two evils.

"Right. Well, how about we take a look at what you have so far." I pointed to the empty chair beside him. "May I?"

He didn't have to answer. The look on his face made it loud and clear he doubted he had a choice.

I frowned at Trey. *Me neither, kid.*

It didn't take long to read the two pages Dee had written. Though short and choppy in a few areas, the essay demonstrated a strength I hadn't expected to find. "You have a great imagination." If he focused on word painting instead of vandalism, he could actually go places.

Dee peeked up from under his hat. "You think so?"

The stoic tone in his response couldn't compensate for the energy flowing back to his eyes with a glimmer of hope that few, I guessed, took the time to notice.

In an unguarded moment, I saw past the mask of a reputation. Past my own assumptions. Same as most of the kids here, Dee likely didn't have anybody in his life to help him see his potential.

A pang of reproach for how I'd treated him clipped into my side. Maybe he'd had a hand in the fire and the graffiti. Maybe he hadn't. Either way, he probably came to the center looking for acceptance. And instead, I'd accused him. No wonder he said he was making a mistake being here—a mistake in hoping we'd be different from what he was used to.

My heart winced. I swallowed and reached for his textbook before my response showed. "Let's go over a few of these grammatical changes I made."

He scrambled to intercept the textbook. A piece of paper that looked like it'd been torn from a sketchpad tumbled out of the book's cover. Dee snatched it, nearly crumbled it into a ball, and shoved it inside his book bag.

"Was that a picture of the basketball court out back?"

He tossed his bag underneath his desk. "It's nothing."

"O-kay."

Whatever minuscule opening I'd gained, I lost in a matter of seconds.

With a quick scan through the table of contents, I noted a handful of page numbers. "Here. Why don't you review these sections and try revising a few of these sentences?" My chair legs scraped against the tile. "Let one of us know if you have any questions, okay?"

Dee's head twitched in a nod.

Leaving him to it, I made my way to the door. Trey and Mr. Brake had already slipped out. I stopped over the threshold and peered behind me at the room full of kids who'd captured my heart and given me purpose these last several months. Seeing Dee seated among them took Trey's perspective maxim to a completely new level.

Still shaking my head, I returned to my work in the

office. The guys weren't there either. It sounded like the rain had stopped. Maybe they were out back.

Trey came through the front door as I was leaving some voice messages on his desk.

"Is Mr. Brake still here?"

Trey pointed behind him. "Just walked him out."

"Everything good?"

An ambivalent shrug answered for him. It was probably too soon to tell. Not that it swayed Trey's positive outlook. Just like the kids' backgrounds didn't sway his belief in their futures. If I gained even half his power of perspective while working here, it would change my life.

I chewed on the corner of my thumb. "I'm sorry for earlier. The way I acted with Dee."

Trey leaned his shoulder into mine. "I know what you must be thinking, but I wouldn't have let him in if I thought there was any chance he'd try to hurt you."

He looked behind him toward the sound of kids stirring in the other room, each with a story as unique as the next. Seen through Trey's eyes of unconditional acceptance, Dee was no exception. After the glimpse I caught a few minutes ago, he was probably right.

"What do you know about him?"

He released a sigh. "Diego Mendierez. Pops bailed on him when he was two. Mom's a struggling single parent. Kid turned to the wrong crowd." The pain of recurring circumstances creased his face. "I can tell you one thing. That boy's got some guts coming here. Tito isn't gonna give up one of his crew members easily. First Dee dips on him, then shows up here?" He shook his head. "Not gonna go over so well."

"And why exactly is he here again?"

My uncertainty didn't faze Trey in the least. His smile held the same sense of fatherhood I'd seen guide his actions time and again. "I think he's searching for something he's been needing for a very long time." He dipped his head at me. "Hope."

"He's lucky you're equipped for the task."

He let out a low, telling laugh. I didn't want to ask what he was thinking.

A swarm of kids filtered through the office. Some raced toward the basketball court. Others headed home for the day. A. J. trailed at the end of the group. "I'll meet you out front in two," he called to me from above the clamor of conversations.

The screen door swung behind him and blew a look of exhaustion over Trey's face.

I crossed the room. "I don't know how you do it."

"You and me both. I'll tell you this much. I couldn't do it without people like you."

He'd likely change his mind about that once he saw the message from our landlord that I left on his desk along with this past month's bank reconciliation.

Sure enough, after glancing over the note, Trey eased his square-shaped glasses off and squeezed his forehead.

I tugged on the door. Each *creak* clothes-pinned my heart in a squeeze of its own. I stopped halfway through and turned.

"Don't worry," he said before I could voice my concern. "All the Success Foundation will have to do is take one look at the difference you're making here, and they'll sign on."

"The difference *we're* making."

One of our seven-year-old girls snuck in the back door and ran across the office, beaded braids flapping as she went. "I forgot to give Miss E a hug goodbye." She whirled her skinny arms around my neck.

Trey shot me a pointed look. "You were saying?"

I kissed her cheek and sent her off. "Yeah, yeah."

"Mm-hmm. Now, go on and get outta here before you get sick of this place and stop coming."

"Never." I winked at him on my way out.

At the end of the walkway, someone stepped in front of me from around the corner. I jumped backward. My pulse jackhammered until I saw who it was. "Dee? What are you still doing here?"

"Aw, sorry. Didn't mean to scare you." He scuffed his Nikes against the sidewalk while keeping his hands in his jacket pockets and his eyes on the pavement.

I dragged the pearl along my necklace, not sure what to say.

The same SUV from earlier zipped up to the curb. Did he forget something? Mr. Brake circled around the front bumper. He stopped long enough for a judgmental glare to connect Dee to the graffiti left on the wall beside us and kept trekking for the door.

Dee nodded at the bricks. "It wasn't me. Not sayin' I never tagged nothing. But not here."

The presumption in Mr. Brake's eyes carved a hole in my gut with a reflection of how calloused I'd been before. "I shouldn't have accused you."

When he shrugged like it was nothing less than expected, the look in his eyes took me back to the look in Jamal's when his aunt had automatically assumed he was to blame for the fire. The memory widened the ache in my chest.

Dee hung his head so low the front of his jacket muffled his voice. "I just wanted to say I'm sorry. You know, for that night. It was stupid. Tito can be a real a—"

However forcefully the expletive entered his mind, he seemed to have enough restraint to stop from saying it in front of me.

Of all moments, Jaycee's sticky notes soared to mind. I rested my hand on Dee's arm. "I forgi—"

A. J. closed in from the opposite end of the walkway. Dee shot him a chin flick without any hint of fear or question. It wasn't until his eyes met mine that they took on a look of perplexity. Was he so tormented by guilt that grace was harder to accept than judgment?

Mr. Brake hurried past us again with a folder in hand. His SUV pulled away from the curb and opened a view to Tito leaning against the building across the street. His stare nearly pinned me to the wall with the same force his forearm had the night he'd attacked me.

A younger version of himself hovered at his side this

time. Probably his brother from the looks of it. What kind of person dragged an elementary kid into a gang?

Tito flicked a cigarette on the ground and pushed off the bricks. On command, a bright green, lowered Mazda 6 with black rims crept out from a side street and tailed Mr. Brake's SUV. They'd been staking out the place, following people who visited? No wonder they knew who our grant contacts were.

Tito flaunted a dark grin as he strutted away, his brother on his heels.

Dee flew around the corner, looking ready to chase him down.

I ran after him. "Dee, wait."

He snatched a bike propped against the wall. A second after getting on it, he slammed his fist against the handlebars and huffed something in Spanish.

I followed his eyes to slashed tires and bent rims.

He shoved the whole thing into the building and strode down the street before I could utter a word.

He couldn't just leave. If Tito jacked up his bike, he could do worse to Dee. I started to go after him, but A. J. caught my hand. "Let him go."

The farther Dee strutted away, the farther the gap between us expanded. Trey was right. The kid needed hope. But if he really did pull out of Tito's gang, what did that mean for him? For the center?

15

RIVALRY

FOUR DAYS of cramming for my corporate finance exam hadn't erased the mark Dee's eyes had left on my heart. Even a night out with my friends lacked the potential of curbing it.

Jaycee opened her closet. "Have you told Riley about the assault yet?"

I looked up from my desk. Where'd that come from? "I don't want to bring it up."

She sifted through a row of hangers. "Have you thought about why that is?"

Nothing like having my own personal shrink. "Jae..."

"I'm just saying." She tugged a knit sweater over her head and smoothed out her hair. "If you lose honesty in your relationship, you lose everything."

"He doesn't need me to be honest. He needs me to be strong."

She turned. "Are you hearing yourself right now? He needs you to be *real*."

I chucked a pencil into the crease of my textbook. "I don't want to be the clingy fiancée who can't make it through anything without him."

"Do you honestly believe he's going to think less of you because you need him? That's how love works, Em. You're there for each other through everything. You know, the whole 'for better or worse' thing?"

"What about putting each other first?" I straightened as if a stiff back would somehow make my voice sound less pathetic. "I want to give him the space he needs while he's there."

Jaycee set her brush down. "The guy already has two thousand miles of space. Trust me. He doesn't need any more. With that much distance, what he needs most is to know he's not losing you."

Me? "I'm not the one who left."

And there it was. The wound I hadn't fully surrendered.

I winced with frustration at myself. If knocking the truth into my head with my book might've helped, I would've tried. Love didn't abandon. I'd already learned that. Why was I still hanging on to the belief that it eventually would?

"Sorry. I shouldn't have—"

"Been real?" Jaycee tilted her head at me. "I wouldn't want you to be anything else. And neither would Riley."

The lines around her eyes softened when mine

pinched at her words. "I'm sorry, Em. I'm not trying to be harsh about any of this. I just don't want you to forget that part of loving him means giving him the chance to love you back, even when you're afraid he won't."

I twisted my engagement ring, remorse spiraling. As usual, Jaycee knew how to shine a light on things that hurt less when kept hidden in shadows. Truth was, I'd wanted to love Riley by putting his needs above my own, but I was still getting it wrong.

Accusations darted in my spirit. Steeling myself against them, I clung to the grasp I was losing and prayed grace could still find me, even in the very place where my faith had faltered.

Following a deep exhale, I pushed up from my chair. "You're right. I should've told him. I'll fix it the next time he calls."

"Good." She finished clasping on her earring, clearly putting an end to the sappy pep talk. "But don't go worrying about it all night. You know Trev's been looking forward to this game all semester."

The flyer on my dresser sent one source of dread chasing another. I'd almost prefer sappy over fanfare. At least it was distraction. I lugged my college hoodie over my head and glowered at Jaycee. "I still can't believe you're making me go. I don't even *like* football."

She gaped at me. "First of all, that's an abomination. Second of all, it's not about liking football. It's about having school spirit and hanging out with your friends."

I straightened the front of my sweatshirt and

pointed to the words, REED COLLEGE. "Ahem. Sporting school spirit right here, thank you very much."

Eyes rolling, Jaycee nudged me into the hallway. "Nice try." She tossed me a pair of fleece gloves. "Here."

I looked up at her. "It's September."

"The *end* of September." She shrugged. "It might get cold after the sun goes down."

Perfect.

I affixed a permanent smile on my face for her sake. And for Riley's. He'd probably include attending football games as part of the *"enjoy your senior year"* plea he'd made me.

Outside, Becky pounced on me with her usual bubbling-over cheer. A side braid bobbed against her shoulder as she curled an arm around mine. "Looks like the two of us have a date tonight."

A date? She motioned to A. J. and Ashlea standing face to face beside the curb. Right. That left Becky and me as the odd ones out of the group. Guess it was better than being the *only* single one.

She skipped down the walkway, tugging me along.

Ashlea stroked her finger over the line painted down the middle of A. J.'s face—white on one side, maroon on the other. He could've passed for a warrior preparing for battle.

I spun in the opposite direction to hide my laugh. Apparently, not fast enough.

A. J. turned me back around. "What's so funny?"

Seeing him head-on only made it worse. "Nothing. You just look really, um, spirited."

Ashlea butted between us like a linebacker blocking him from an opponent. "He looks perfect." She perched her nose in the air. "We're playing our rival school, Emma. It wouldn't hurt you to have a little more spirit yourself."

I pointed at my college sweatshirt again. Was I the only one who could read? Something covered the top of my head from behind.

"She can borrow some of mine." Trevor popped in front of me and flaunted a mischievous grin while straightening what must've been a Reed College ball cap he was lending me for the evening.

Offering me a furtive wink, he called behind him, "Looks like we're ready now." He draped an arm over my shoulders. "Come on, Cheer Captain. Let's go show these punks what it means to ball on our turf."

I tugged on the bill of the hat as we walked. "Thanks. For a minute there, I thought you were going to give me a glow-in-the-dark necklace or something."

He tapped the inside pocket of his coat. "Have no fear, Em. I wouldn't dream of letting you down."

Ignoring him, I peeked over my shoulder and laughed all over again. We looked like a group of misfit soldiers marching into a battle zone with flaunted valor.

The closer we got to the field, the louder the school band's fight song blared from the stands. Our mascot danced along the edge of the track, cueing each section of fans for their turn to cheer. Flags and noisemakers circled above droves of maroon and white shirts and faces while the odor of greasy concessions and sweat blew in from the sports field to top it all off.

"Jae, you're seriously trying to kill me, aren't you?"

She slipped on her gloves. "Stop whining before we make you go dance with Griffin Boy over there."

Fat chance that was happening.

With Trevor bulldozing a path through the crowd, we found an opening on one of the bleachers with enough space for us to fit as a group. Of course, that meant climbing over a couple of guys to get to it.

The pair forced their legs to the side as we each squeezed by, apologizing profusely as we went. The burly one turned at the perfect moment. I tripped over his knees and grabbed his shoulders to keep from landing smack into his lap. He steadied me at the waist with two groping hands. A grin slanted beneath blond hair with more grease than the half-eaten hotdog beside him.

I scurried into the empty seat and let the cold bleacher beneath my legs drain the heat from my face. A. J. sat next to me with Ashlea hovering closely on his other side.

So much for Becky and me rallying together.

I pulled my sweatshirt hood over my hat to blind my peripheral vision. If I could get into the game long enough to block out questions about Dee and concerns about how Riley would react to the truth, maybe I'd stand a chance at enduring the night.

Fifteen minutes of trying to follow the calls from the field killed that possibility.

A sideways glance caught A. J. demolishing a tub of popcorn. With his attention fastened to the action, he sustained a continual circular motion from the bowl to his mouth.

"You better slow down before you wear out your bicep." I pointed at the mascot still cheering on the crowd. "Never know. He might pick you to throw a pass at halftime."

Either A. J. didn't hear me, or he was flat-out ignoring me. Were we back to the cold shoulder thing again? Or was it because Ashlea was here?

Without warning, something nailed me dead in the face. A single piece of popcorn bounced into my lap. "Cute, A. J."

"What?" He cupped his hand around his ear and chomped with extra gusto.

I launched the rogue piece of popcorn back at him.

He blocked it with his palm. "Oh, you don't want to start this."

Before I could respond to the challenge, a handful of popcorn flew at me. It took me a second to shake the kernels from my hair and the stunned look from my face. I reached for two fistfuls from his tub. He pulled away, forcing me to climb over him to get to it.

Ashlea blasted to her feet. "I'm going to get a soda,"

she practically yelled. A silent scold edged me back into my designated seat as she clambered over us.

I slid my hands under my legs and gripped the ribbed bleacher. It seemed colder than when we first sat down.

"So," I said once she made it down the stairs. "You and Ashlea, huh?"

A. J. scratched his chin. "Yeah, I've been meaning to have a talk with her about that."

"What do you mean?" I faced him, but his stare didn't budge from the field.

"Ashlea's great. I just don't think I can give her what she wants." He set the popcorn tub down. "I'm not looking forward to having that conversation."

Couldn't blame him. Especially after he'd been on the receiving end of a similar one last year.

The reminder of that night in the gym when he told me he loved me pulsed from a scar that hadn't healed.

"I'm sorry." *For so much.*

Letting out a low chuckle, he prodded me with his elbow. "At least we know there'll be survivors, right?"

My face fell.

He laughed. "Aw, c'mon. I'm teasing, Em. Just trying to keep things from being awkward."

"Um, you might wanna try another game plan." I shouldered him into the empty space on his other side.

He stayed hunched over, rubbing his arm and laughing harder. I reached for the popcorn again. Scrambling to block me, A. J. accidentally bumped into the students in front of us. Two freshman boys decked out in

Reed fanfare pivoted in their seats, about to stand up. One look at A. J.'s size must've made them think twice.

A senior girl wearing a student council blazer whipped her long blond ponytail around. Though she didn't make a peep, the reprimand in her expression blared louder than the band's horn section.

I leaned into A. J. "I'd take on the guys over Blondie, if I were you."

He pressed his shoulder against mine. "Good call."

I smiled. It felt good to be at ease with him again. Good to have a friend beside me. But the moment Ashlea slinked back through the narrow space in front of us, she drew the feeling—and our conversation—to a standstill. A. J. and I zipped face forward and fixed our attention on the halftime show instead.

In perfect sync with the setting sun, a glow-in-the-dark necklace waded down the row. I ignored A. J.'s not-so-subtle smirk as he handed it to me. I clipped it around my neck and brandished a half-smile at Trevor's cheesy grin beaming from the end of the bleacher.

"Very techno," A. J. said from the corner of his mouth.

I elbowed him. "Oh, shut up, Mr. Finger Paint."

He flashed me an incredulous look. "Why you keep startin' somethin' you know you can't finish?"

"Psh, please."

That did it. A. J. maneuvered past my flailing hands and the bill of my hat and almost got close enough to wipe face paint from his cheek to mine. He squeezed my side. I squealed right as Ashlea passed a phone to me.

Riley's number glared at me from the screen. My stomach tightened. I eased back into my seat, swallowed hard, and lifted the phone to my ear. "Hey."

"You all right? You didn't answer your phone, so I called Jaycee's."

I patted my pockets for my cell. "Sorry. I must not have heard it."

"Too preoccupied?"

What was that supposed to mean? Like he was one to say anything about missing calls anyway.

"We're at a football game. It's kinda loud." And definitely not the right time or place to tell him about the attack. "Can I call you when it's over?"

He didn't answer at first. "I'm about to go into a rehearsal. I'll call on my next break."

"Okay." Not that I'd be ready then either. Holding the phone with both hands, I stared at my lap. This was going to be even harder than I thought.

A. J. shifted on the bench and straightened out his jeans at the knees. "Everything all right?"

Nothing seemed all right anymore. I passed off a smile and Jaycee's cell. "Yep."

I tucked my hands into my hoodie pocket and tried to focus on the game. At least I could put off the call a little longer.

After far too many drawn-out plays, the football spiraled down the field. I inched to the edge of the bleacher and lunged to my feet at the same time as everyone else. Holding our breath, we all tilted toward the end zone. The ball skimmed past the defender's hands and landed in our running back's secure grip.

Between all the jumping and hollering, I could barely see over the student in front of me. Not that I needed a direct line of sight to the field to know we'd just scored a touchdown.

The stands erupted in chaos. The sweet taste of victory sent all Reedies toppling over each other. At least, everyone but A. J. and me. I didn't dare hug him with Miss Ice Queen standing guard on his opposite side.

A tap on my shoulder drew me toward the devilish grin of the burly guy I'd tripped over earlier. His eyebrows bobbed with an open, and entirely too eager, invitation for a hug.

On instinct, I slid toward A. J. and wrapped my arm around his. He peered toward the source of my reaction and laughed against my hair.

Great. What was I thinking? He'd probably throw me into the ghoulish-looking guy's arms as retaliation for the face paint crack I'd made. I grounded my feet, but A. J. draped his long arm over my shoulders instead.

He must've given the guy a look that told him, in no uncertain terms, to back off. When I braved another peek in my seatmate's direction, he looked as if an invisible neck brace prevented him from turning his head at even the slightest angle toward me.

I offered A. J. a grateful nod and prudently backed out from under his protective arm. No need to add to whatever suspicions Ashlea seemed to be brooding over. In all honesty, she had no reason to be jealous. A. J. and I teased each other as much as Trevor and I did. That's what friends did.

As if proving my point, Trevor squeezed to the end of the row, grabbed my shoulders, and prodded me into the crowd. "Let's roll, guys. Emma can lead the way with her necklace. Kinda like Rudolph," he added with an obnoxious laugh.

He was lucky I didn't have antlers.

Our small group of friends navigated through the throng of fans and snuck off to the less crowded path wrapping the long way back to our apartments.

Becky looped arms with me. "I'm sorry we didn't get to sit together. Maybe we can—"

My phone rang from my pocket. I untangled my arm from Becky's. The number on the screen rooted me in place. No putting it off this time. All the different ways I'd come up with to tell Riley about the assault twisted into a ball mounting in my throat.

A. J.'s hesitant glance met mine, but Jaycee corralled everyone forward. "C'mon, guys. Emma will be along in a minute."

If I made it through this.

16

LOST AND FOUND

RILEY WHIZZED past the waver in my hello. "Is this a good time?"

Would it ever be?

"The game's over now." I scurried up the sidewalk away from the racket still brewing on the field.

"Sorry for being short with you earlier. I'm just..." He released a long, knotted breath. "Overtired, frustrated."

Join the club.

"I've had a hectic day—weeks, if I'm being honest. I feel like I'm sleepwalking most of the time. Jess wants me to write a couple songs with piano to add more diversity to the album, but I keep hitting this block. All week, I've been up half the night working on this one song."

The strain in his voice tore at my heart. He was already dealing with enough pressure without my heaping on any more. I broke off a tiny branch from the bordering shrubs and fiddled with it as I walked. Was honesty really what he needed right now?

He sighed again. "Sorry. I called to hear your voice, not to complain. How was the game? Did we win?"

"Yep, thirteen to seven," I said with more pride than I expected. "Things got a little rowdy at the end."

"I bet. Gotta say, I'm impressed your friends coerced you into going to a game."

"You and me both." I spun the plastic tube around my neck. "I'm even rocking a glow-in-the-dark necklace."

"Let me guess. Trevor's handiwork?"

"Like you have to ask."

Riley's laughter cuddled around me like one of his fleece pull-overs. Soft, comforting. Its warmth amplified my longing to be with him.

A moan seeped through his end of the line. "Wish I could be there. Honestly, I think that's part of why I snapped when I called earlier. I hate missing these moments with you. Hate not getting to talk all the time."

"Me too." An acute pain followed my confession. Riley wasn't down the road at his apartment. He was in another state. Phone calls weren't enough to fill the hole of his absence.

I sat on a thick patch of grass in front of the creek and pretended he was right beside me, rather than hundreds of miles away. At least we had right now.

He exhaled, probably trying to shake it off too. "What else have I been missing?"

I faced the sky. *Please help me through this.*

"Actually…" I curved the twig in a semicircle. "Listen, don't be mad, but there's something I need to tell you."

An electric pause surged.

Courage, Em. "Earlier in the semester, I was working late on my Wednesday shift, and Trey had to leave early, so…"

"What happened?" he said, each word measured with caution.

I drew swirls in the dirt, stalling to find the words to tread lightly over the dark memory.

"I had to run out to your car to get my charger, and when I turned around there were some guys waiting for me."

"What do you mean they were *waiting* for you? What guys?"

"Some teenage thugs from the neighborhood."

Riley's breathing turned choppy. "What did they do, Emma?"

The creek flowed peacefully downstream. Why wouldn't words come as easily? There had to be a way to be honest while defusing his reaction at the same time.

"They cornered me. I almost got away on my own, which reminds me. I need to thank Austin for all the wrestling lessons he gave me. But everything's fine. Don't worry, I—"

"Don't worry? You tell me you *almost* got away from a group of thugs, and you ask me not to worry?"

"You didn't let me finish. I said I almost got away *on my own*. A. J. showed up before they could do anything."

"A. J.? What was he doing there?"

It hit me that I'd never told him A. J. took the job as coach. I picked at a snag on the side of my Converse sneaker. "He works there now."

Riley's pause shouted everything he didn't say.

I tried to brush past it. "He took the guys down without either of us getting hurt and brought me home safely. I only had a mild headache for a few days. It was nothing."

"How can you say that? You could've been hurt. You could've been—"

"But I wasn't. And there's no way A. J. and Trey are letting me out of their sight again."

"You should have told me."

The reproach in his tone set off a pang of defense across my shoulders. "And what if I had? Would you have been on the first plane here?"

"That's beside the point."

"No, that's exactly the point." I snapped the twig in half and flicked it into the creek. "This is why I didn't tell you. You can't rush back here just because I run into some trouble. You have a lot going on in your life right now. You don't need any distractions."

"Stop it, please. When will you understand you're the most important part of my life?" He released a hard breath. "Of course I'd drop everything and come home if you needed me. I should have been there. I should be the one to take care of you. Not… A. J. Bowers."

"Riley." The damp earth soaked through my jeans

with the sting of regret. "I'm sorry. I should've told you, but I didn't want you to worry. And A. J. was just being a good friend."

A harsh laugh raked across the line. "Don't be gullible, Emma."

Me? I dug my fingers in the grass. "I'm not allowed to work with a friend, but you can go clubbing with your manager every night?"

He didn't respond. Didn't need to. Guilt stabbed on its own.

"I'm sorry. That was out of line." And immature.

The silence stretched past excruciating.

"Riley?"

"It's getting late. We should both get to bed." The miles between us didn't diminish the hurt his voice carried or buffer my heart from splintering like the broken twig.

He'd finish talking about it when he was ready. There wasn't any more I could say tonight, except for one thing. "I love you."

The words throbbed in another pause, a question begging for a response.

"I love you too. Good night."

His hollow tone swallowed the assurance I craved. Tears pushed through my closed lashes. Every one of our calls ended with dissonance. What was happening to us? To me?

Water lapped against rocks in the creek bed, the wavering against the unwavering. I yanked off Trevor's hat and threw it on the grass. Gripping my hair between my fingers, I faced the heavens and prayed for some measure of direction, for one whisper of what I should do. "I'm scared. What if I'm losing him?"

The longer I waited, the deeper the clouds shrouded the stars and the clarity I used to be able to find out here.

Alone on the bank, I stretched my hoodie over my legs. The campus transformed this time of night. The crickets' hum replaced the voices clamoring from the stadium. Shafts of lamplight swayed along the water's current. Even the rain-scented mist rising from the grass exuded peace, but it all felt outside my grasp. Still, I kept waiting until the dampness finally crept under the lining of my sweatshirt and prodded me to my feet.

My body froze at the sight of someone gaining ground on me. I darted a glance down the opposite side of the trail toward the fleeting hope that other students were nearby. After the run-in with Tito, I promised myself I'd never end up in a similar circumstance again.

The hot sting of fear pricked my skin with an imprint that'd always be with me now. The suspicions, the adrenaline. I backed to the edge of the path and bumped into a lamppost. *It's fine. We're on campus. Nothing's gonna happen.* I crouched and pretended to tie my shoe. He'd probably pass right by me.

"I thought we talked about you not being out at night by yourself." A. J.'s grin beamed above his outstretched arm.

An elongated exhale released my unwarranted panic.

I grabbed his hand and rose with relief. "I think our campus has a slightly lower crime rate than downtown Portland."

"You can never be too careful. Especially after we just beat our rival school. Never know who might be lurking around, ready to take vengeance."

I dusted off the gravel from my hands. "Come to think of it, I might've heard of some sketchy basketball players sneaking up on innocent girls in dark parts of campus." A sassy grin latched on to my mock accusation.

"Guess we better get you back to your apartment, then. I hear those basketball players can be quite charming. You'd never see it coming."

"Is that right?"

"It's their greatest weapon. One dashing smile, and it's all over after that." He flashed a spread of brilliant white teeth.

I exaggerated an uninterested yawn. "Good thing that kind of charm doesn't faze me."

"Heart of steel you got there." His laugh soothed. He nodded to the trail. "C'mon, I'll walk you home."

In a pair of mesh basketball shorts and a hooded Nike sweatshirt, he must've been headed for the gym. Maybe I wasn't the only one in need of a stress reliever.

A. J. tucked a basketball against his hip. "You seemed kinda tense on the phone back at the game. You sure you're good?"

Only if falling apart counted as good. I nudged a rock

into the grass with the tip of my sneaker. "I told Riley about that night with Tito."

Understanding touched his eyes.

"The strain of being apart… It's too much sometimes. I just want it all to be over, you know?"

He kept his focus ahead of us. "I know," he said softly.

Unlike Jaycee, A. J. wasn't quick to offer advice. Didn't press. We simply walked. The tension lessened with him nearby, even in silence.

Every few steps, I slid a glance his way. The lamplight caught flakes of white face paint left in the whiskers along his jawline and in the bits of brown hair peeking out from under his backward hat.

"I like your beard, by the way."

He balked. "It's not a beard. It's scruff."

"Scruff?"

"Adds to my rugged mystique." He ran his knuckles along his cheekbone.

I bit my cuff, barely squelching a laugh. "How's that working out for you?"

"Considering the girl I'm walking home is laughing at me, I'd say not too well."

I shoved him forward. "With a girl like Ashlea hanging all over you, I'd say you're doing just fine, buddy."

He scuffed his Nikes along the concrete while keeping his head down and whatever he wasn't saying hidden.

"I really tried," he said a minute later. "With Ashlea.

But something's missing." He spun the basketball in his hands. "Trev told me to go for it. To *let* myself fall in love with her. Guess we both know it doesn't exactly work that way."

Did he always have to say stuff like that?

Branches of nearby trees rustled in the wind with an excuse to look away from him. Blackberry stains covering the sidewalk passed under our feet. I had to believe I could undo the stains I'd left on our friendship as much as I had to believe A. J. would find the right girl.

"Give it some more time," I said. "It can be hard to know when you're really in love if you're afraid to find out."

The breeze carried an echo of his soft laughter ahead of us.

"What's so funny?"

He stopped and faced me. "Actually, I think that's *how* you know you're in love. When the feelings inside you are so overwhelming, they literally scare you."

My gaze strayed away from the intensity in his.

He lifted his hat, ruffled his hair, and slid it back on. "Ashlea's great. We hit it off. That should be enough, but..."

"It's not." I knew exactly what he meant. "It's like music."

"Music." His forehead crumpled. "You're not getting all Dr. Phil on me, are you?"

I stole the ball from him. "Okay, smarty pants, just think about it. You like all the songs on your favorite album, right? The lyrics, the energy, the riffs." I tossed the ball around as we walked. "But there's always that *one* song that stands out from the rest."

A. J. stopped behind me.

I turned. "What?"

He lowered his head, swallowed. "Nothing." He rubbed his scruffy cheek. "Sorry. I don't know why I even brought any of this up."

Reaching him, I rested a hand over his. "Because I'm your friend. You can talk to me about anything."

His eyes blazed under the streetlight.

This time, my whole body strayed away from the look in his eyes. A whisper came from behind me. "Some things you don't want to hear."

He was probably right. I kept walking.

He jogged to catch up and hopped in front of me. A mischievous grin reemerged. Following a Michael Jackson spin, he bowed and extended his arm toward my apartment. "Thank you, Miss Matthews, for using the twenty-four-hour Bowers' Protective Detail Service. You've been safely escorted to your home."

With his face inclined toward the ground, he hovered in position until my lack of movement solicited an upward glance. He hesitated, probably debating over which of us had more resolve.

I perched a fist on my hip and wasted no time mimicking his arched brow. "You didn't happen to come out just to look for me earlier, did you?"

His gaze drifted from my hand to my foot tapping the

sidewalk. A guiltless expression took over. "Now, why would I do that? I was minding my own business on my way to the gym when you happened to show up on my path." His feisty smile edged closer. "Sure *you're* not the one following *me*?"

Ignoring his loaded comment, I thrust the ball into his arms and made it halfway to the door before calling over my shoulder. "Thanks for the protection, Agent Bowers. Looks like it was a narrow escape, after all." I shuffled backward. "I wonder how those charming basketball players get around with such inflated heads."

He stood at the curb with both hands stowed inside his sweatshirt's front pocket. His grin nearly surpassed the width of the ball snuggled under his arm. "One of our many talents."

"Clearly." I turned in time to hop onto the stoop.

"Night, Em."

I waved behind me until I caught a glimpse of his reflection in the windowed door, looking at me the way he used to. A part of me swelled with relief for regaining what I'd lost. Another part had to know what had changed.

"A. J., wait." I jogged back down the sidewalk. But once in front of him, I didn't know how to ask. "This summer... You were so distant."

"I know." He lowered his head again. "Guess I wasn't as strong as I thought I was."

"And now you are?"

"No." He looked up slowly. "Just tired of pretending to be."

Pretending. The word carved an outline around the hole in my chest. "Sometimes pretending is your only choice," I whispered.

A smile tugged his lips sideways. "Heart of steel. You know, if you ever let your guard down, you might be surprised by what you find."

Or terrified of what I'd lose.

17

LABELS

IT WAS EASIER to stop pretending at the center. Something about the place girded me with a sense of courage I wasn't convinced was my own. After not hearing back from Riley for two days, I needed all the help I could get.

His sun-warmed car door pressed into my back while a city bus zipped down the street. Someone hustled toward me through the charcoal cloud of exhaust.

"Miss E, wait up." Dee skidded to a stop in front of the bumper. "Can I ask you somethin'?" He wound the ends of his backpack straps around his fingers and stared at the pavement as though it would answer for me. "Why did you stop him the day in the hall? Mr. A. J., I mean."

"You wanted me to let him hit you?"

"He was just doin' what was right."

Was that what he thought? Same as my initial

response, A. J.'s reaction had added another defining mark to the stigma every kid in this neighborhood carried.

Someone opened a back door a little way ahead of us and dumped a bucket onto the street. Water gushed down the storm drain, the steady flow pulling my heart with it.

"Just because you're used to being treated a certain way doesn't make it right. Labels don't define you." No matter his past, he deserved a second chance. We all did.

Years of skepticism tarnished his expression.

There had to be a way to break through.

"You punish yourself enough for the attack as it is." I squeezed his shoulder. "I forgive you, Dee. I think it's about time you do the same."

A slow blink lifted his eyes toward mine. "You really believe the stuff they teach us here, don't you?"

Two guys from Tito's gang strutted around the opposite building right as I reached for Dee's hand.

The one with tattoo sleeves hurled a groping stare up and down my body. "No wonder you bailed on us, Dee. Getting a little private tutoring on the side?" He clasped his companion's hand and laughed. "C'mon, bro, you can't be hoarding all the goods to yourself like that. Thought we was *hermanos*."

With my arm secured around Dee's back, I prodded him to the center without glancing backward until we made it around the side of the building. Thankfully, the punks didn't follow.

Dee stopped just beyond the doorway. A look of shame weighed down his whole demeanor again.

It killed me to see the bars of his circumstances hold him prisoner. "You're not like those guys."

"How do you know?"

"Because you're here." Trey was right. It took guts for him to come to the center. I lowered my head to meet Dee's eyes. "Your life has promise. You've just gotta be brave enough to believe it." Same as I did.

"Sometimes you need to recite it to yourself." I circled my hand in the air. "Come on. Let's hear you say, 'I am courageous.'"

His blank stare swept from me to the door and down the walkway on either side of us. With no one else around, he mumbled the words.

"How about with a little more conviction next time?"

An unguarded smile slipped through his cover. "Miss E?" He spun his black ball cap around, bill at a slight angle. "Can I show you somethin'?"

"Sure."

He dropped his bag from his shoulder to his forearm and withdrew a medium-sized sketchpad. After a moment's hesitation, he handed it to me and looked away.

Exquisite detail captured in pencil came to life on page after page of off-white canvas. *This* was what he'd been hiding in his backpack? My gaze shifted between the artwork and Dee's shadow squirming on the sidewalk. "You drew all these?"

"Yeah." He slung his bag over his arm and shrugged.

I lifted my necklace to my chin. "Dee, these are amazing. Have you ever thought about pursuing this?"

"My cousin mentioned somethin' to me 'bout maybe doing graphic design, but I don't know…"

"There are a lot of things you can do as an artist. Besides tagging old buildings." A pointed look followed my elbow nudge. "See, this is exactly what I'm talking about. You have too much potential to throw away."

Chin lowered, he drew an imaginary line along the concrete with his sneaker. "Maybe you could, you know, help me with some college apps."

It was a good thing he had his head down, or he would've seen the sudden rise of emotion racing for my eyes. "I'd love to," I managed to say without my voice cracking.

He squeezed the bill of his hat. "And, uh, you think you could help me study for the PSATs?" he mumbled.

"We all will," A. J. said from behind us. "I owe you an apology, bro. I'm sorry I jumped to conclusions without giving you a fair shot."

"It's cool." Dee gave him one of those half-handshake-half-hug things that had some inexplicable way of mending all guy arguments.

"Miss E's right. You've got potential." He tapped Dee's bicep, lugged an arm around his neck, and steered him inside like a big brother. "Why don't you show off some of those mad skills on the court. I could use a helper today."

And I could've used a box of tissues between the pair of them pulling at my heartstrings.

A renewed sense of purpose followed me into the office. Maybe Trey was right about hope after all.

The front door opened as I booted up my computer. A couple stepped inside—Mr. Brake and a woman who must've been his wife. Side by side, they looked like they could've walked right off *Celebrity Apprentice.* Was she holding a Chihuahua?

A cautious glance from behind designer glasses bounced from one side of the room to the other. In a long, black dress coat, Mr. Brake lowered his briefcase to the floor and extended a hand toward Trey. "We were passing through so thought we'd make a quick stop." He motioned to the woman. "My wife, Mindy. Mindy, Trey Williams."

If her hair wasn't wound so tightly, her face might've relaxed enough to release a smile.

Trey offered her a handshake, nonetheless. "Wasn't expecting you today."

Jim picked up his briefcase and dusted off the bottom. His curt laugh sounded painfully out of place. "We believe check-ins should be spontaneous. Gives us a more... authentic view of things." He slid his hand down his wife's back. "Think of us sort of like Social Services."

Did he seriously just say that?

I coiled the wire to my mouse around my finger and kept my mouth shut.

Trey's reservoir of grace must've run even deeper

than I thought. He motioned in front of him. "Let me show you out back since it's not raining today."

A group of preteen girls ran in from the basketball court with Brandon on their heels.

"Ladies, you know how I be joking." He stopped in front of Dee and leaned over his knees. "Help a brother out."

Dee raised his shoulders. "You're on your own, bro."

The girls skimmed past the couple on their way out the door. Mindy clutched her purse and slinked behind her husband as Brandon jogged after them. A tiny snout baring extra-white teeth peeked around her shoulder.

Mr. Brake nudged his wife toward the exit. "Why don't you wait in the car, dear? Baxter will keep an eye on you." He ruffled the dog's ears. "Isn't that right, pookie?"

"Pookie?" Dee mouthed from the corner of the room, his face scrunching like the dog's.

I knocked my pen on the floor and crawled under my desk so the couple couldn't see me laugh.

Trey cleared his throat. "Ready?"

The snaps to Mr. Brake's briefcase clicked open, followed by some papers rustling. "We won't take up too much of your day. Just want to make a few observations to report back to the board. We don't take our investments lightly…" His twangy voice trailed onto the court. He obviously wasn't a Portlander.

I mounted my chair in time to watch A. J. follow them out. Truth was, it didn't matter what I thought about the guy, or his dog. If his foundation was the key to funneling grant money into the center, I'd polish his oversized dress shoes if I had to. At least he was giving us a chance.

Less than ten minutes later, a high-pitched scream echoed a blaring car alarm. Dee and I exchanged a nervous glance. We bolted out front, the other three right behind us. Baxter scratched from inside the Lexus RX's tinted windows. Mindy raced out of the car into her husband's arms, as if escaping a fire.

My stomach pinched. Dread chased every glance around the car for evidence of damage.

A. J. hustled across the street. "Trey," he yelled.

We all followed. A spray-painted symbol dripped down the quarter panel of Trey's Honda onto shards of glass piled beneath a busted side window.

Guilt collided with relief that it was Trey's car and not the success couple's.

Jim cuddled his overly traumatized wife to his side. "This is exactly why we do random check-ins. To see what really goes on here."

He was two seconds away from getting his wool cap shoved down his throat. "And what exactly do you think is going on here?"

Ignoring me, he shot Trey a wary stare. "I'd be careful who you let into your place." His gaze slanted to Dee and back. "I saw him by that fresh graffiti the other day."

He saw what he wanted to. Same as I had at first. Remorse took another stab. With one scathing look, he'd refuted everything I'd told Dee about being more than a label.

I stepped in front of Dee. "He was inside the office with me."

Without a reply, Jim escorted his wife over to their car. The warning on his face sliced through me with the wind. If we lost the grant over this...

A. J. pulled out his cell. "I'll call a tow truck."

Trey stopped him. "Let me take care of this. You guys go on." He peered behind him at the center. "I think we've had enough action to call it a day."

My head told me not to argue. My heart kept my feet cemented to the ground. Trey motioned for A. J. to intervene. With his arm around me, he led me to Riley's Civic. I snapped my seat belt on, heart still heavy.

A. J. leaned against the door rim. "Trey's got this."

That didn't make it any easier to swallow. "I know."

"Meet you back at campus?"

"I'm gonna stop at Starbucks first. Clear my head for a while."

"Text me when you get home." He closed the door and waited for me to take off.

As I'd hoped, an hour of soaking in Starbucks's calming atmosphere eased the tension. Until the silence filling the car on the way home brought it surging back again.

Was the success couple really that sheltered? They had to know not all of downtown Portland was like the Cultural District. Or maybe everything was about upholding pretenses. If that was what it'd take to keep us from losing this contract, then A. J. and I had to come up with a plan, and fast. Trey had too much on his plate. If we could just—

My cell buzzed from the passenger seat. I swiped the screen. "Trey?"

Concern cloaked the fatherly tone he wrestled to keep in place from the second he started talking.

"Wait, what? Are you serious?" I glared in the rearview mirror. "I'll be right there."

18

SPLINTERED

I WHIPPED the car into the same parking spot I'd left an hour ago. In my rush to get out, I couldn't get my seat belt off fast enough. My keys dropped to the curb. I wrenched my arm free, crammed the tangled seat belt inside, and pushed the door closed. With my hair shoved out of my face, the center tunneled into focus.

My palm scraped along the bricks as I darted around the corner. Trey stood at the end of the walkway, head down, a charcoal beret shadowing his face. I slowed. "Trey?"

"I didn't mean for you to come back." The porch light's buzz almost drowned out his gravelly voice.

"It's fine. I was only halfway home."

"Me too." He tipped his head at the building next door. "I got a call from Mr. Jenkins. Said he heard some ruckus."

"Ruckus?"

His pinched brow intensified the dread that'd been festering in my stomach since his call. His backward step equaled my forward stride. He reached for my shoulders and braced me a foot away from the basketball court. "Emma, you don't need to be here."

How could he say that? "Yes, I do." I pushed around him, but the caved-in fence stopped me short.

A metal trash can lay in the center of the court on top of layers of garbage covering the ground. The basketball net hung in frayed threads from a bent rim.

"What is all this?"

"Another warning." He nodded toward the same spray-painted symbol from his car tattooed over the back of the building.

Staring at the wall, I climbed through the broken fence. Wads of paper and foil and who-knows-what-else crinkled along my sneaker-driven path toward the graffiti. Thoughts screamed until one name superseded every other sound. I spun around. "Is Dee okay?"

"He's fine," Trey said, already right beside me. "I checked in with Ms. Mendierez."

Of course he had. Even in such a short time, it was obvious Dee revered Trey as a father, and, no doubt, Trey felt likewise. Dee was family now, and this was his home. It was all of ours.

I snatched up a piece of garbage and clenched it in my fist. "I don't know what kind of hold those punks think they have over him, but—"

"You're exactly right. You don't know."

"What?" I lost my grip on the wadded-up ball and my crumbled sense of belonging.

Trey picked up the garbage. "I didn't mean that the way it sounded. It's just..." He rocked the trash can upright and dropped the paper inside. "These guys are reckless, Emma. Dangerous. You think if they weren't afraid to torch Jamal's house that they'll bat an eye at doing worse?"

"Wait, you know for sure Tito was behind that?" Heat rose in my cheeks, this time by my sheer naïveté. *Everyone* probably knew. "Why is no one turning him in?"

The look on his face reiterated how little I understood about how things worked around here. "Guys like Tito command loyalty or fear. Usually both." He leaned onto the can's metal edge and let out a tension-filled wheeze. "Look, Emma, I didn't call to bring you back into the middle of all this. I called to make sure you'd made it home safely."

Chin lowered, he looked like a homeless man hovering around a barrel of fire, worn and weary. "You got lucky last time. What if you're here, and A. J.'s not around? What if I'm not?"

The implications marched me backward into the wall and into a choice I had to make.

Vivid scenes from the assault crashed through my defenses and pummeled me with the vulnerability that reliving them always triggered. The helplessness I'd felt that night, the fear of what I could've lost. The bruises on my wrists might've faded, but the memory never would. It'd always be in the background now, lurking in the shadows.

Eyes closed, I clung to my necklace and breathed in until a gentle whisper strengthened my resolve. The risk of being hurt while at the center was as real as the scar Tito's ring left under my chin. There was no denying that. But so was the risk of all we could lose by giving into fear.

I looked around the court. Tito could turn the place into shambles if he wanted, but I wouldn't let him do the same to the kids' lives. Or to mine. Like love, purpose took commitment and sacrifice. We couldn't lose our last grant lead. I'd do whatever it took.

I kicked off the wall and stood tall before Trey. "Dee's worth the cost. All the kids are."

Parenthesis-shaped wrinkles bookended a smile that looked pained. "You're a treasure, Emma." He swallowed something unsaid and turned. "It shows in the performance review I just submitted for you. They'd be crazy not to give you an A."

His voice betrayed his light tone.

"I don't care about any of that."

He stopped and faced me. "You should. You urge Dee to protect his future, but what about yours?"

My throat constricted. "What are you saying?"

"I'm saying maybe we should end your internship a little early. You've certainly earned your experience." He waded through the debris toward the utility closet.

My mind sprinted ten steps ahead of my frozen body. "What? You...? No." I ran after him. "Trey, no. I'm not doing this for experience. Or grades. Or even my future. This—this place, the work we're doing here—this is my life right now." The one constant. "I won't work past six. I'll always have someone walk me out." I rested a hand over his and nodded. "Please."

He squeezed my fingers. "You're brave, kid. I'll give you that." He retrieved a broom from the closet.

I stole one for myself and squared off beside him. "Thought I was stubborn."

His throaty laugh billowed across the open-walled court. "That too, my dear. In full spades. I tried to warn Riley."

The chain fence rattled. Trey swept in front of me like a bodyguard.

On the sidewalk, A. J. reached for his mouth. "What the—?"

"Tito, that's what," I said from behind Trey's shoulder.

A. J.'s knuckles whitened around the fence links, his face the exact opposite shade. "What are we still doing here? Those thugs could be nearby."

The fence shook as he pushed off it.

"Stop." Trey strode forward with the authority of a commanding officer. "This isn't your fight."

A. J.'s glance bounced from me to the vandalized court and back. "The heck it isn't." He jerked toward the street again. "I let those two kids get away last time. Not again."

Trey slid in front of him. "There were only two of them last time. Not a whole gang."

A. J. turned. "We don't know how many are out there."

"Exactly," Trey said.

He squeezed the fence again. "So, you're just gonna let them win?"

Trey set a solid grip on A. J.'s shoulder and held out a broom. "Not all fights are won with your fists."

He examined the broom, as if Trey had handed him something from outer space. "You want me to win this fight by cleaning? You can't be serious. They might be watching us right now."

Trey turned. "Oh, I'm counting on it."

A. J. lumbered onto the court behind him. He tossed his hat on the ground and raked his fingers through his hair. "You've got a strange way of looking at things, man."

The sound of footsteps from the walkway butted into Trey's husky laugh.

This time, two bodyguards stood post in front of me.

I pushed through their shoulders. "Dee? What do you think you're doing here?"

He shrugged. "My mom told me what happened."

"You can't just come parading down the streets at night. You could've been hurt."

Dee shook his coat off his shoulders, baring his stocky muscles. "I can handle myself on the streets."

Were he and A. J. like brothers, or what?

Dee flicked his chin at the mess around us. "Trashing your car wasn't enough for Tito?"

Trey swept up a small square of debris. "Apparently not."

Dee mumbled something in Spanish and hit the fence.

"Hey," Trey yelled. "You wanna flex those muscles? Here." He shoved him his broom.

A. J. laughed at Dee's expression and rubbed a hand over his head. "Don't argue, bro. Trust me."

Trey retrieved trash bags and dustpans from the closet. The four of us paired up and got to work on opposite ends of the court.

We wouldn't be able to remove all traces of the vandalism before tomorrow, but we'd do the best we could. The kids deserved that much, and we couldn't afford to let the Success Duo see any more of Tito's handiwork.

Dee dumped a dustpan full of litter into a bag. "I'm sorry, Miss E."

"It's cool." I angled a thumb at A. J. "You should've seen Mr. Macho's reaction when he first got here."

"No, I mean for this." Dee motioned toward the middle of the court and the wreckage covering it. "This is my fault."

"Oh, really?" I leaned on my broom's wooden handle. "You ordered Tito to do this?"

"No, but—"

I raised a brow. "That's what I thought. We each make our own choices. You know that."

He twisted two sides of a black trash bag and compacted the garbage with his knee. His gaze swept around the court and landed on Trey. "He's not gonna press charges, is he?"

I pushed the sweaty hair away from my forehead with my sleeve. "Like I said. We all make our own choices."

Dee tied the ends of the garbage bag into a tight knot. "He's right. Fighting with Tito ain't gonna change nothing. I should man up and talk to him. Show him how different things could roll if he came here."

"Oh, Dee, I don't think that's a good idea." This was about the center, but it was personal too. He could be hurt or worse.

He rose. "You guys took me in. Why not him?"

My palms dragged down the chipped broom handle. Was he kidding?

"You aren't Tito." I picked at a splinter on my thumb. "You're different."

He shrugged. "Not really."

"How can you say that?"

He heaved the garbage bag onto his shoulder. "'Cause it's what you taught me. We all need grace, right?"

In such a short time, I'd watched the anticipation of believing things could change replace the doubt that had caged him. Every moment spent with him exposed how little I really understood about courage.

The splinter in my skin didn't come close to the one digging into my chest. The chime of an incoming text pushed it in even deeper. I knew Riley would need some time to think after our last conversation. He had more to process than just the fact that I'd been bruised up by gang members. He had to process through the reason why I'd waited so long to tell him.

I swiped the screen. My heart plummeted at the sight of Jaycee's name instead of Riley's.

You ok? Where are you?

She expected me home an hour ago. No wonder she was worried. I typed a quick reply and pocketed my phone again.

The day's stress soaked into the darkness overtaking the back corner of the court. *"We all need grace."* Dee's words settled over me. Would that same grace cover Riley and me too? I faced the night sky for an answer. But the truth was, some things were easier to believe in daylight.

19

BRUISED

LAST NIGHT'S manual labor ached in the muscles my usual workouts at the gym obviously missed. Sitting in this stiff office chair all afternoon sure hadn't helped either. Stationed at my desk, I rotated from side to side to stretch out my back.

At least Trey had agreed to let me stay on—with constant supervision, of course.

My cell sat on a notepad beside me. No notifications. I tapped the side of my keyboard, debating whether I should call Riley. Would he even answer? But what if this whole time *he'd* been waiting on *me*? I scooped up my phone, swiveled toward the wall, and waited while one ring led to another. His all too familiar voicemail stood in for him.

My voice dropped with my chin. "Hey, just, um, wanted to talk." Wanted to make sure there was still something to talk about. The screen door shuddered behind me. "Call me when you have time."

I hung up and turned right as little Andre came toppling into the office from the basketball court. He bounded headfirst into A. J.'s legs. My pinched lips wouldn't have held back my smile if I tried. Achy muscles were nothing compared to my return on investment with these kids. Same as studying for the PSATs with Dee would be. They were worth focusing on. I shut my cell and questions about Riley in a side drawer for now.

On his desk phone, Trey stared into his mug and swept off his cap. The overhead light caught a few silver hairs I didn't remember seeing before. He took a sip of coffee that had to have trespassed way beyond the lukewarm stage by this point in the day.

He clamped the phone to his ear with his shoulder and massaged his temples. "Yes, sir, I know when the rent is due. I—" He pinched the bridge of his nose. "I understand, Mr. Glyndon. I hate putting you in this position too."

His chair creaked upright. "Mm-hmm." Trey leafed through a pile of bills I'd given him earlier, dropped them back on his desk, and shook his mouse. Poring over the computer screen, he adjusted his glasses. "I promise to have a payment to you by the end of the week." He pulled a pen cap off with his teeth and jotted something down. "Yes... yes, sir. Will do. We'll see you then."

The handset clicked into its base. Trey unwound his finger from the spiraled cord, but the stress on his face didn't come close to unraveling as easily. He met my anxious eyes, directed my attention toward Andre, and shook his head as if to say, not now.

The side door opened. Dee slipped in with his hood pulled over his hat.

The repercussions of Trey's phone call could wait a little longer. I unburied a booklet from beneath a pile of paper. "Hey, I was just thinking of you. Ready to tackle the PSAT prep course?"

Dee started for the classroom without lifting a glance my way. "I'm not taking them."

"What?"

Trey and A. J. both returned my confused stare.

I headed after him. "Dee, wait."

Keeping his head down, he tugged on the bill of his hat to shield his face. I cut him off at the door, but he pulled his arm away from my hand. "Just forget it, a'ight? It's not gonna happen. Never was."

"What are you talking about? I don't understand. I thought—"

"You thought wrong." He looked at me then. The light caught the sheen of blood on a gash in his lip that had barely started to scab. Dark bruises discolored the skin swollen around his left brow. More than any physical wound, the fractured look in his eyes cut the deepest. Whatever fight he'd been in, he'd taken my heart through it too.

I covered my mouth and reached for him. "Dee."

He flinched from my touch. "I'm a thug, Miss E. The streets is where I belong. Not some college."

How could he say that? Crestfallen, I turned to Trey.

He nodded and lifted Andre onto his hip. "How 'bout we work on that dunk you've been practicing?" He motioned for A. J. to follow them out back.

The room fell quiet again. "You went to talk to Tito, didn't you?"

Dee kicked the baseboard and let out a rueful laugh. "Naw. He sent Hugo and Mark to pay me a visit. Roughed up my pad. If my mom had been there..." He yanked his hood off and mumbled in Spanish. "They said Tito was doin' me a favor. Remindin' me who I am. Where I belong."

I brushed my thumb over the cuts on his knuckles. He winced but didn't pull away. "You can't let them bully you."

"You don't think I'm trying?" He backed up and shook his head. "You don't know nothin' 'bout how things roll here."

I swallowed the sting. "Maybe not, but I know you." I lifted his chin until he met the certainty in my eyes. "And I believe in what I see."

A rap at the door drew us both around.

Mr. Brake stepped in, slid his Newsboy cap off, and scanned the room.

What was he doing here? Taking some kind of inventory again?

"Trey's out back." I started for the door. "Let me grab him—"

"Don't bother. I'm not staying." He strode past me. "Someone broke into my daughter's car last night. Used the same M. O. as with Mr. Williams's car." He peered outside toward the frayed basketball net.

My blank stare trailed from him to Dee and back again.

"She saw the bastard from her apartment window. Said he looked like he'd been in a fight." His brown eyes paraded over Dee's broken face. His knuckles whitened. Trembling, he took two strides toward him. "If you ever come near my daughter again, so help me."

Dee looked backhanded. "I didn't do nothin' to your daughter or her car."

Jim released his balled-up fists and visibly strained for enough composure to straighten his tie. "I told Mr. Williams to be careful who he let in here."

My nails dug into my palms. "Excuse me?"

His briefcase brackets clicked open. He laid a piece of paper on Trey's desk, business-mode taking over again. "We only support organizations that set up the next generation for success." He flicked his chin in Dee's direction. "Not ones that perpetuate failure."

I blinked. Twice. Voice lost.

Dee's busted lip twitched beneath glassy eyes. He tugged his hood back on and grazed Jim's shoulder on his way out.

"Dee, wait."

Mr. Brake stood in my path and motioned to the rejection notice he'd left on Trey's desk. "I trust you'll make sure Mr. Williams gets this?"

My temples throbbed. I glared at him. "You don't know a thing about this place, about these kids."

He secured his cap over his balding head. "I know they just cost you a grant."

I started to shake, angrier at his arrogance than at Tito's. "Get. Out."

The screen door swung open. Mr. Brake nodded to someone behind me and backed out the way he came in.

I turned, and A. J. caught me in his arms. Trey blurred out of focus in front of me.

Perpetuating failure? That pompous jerk had some nerve. I didn't care how it looked. He should've gotten the facts first. Why'd he bother flaunting a chance of success if he'd discounted the kids at first glance? *He* was the one perpetuating failure. Not Dee.

Dee. I pushed off A. J. "I have to find him."

"Em—"

Trey grabbed A. J.'s arm. "Let her go."

I ran outside and down to the main street. Beside a metal trash can in front of our neighbor's, Dee sat on the curb with his head in his hands. I inched toward him, not knowing what to say except that I wanted to make it all go away—every bruise, seen and unseen.

I joined him on the curb and rested my arm against his in place of words that wouldn't come.

He rubbed his cuff under his nose. "Don't worry 'bout it. It ain't nothin' I never heard before."

"That doesn't mean it's true."

A view of the sun disintegrated behind the building opposite us. In the distance, I could see a glimpse of Jamal's old townhouse, now fully rebuilt. Something about the image brought Trey's words back to mind. Maybe some people truly did fear love. But while sitting here on this street corner with Dee, it was hard to give up on grace.

A smile gradually found its way through the silence onto his face. "You're going to make me say courageous, aren't you?"

"You know I am." My laugh petered into a side hug. I still didn't understand why God had led me to the center if I couldn't even succeed at securing us grant money. Honestly, I still didn't understand why something I was so sure He had His hand in would be this difficult. But even if nothing else made sense, I knew this kid beside me was part of the reason I was here. And he was counting on me.

I peered across the neighborhood to the remodeled townhouse—once left for ashes, now restored—and squeezed Dee's shoulder. "Things are gonna work out," I whispered.

Somehow.

20

SWAGGER

SITTING through my Monday classes should've sped up the hours keeping me away from my internship. With Mr. Brake's bombshell from Saturday still lurking in the background, it was hard to focus on anything else. I'd even stopped checking my phone for texts from Riley. I couldn't take more than one hurdle at a time.

Thankfully, Trey managed to scrape enough funds together to appease our landlord. For now.

I breathed a little lighter once I settled in at the office.

Trey traipsed by my computer monitor. "Scoping out a new college to transfer to?"

"Funny. I'm researching schools with good computer graphics programs. I promised Dee I'd help him look into some colleges after he takes the PSATs."

Trey sorted through a handful of mail. "Aren't those coming up?"

"Mm-hmm." I tapped the applications I'd printed off

into a stack. "Which is why I'm going to have these ready for him when he gets his results."

"You seem pretty confident. Think he's ready?"

"Shoot, after the top-notch tutoring course I'm giving him, he better be." I laughed, moved a pile of papers aside, and leaned on my arms. "To be honest, I don't think it'd hold him back even if he failed them. There's something special about him, Trey. He has this quiet strength that pushes the status quo, even with everything in his life trying to confine him to it."

"Not everything in his life." He lowered his glasses and gave me that infamous father-look. "He pushes boundaries 'cause you've taught him to hope in a future."

"You're giving me way too much credit there, buddy."

Trey held his ground. "He looks up to you."

I stared out the window into memories of how terrified I was when he'd first shown up. So much had changed. "It's kinda crazy. Dee's the last person I wanted to build a relationship with. It's almost like I had to be willing to face my own fears before he was able to do the same."

My chewed-up pencil dropped onto my desk. "Wait a sec. You knew, didn't you? That's why you paired us up from the beginning." I waved a finger at him. "You so planned this."

At his desk, Trey angled his bifocals to read the monitor. "Restoration is always a worthy plan," he said in his sage-like manner. "As far as what follows what?" He shrugged. "That can go down a whole lot of ways. But if you want to cast out fear?" His eyes flickered to mine. "The starting point's always love, Emma."

Whether his eyes or words held me in place, I wasn't sure. All I knew was that something about what he'd just said wasn't ready to release me.

A roar of high-pitched yells from out back ransacked my attempt at a response. With our gazes still connected, Trey and I both flew to the basketball court.

Darius's nose almost touched Mark's. "Man, I do circles 'round you."

"Wha?" Mark shoved him. "Don't make me Kobe Bryant your sorry—"

"Hey." I marched through the crowd and separated the two hot-faced teens. "Someone want to tell me what's going on here?"

"Mark and Darius is fightin' over who's the best baller." A young girl with skinny beaded braids wasted no time in tattling.

I crossed my arms. "Is that right, guys?"

Not a single response.

Trey tipped his head at me and returned to the office.

I bolstered my shoulders with borrowed confidence and faced the pair of them. "You're both very talented, but you know the real way to win a basketball game?"

Darius bounced the ball between his legs and dodged my eye contact. Mark smirked at a cluster of boys at his side, already dismissing what I had to say.

"Teamwork," I said anyway. "If you two work

together, you might actually learn something from each other."

Darius and Mark exchanged an abhorring glance, the possibility out of the question.

"She's right." A. J. strode out of the utility closet with a basketball in hand. "Maybe we can play a little two-on-two—you guys versus Miss E and me."

No he didn't. My dazed look blended right in with the cluster of blank faces staring back at A. J.

It took less than five seconds for a stream of questions to gush out, one after the other.

"Hold up? Miss E can ball?"

"You just messin' wit' us right, Mr. A. J.?"

"Miss E, you been holdin' out on us?"

Their expectant eyes cornered me. I would've sworn the basketball net reached its stringy arms out and tangled my stomach inside it. Playing for fun was one thing. Being on display in front of all these kids—who lived, breathed, and dreamed basketball—was another thing altogether.

A. J. strolled into the middle of the huddle, his eyes not releasing mine. "You don't want to mess with Miss E. She can throw it down on the court. Don't let her hustle you. Actually..." He rubbed his jawline, an idea visibly forming. "You wanna know what she's really good at?"

Every muscle in my body tensed at the possibility of what could leave A. J.'s mouth.

He crouched to the kids' level and stoked their

curiosity like a dad about to tell a ghost story at a camp-fire. "Miss E can play the guitar."

He might as well have hurled the ball into my gut.

His disclosure unleashed another shockwave throughout my now-attentive audience.

"Miss E, you gotta play for us."

"Please!"

"I always wanted to learn how to play the guitar."

"Oh, Miss E, you gotta play. Please, please!"

One adorable face to the next zeroed in on my medi-ocrity as a musician.

"Trust me, guys, you don't wanna hear…"

The stare from someone in the back of the group cut off my refusal. With a mischievous smile rivaling A. J.'s, Dee mouthed the words he'd obviously been waiting for the chance to make me eat. "I am courageous."

Perfect. Now I really had no choice. I lifted my palms in surrender. "Fine. Okay, okay," I shouted over the bellow of petitioning voices. "In a couple of weeks, all right? After the PSATs. Promise."

Appeased, the boisterous mob disbanded into pairs of friends, each chatting about their own hidden talents. If nothing else, thankfully the topic had sidetracked them from A. J.'s two-on-two suggestion. Though, I honestly wasn't sure which was worse.

I dropped onto the stone bench beside him. "I'd wipe that smirk off your face if I were you. Two weeks is a long time away. I can still get out of it."

A. J. shot a dramatized look of surprise at Dee and

flung his hand over his chest, as if I'd blasted an arrow through it.

He was lucky I didn't have a real one. "Uh-huh. I might be locked up by then once they find out I killed you."

A. J.'s dimples barely contained his smile. "Oh, c'mon. Be a good sport. For the kids."

"Right," I said. "For the kids. You're completely innocent in this whole little scheme."

He held up his fingers. "Scout's honor." Grin toppling, he leaned his burly arm against my shoulder. "Seriously, Em, when was the last time you actually played your guitar?"

"I… I…"

He crossed his ankles in front of him. "That's what I thought."

I sat against the cement wall, arms laced.

A. J. twisted toward me. "Playing used to make you happy. You shouldn't let that die just because…"

The look of warning in my eyes must've dissuaded him from finishing. He stood up and pulled his cell from his pocket instead. "You know what you need?"

"Oh, no. Here we go."

He ignored my response. "You need to let your hair down. Have a little fun," he added with a wink.

A twangy pitch of banjos and fiddles took over the basketball court. Dee's head sprang up from his lap, his face mirroring the same look of horror overtaking my own.

A. J. extended a hand toward me. "Come on. There's nothing like a little country music to help you loosen up."

I uncrossed my arms. "You do *not* like country music."

"Everybody loves country music." He lugged me up from the bench. "Me and…" He stole a peek at his phone. "…Blake Shelton, here, are just trying to help you get in touch with your country side."

With both my hands in his, A. J. swung my arms back and forth until my whole body swayed against my resistance. "There you go. Let it out."

He belted the chorus after one time through, taking extra measure to yell the words "hillbilly" and "yee-haw" at a decibel even more obnoxious than the music itself.

Dee came to my rescue and wrestled A. J. to the ground for his phone. "Bro, you're killin' me. If you're gonna show her how to dance, you at least gotta have real music."

"All right, Deejay Dee." A. J. egged him on. "Why don't you show us how it's done?"

Dee scrolled through to find a suitable station. After stealing a minute to feel the music, he moved in sync with the bass like one of Usher's backup dancers. "You gotta lower your hips, Miss E. Like this. Dip your shoulder into it. Yeah, but you gotta add swag to it."

"Yeah, Em," A. J. said with a grin I almost smacked off his face. "You gotta add *swag*."

I glared at him over top of Dee's head. "I hate you."

A. J. laughed. "You love me."

"No. No, I'm fairly certain I hate you right now."

"C'mon, Rosy. Who else is going to show you how to have fun?"

"Is that what you call it? Because I was thinking more along the lines of humiliation." My lips scrunched together, refusing to give in to the pull luring them in the opposite direction.

One look at Dee's face, and that was it. I lost it. We could definitely rule out my career in dancing. Comedy Central, on the other hand, could be a very plausible destination. At least my disgrace gave us some levity.

I shook my head at A. J. Here he was, once again teaching me how to live with my eyes and heart wide open.

Riley's ringtone clipped into the music. For a moment, I hesitated to answer.

"Having a party?" Riley asked.

I glided over to a corner of the court, away from the noise. "Dee and A. J. were trying to teach me how to dance. You know what a disaster that can be."

A. J. mimicked Dee's moves, and my laughter spilled out again.

An edge pulsed in Riley's delayed response. "You're dancing," he said slowly, "with A. J.?"

"It's not like that. All *three* of us are messing around on the basketball court. Friends having a good time. That's all. You wanted me to enjoy my senior year while you're away. I'm trying." I clenched the fence and pressed my head to the back of my hand.

Another wrenching pause.

"You're right," he said. "It's good to hear you laugh."

"Riley, I didn't mean that the way it sounded."

"It's fine. I won't keep you. I just wanted to say I'm sorry for the way I ended our last call. I needed some time to think. As much as it kills me not to have been there to protect you, it hurts more to know you were afraid to tell me what happened."

"I shouldn't have kept it from you. This whole being apart thing…"

"I know," he said softly. "Listen, I've been wanting to tell you… There's a chance I might be able to come home early. It's—"

"You ready?" someone asked Riley.

"In a sec," he answered her. "Em, I'm sorry, I have to—"

"You have to go."

He sighed. "I have to test out some new songs with Jess before we pitch them to the rest of the team."

The way we'd talked about doing before he left? He hadn't played for me since he first got there. But I understood. Music was easier to share with someone in person. Same as every part of a relationship.

"It won't always be like this, Emma."

But what would be left by then?

A girl's nasally voice haggled in the background again. I said goodbye before he heard the quiver in mine.

Maybe it was time we stopped making each other promises we weren't sure we could keep. I launched off the rickety fence. With my gaze dragging along the ground, I almost bumped smack into A. J.

"Trouble in paradise?"

The fence rattled behind me. "No."

"Good." He stretched his long arm around my shoulders. "Because we wouldn't want any distractions hindering the little performance you've got coming up."

I popped him in the stomach. "Thanks for the reminder."

"You've conquered worse. It's just a guitar."

Wrong. It was another fire I wasn't ready to face.

21

FRICTION

MY BEDROOM DOOR closed behind me. I stopped two steps inside. Outlined in a thin layer of dust, my guitar stared at me from the opposite corner of the room. Putting this off for two weeks hadn't made one bit of difference.

I turned, frozen with my hand on the light switch and A. J.'s voice in my mind. *"It's just a guitar."* I shook my arms out at my sides and convinced my Converse sneakers to do an about-face to end the unwarranted standoff.

It took a few minutes for the guitar to lose its awkwardness and feel at home again. My transitions weren't the smoothest. I'd probably never touch people the way gifted musicians could. But in that secluded moment, none of that mattered. With all apprehension dissolved, nothing could squelch the joy of remembering music was a gift meant to give away.

If Riley could be brave enough to offer that gift to the world, then I could be brave enough to offer it to kids who'd given me more than they'd ever realize.

A. J. had nailed it. Again. Playing was exactly what I needed.

"I thought I heard you in here." Jaycee flitted through the door and slumped onto her bed across from mine. "I've missed hearing you play. It's soothing."

I set the guitar aside. "Uh-oh. Wedding plans got you stressed out?"

"Girl, please." She crossed her legs, kicking the apparent insult into oblivion. But when she looked at me again, the original strain in her expression fractured the confidence in her eyes.

"It's my mom. She keeps getting sick. Each time, it's harder for her to recover. I'm kinda starting to freak out about it."

The one word in the English vocabulary I loathed more than any other sprang to mind. Cancer.

"How did you do it?" The beginning of tears coated her voice. "How did you keep yourself together when your dad went through this?"

"Jae, we don't know if it's that serious."

"But what if it is?"

I ran my fingers down the neck of the guitar in search of the right thing to say. "It's not always something you understand while going through it, but I think we're given a special grace in the times we need it the most."

More than a platitude, it was a statement of conviction I'd gained through experience. Even now, I depended on the indefinable strength that had girded my family during that season.

Jaycee stared at the floor. Unspoken "what ifs" entwined with the carpet threads. "I'm glad you're here, Em."

If I'd gone to Nashville, I wouldn't have been. A surge of gratefulness joined the warmth of the afternoon sunshine painting our bedroom in golden streaks.

"Will you keep playing," she asked, "for a little while longer?"

I set the pick on my mattress and let the strum of my fingertips release comfort into the unseen places only music could touch. With a companion this time, I returned to a world spun by the guitar's soothing melody.

WHAT I WOULD'VE DONE to hang on to that same sweet peace the rest of the day.

My nerves competed with the car's throttle the entire ride to the center. When Dad had played for me, he could've made a hundred blunders, and it wouldn't have mattered. I was too fascinated at the way his fingers mastered the strings and too untrained to notice any minor dissonance. Maybe the kids would feel the same, even if I accidentally mixed up a couple of chords. It would be fine. Right?

Wrong.

One foot into the office, and the weight of my guitar dragged my self-confidence straight to the basement. My pulse echoed the second hand on the wall clock. Wait. When was it ever quiet enough to hear the clock ticking?

I swept a glance around the empty office, then plodded onto the deserted basketball court. Where was everyone?

The distant hum of traffic replaced the court's usual commotion. Knowing A. J., he'd probably planned on giving me time to warm up. Figured.

I sat on the stone bench, stretched my neck from side to side, and tested out a few chords. It didn't take long for the beginning of a song Dad had played for me when I was about the age of the kids here to unlock the same peace I'd found in my bedroom earlier. I faced the open sky. "Thank you," I whispered.

My cell vibrated in my pocket.

"Thought I'd lost her," A. J. said from the doorway.

Jumping at his voice, I caught the guitar before it slid all the way off my lap and ignored my phone. "Who?"

He crossed the short distance between us. "That girl I saw on campus a year ago—off by herself in a moment no one could steal from her."

I shook my head at him. "I don't know how, but it's like you know what I need before I do."

He sat beside me and stared at the top of the basketball court. "Things are easier to see from the outside."

Always were.

"Thanks for your friendship, A. J. Your stubborn, witty friendship, that is." I laughed. "I'm starting to wonder what I'd do without it."

He turned slowly. "I told you I'd always take care of you." His eyes locked onto mine and ushered a volume of thoughts through the silence. Memories from the night we danced in the city last Christmas overtook the court.

Before I found my voice, a stampede rushed onto the court from inside. Trey must've had everyone holed up in the classroom.

A. J. hopped to his feet as though no more fazed by whatever had just passed between us a second ago than by the throng of kids now surrounding us both. "All right, guys, it's the moment you've been waiting for. Everyone take a seat."

The kids congregated on the ground in uneven rows. A spotlight of eyes beaming with anticipation fell on me.

No matter how many times I rubbed my palms over my jeans, the guitar kept slipping free. My dry mouth made it impossible to speak—forget singing.

Of all moments, A. J. disappeared. The screen door shut behind him and sent an echo into the empty space beside me on the bench. One forced swallow followed another until the door squeaked again.

A. J. dropped back into his spot. He flipped a small

plastic trash can upside down between his legs, tapped the makeshift drum, and winked. "Ready?"

He always knew how to put me at ease. By the second time through the chorus, the joy of watching the kids' faces light up trumped my nerves. I never should've doubted the way music could cross any barrier.

My cell buzzed again in the middle of the song, but I couldn't answer while playing.

On the last row, Dee shifted his focus back and forth between something in his lap and me.

The memory of Dad's voice swelled in my heart. *"Life's a lot like being an artist. It's not as much about mastering technique as it is risking the cost of opening your heart to the song you're meant to share."*

I peeked toward the heavens and smiled. *You're still teaching me how to open my heart, aren't you?*

One of our preteen girls sat on her knees and reached for my guitar the second we finished. "Can I try?"

Petitions rose as the seated audience turned into a jumping mob.

"Relax, guys." A. J. towered above us. "I brought an extra guitar so you can take turns."

He thought to bring a spare?

A. J. raised his brows at my expression. "Always a look of surprise."

He had me. All I could do was laugh.

Once the chord plucking began, I escaped to the office. I'd take balance sheets and profit loss statements over guitar spotlights any day.

It was six o'clock before the outside serenading transitioned back to the center's normal buzz. A whirlwind of data entry and emails had carried me through the rest of my shift.

I condensed the remaining stack of bills on my desk into a thin pile and crossed the room to a metal filing cabinet. I did a double take out the back screen door.

On A. J.'s shoulders, Andre gripped a basketball between two pudgy hands. A swarm of animated kids below him chanted and cheered. But even with his arms stretched as far as they would go, he couldn't clear the rim.

With the extra lift of rising on his tiptoes, A. J. closed the gap separating Andre from the glory of his first ever slam-dunk. He took off jogging with Andre on his shoulders like a champion who'd just scored the winning point in a tournament game.

King of the world, the little guy squealed and pumped his fist. A. J. had barely set him down before a group of amped friends swept him up and carried him through the chain-link fence toward their neighborhoods.

The sun followed them and cast an orange glow over the few fire-red leaves left on the maple tree between our building and our neighbor's. It seemed colder than it should have for the middle of October.

I leaned against the doorjamb and watched A. J. slip a pair of earbuds in before collecting the equipment scattered behind. His long-sleeved, off-white T-shirt and worn basketball cap took me back to the first night we met. His boyish grin was as endearing now as it had been then.

The strength and tenderness he offered the kids made me proud to be his friend. Proud to serve alongside him. Why couldn't enjoying the rest of my senior year be as easy as enjoying my work here?

I snuck up behind him on the now-deserted court. "Told you you'd make a good coach."

He tossed a basketball into the netted bag slung over his shoulder and tugged on his earbuds. "You think so, huh?"

"Yep." I picked up one of the balls and toed the free throw line. "Maybe you can give me a few pointers."

His dimples sank into his cheeks. "Thought you said the moves the kids taught you were supposed to leave me dizzy."

Without moving my body, I met A. J.'s impish grin, returned my focus to the basket under the floodlight, and released the ball with one swift wrist flex. I kept my arms in the air until that glorious *swish* sung an anthem of praise. "Oh... nothin' but net!" I strutted toward him. "You're right. Maybe *I* should be the one giving *you* some pointers."

"Oh, yeah?" A. J. swiped the ball, cut across the court, and nailed an impressive backhand layup. He slid me a smile. "Ready for that rematch, are we?"

I whirled my hair up into a half ponytail, half bun. "You're on."

He crouched in front of me. "Bring it, chica."

His long arms loomed over me every time I tried to make a basket from inside the paint, but I wasn't about to give up. I waved at the fence behind him. "Hi, Dee."

A. J. turned, and I made a solid jump shot from the perimeter. He spun away from the empty fence toward my guilty-slash-gloating smile. "Playin' dirty. I see how it is."

He trumped my moves without any diversion tactics necessary. Faking a shot, he had way too much fun watching my pitiful attempt at leaping in the air to block him. With the sun gone and wind picking up, my frozen hands probably would've dropped the ball anyway.

He scooted me backward and boxed me out inch by inch. The bottom of his sweaty shirt pressed into my palm. "Need that ten-point advantage?"

"You're really enjoying this, aren't you?"

He tossed his head back. "You have no idea."

I reached around and smacked the ball out of his hands. Pivoting on the tip of my foot, I sidestepped around him, stole the loose ball, and skirted to the perimeter again. "It's true what they say, you know. Pride comes before the fall."

He tipped his head. "Spoken by an expert."

A curt smile preceded a valiant three-point shot. "Oh!"

"Nice." He strutted across the court. "You got mad skills, girl. If I didn't know any better, I'd think you might've been trying to play me again."

"Oh, no you don't. Don't even go there. There was no

hustling involved this time. You knew full well what you were up against." I pulled my hair tie out of what was left of my ponytail.

"Mm-hmm," he said, standing right in front of me now. "I guess it doesn't really matter." He rubbed his knuckles against his shirt. "Since I won and all."

My lashes fluttered off his gloating. "Okay, I'll admit, you're not *half bad* on the basketball court." I deliberately choked over the words.

"For the record?"

I nodded a begrudging yes.

"That's very generous of you." He brushed away a film of hard-earned sweat from my temple. "You're not half bad yourself, Rosy."

With him this close, my heart rate picked up faster than it had in the game. I backed up. A breeze barreled through my damp shirt and chilled my skin. "Well, you only won 'cause my fingers are numb. It's freezing out here."

His brow slanted. "What were you saying about pride?"

I mirrored his expression and held my hands out for proof. He squeezed my frozen fingers.

"See?"

He grinned while rubbing his hands over mine. Friction slowly sparked warmth. "Better?"

I didn't answer. Couldn't. Not with the way heat was spreading from my hands down my body.

In the glow of the floodlight, his unwavering gaze

blurred everything else out of focus as he drew my fingertips to his mouth and blew on them.

An icy pang cut into the warmth and caught me in the gut. I blinked and looked away.

A. J. kept rubbing my hands. "By the way, I finally had that talk with Ashlea."

My head flashed up. "What'd you tell her?"

His enigmatic eyes latched on to mine again. "The truth."

22

SCATTERED

BEING WINDED from the basketball game had nothing on the way A. J.'s words knocked the breath out of me. Honesty could be costly.

He released my gaze but held on to an unreadable expression. "When I told Ashlea we needed to talk, I'm pretty sure she knew it wasn't about flying across the country to meet my folks." He laughed, probably envisioning the scene playing out. "Mom might've bought the act, or at least pretended to. But Aiden Sr.? Not a chance. And he sure enough wouldn't have had a problem calling me out on it."

An undertone of regret, disappointment maybe, laced his usual humor. "Ashlea didn't need to hear the truth from anyone but me. As much as I didn't want to hurt her, I knew what I had to say." He picked up his cell from the bench and wrapped his earbud cords around it. "Even if it doesn't make sense."

"If what doesn't make sense?"

He stared at his cell. "You don't choose who you fall in love with," he said softly. "Like music, remember?"

"Music?"

A. J. pocketed his phone and kicked the basketball up into his hands. "Hey, you're the one who went all Dr. Phil on me with the music analogy. I'm just saying you were right." He nudged me with the ball. "The whole one song thing?"

I teetered on my feet, words feeling even less stable.

Breaths collected in the air as he peered across the court. "You can't explain why it stands out from the rest. You just feel it in your soul, feel chills on your arms every time you hear it." He looked up slowly, eyes full of passion. "You never lose the connection."

My pulse skittered. Looking away again, I twisted the elastic band around my wrist. "Did you tell that to Ash?"

He rubbed out his hair and slid his hat back on. "Basically."

"How'd she take it?"

"She said she understood, hugged me, and walked away."

"That's it?" No pleading? No balls of fire or icy razors shooting through those malevolent eyes? Not even tears?

He scratched his cheek. "You know how proud Ash is."

That didn't mean she wasn't hurt. From the look on A. J.'s face, he knew it too.

"Listen, it may take some time, but the wound will

heal." It had to. I had to believe that with enough time brokenness could heal for good.

He inched closer. "What if the person isn't willing to let go?"

His expression trapped my voice beneath the layers of that unanswerable question.

My arm drifted to my side. I shuffled backward. One foot, then another. Something creased into my calf and almost tumbled over. I turned and batted the orange cone like a bona fide circus performer. Worst part was, even after it finally stabilized, my heart rate wasn't any closer to doing the same.

"It's getting late," I blurted out randomly. "I should probably get going. Just need to grab my stuff from inside."

A. J. smiled, saying nothing and everything.

I made a beeline for the door. Hidden in the office, I slouched against the trim and pressed the heel of my hand to my forehead. What in the world was going on with me?

"Hey, Emma."

I gasped, tripped into a metallic trash can, and caught the corner of the filing cabinet before I ended up on the floor.

Trey flung his palms up in surrender. "Easy, there."

"Sorry, I didn't know you were still here." Thankfully, I managed to maintain my balance on my way to my desk.

A lot of good it did.

"Everything all right? You seem a little shaky."

I powered down my computer and gathered my things from the drawer. "Just winded from playing ball."

Trey plopped down in his creaky chair with the burden of another day resting on his shoulders. "Mm-hmm."

His familiar grunt rang in the office like a phone waiting to be answered.

I wasn't about to ask. Face forward, I headed for the door until a sparkle from a bag at the base of Trey's desk caught my eye. "Is that crystal?"

He peered over his arm at the bag. "Old wedding presents. I'm hitting up the pawn shop on my way home."

Hocking possessions to pay bills? I wondered where he came up with the money for last month's rent. My chest deflated. "Trey, I'm so sorry."

He shrugged. "You do what you gotta do."

Even when it hurt.

I turned to the door again.

"Oh, Emma, I meant to tell you. I heard from Jamal."

I spun around. "Any update on when they're coming back?" Now that their townhouse was rebuilt, it had to be soon.

"Actually, they're staying in Boise."

My heart sank. "For good?"

"Sounds like it." He lowered his coffee mug. "I knew the boys had been estranged from their grandparents, but I never knew why. Evidently, a lot of misunderstandings have kept them apart. Jamal always assumed they didn't want to be a part of their lives. Turns out, they've wanted the kids to live with them all along."

A mix of gratefulness and sorrow tinted his eyes. "Jamal said this is the first time he's lived in a home where he's felt genuinely wanted."

Hearing Jamal's tender heart ring through the words tore at the edges of mine. "You made him feel that way here, too, you know." It was another poignant reminder of why the center couldn't close.

Trey's fatherly smile lifted beneath his glasses. "So did you, kid."

Emotions began to overlap. Tears pricked up my throat. Squelching them, I managed a nod before high-tailing it to the car in vain hope that distance would settle the restlessness in my chest.

The same tug-of-war I saw in Trey's eyes churned inside me. Though I'd miss them, Jamal and Reggie were loved, provided for, wanted—things they wouldn't have found if the fire hadn't driven them out of the circum-stances they'd been trapped in. They'd found where they were meant to be.

Was it the same for Riley? For A. J.? Me?

The scene on the basketball court screened to mind, and the whirlwind of competing thoughts funneled back to the questions that were gnawing at me before Trey's diversion.

I had to be overreacting. A. J. was my coworker. A friend, like Trevor and Trey. I valued his friendship, treasured his connection with the center. That didn't mean it was anything more.

A city bus pulled out a block ahead, leaving a haze of diesel smoke to cloud my certainty. I rifled through my purse for my cell and called Austin before understanding why, other than knowing I had to sort this out. Now.

I skipped the hellos. "Do you have a few minutes?"

"For my little sister? Sure."

I toyed with the keys in the ignition. "Do you think guys and girls can be best friends? I mean, without romantic feelings complicating things."

"No."

"That was a quick answer. You didn't even think about it?"

"It's a simple question, Em. A simple question with a simple answer."

"Maybe for you." I flicked the dangling keys, sending them clinking and clanking into the dashboard. "Sorry, not all of us are as enlightened as you, oh great wise one."

"Aren't we touchy tonight?" Austin reined in a snicker. "It's not like it's some confounding mystery. Just think about it."

My mind reeled. "Trev and I are best friends."

"I doubt that. Close, maybe. But not like spending one-on-one time with Jaycee, baring all your secrets, right?"

I chewed my thumb. "Right." The steam rising from a manhole in front of the car oozed out more gracefully than my begrudging response.

"Why do you think that is?"

"He's my best friend's fiancé." I yanked out a bag of M&Ms from my purse. "That'd be a little inappropriate."

"Well, there you go," Austin said, sealing the argument. I could almost hear the gavel slamming in the background.

I steadied the phone between my ear and shoulder and pinched the top corner of the bag with my nails.

Austin swallowed whatever he was drinking—a venti Americano, no doubt. "And A. J.—"

My tiny incision split the bag straight down the middle and launched M&Ms into flight throughout the car. "What about A. J.?"

Great. As if I needed to add any fuel to my brother's already-blazing soapbox.

"Em, it's obvious your friendships with Trevor and A. J. mean a lot to you. I get it. I'm just saying. It's easy to give away pieces of your heart if you don't guard it. And, trust me, you don't wanna be stuck having to break those heart ties on the back end."

"You speaking from experience?"

"You could say that." He paused. "When I first started dating Hailey, I made a conscious choice to distance myself from my female friends."

"Like Anna?" I'd wondered why they'd lost touch.

"Anna?"

Was he that clueless? "You guys were inseparable at USC." I collected a handful of the candy that had landed on the passenger seat.

He laughed. "We were study partners. It's not like I cried on her shoulder or anything."

Clueless and hopeless.

"That was before I met Hailey anyway. But, yeah, Anna and I talk only by email every so often now."

I picked through the M&Ms for the brown ones. "Hailey doesn't strike me as the jealous type."

"It's more about commitment than jealousy. When you find the right person, you're willing to make sacrifices to protect that."

"And Hailey's the right one?" I'd only met her once over the summer when they'd come to visit, but something about her didn't sit well.

"We haven't been dating that long. I want to give it some time. See what's left after all the love-at-first-sight stuff fades."

I looked at my ring. "Why does it have to fade?" I said more to myself than to him.

He laughed. "This isn't a country song, Em. It's life. And like it or not, life's gonna throw us into fires to see what's real and what isn't."

"Fires. Wow. Thanks for that comforting metaphor. You're really on a roll with the whole sage thing tonight, aren't you?"

"That *is* why you call me." There was that same tone again.

"Yeah well, you don't always have to be so good at your job, you know?"

"Then where would you be?"

Lost, probably. I downed a handful of chocolate, wishing everything he'd said was as easy to swallow. "I should get going. But, Aust?"

"Yeah?"

I let out a tension-filled breath and smiled. "Love you."

"You too."

As usual, my brother's Daily Maxims radio station continued to blare in my head even after I hung up. I knew what he was saying, but A. J. and I'd already drawn lines last year. Clear lines. None of that should have changed.

As soon as I cranked the ignition, my thoughts scattered with the multi-colored M&Ms rattling on the floorboard. A whisper rose amidst the chaotic noise, and I knew. I needed to clear up any uncertainty with A. J. for both our sakes.

I cut the engine and hurried back inside.

A. J. almost ran into me from the opposite direction. "Hey, I was hoping you hadn't left yet." He motioned behind him. "Someone wants to talk to you before you leave."

My slanted glance petitioned him to fill in the blanks, but his lopsided grin offered nothing. Fine. We'd talk afterward. I eased onto the basketball court again.

"Miss E," someone called from the shadows.

My shoulders hit my ears. With one hand pressed to my heart and the other to the wall, I steadied my balance.

"Dee, you really need to stop sneaking up on me like that."

"Oh, sorry."

I joined him on the bench. What was he still doing here?

His smile tenderized my heart and overrode everything else.

"Tomorrow's the big day," he said.

"Ah… the PSATs." I prodded him with my elbow. "You're gonna nail 'em."

He gripped the beveled edge of the bench on either side of his legs. "It's easy to believe that here." His eyes flickered with the same self-doubt that had darkened them when he first came to the center.

He shrugged. "Guess I never had nobody to accept and believe in me like you guys do." He shifted the bill of his hat. "Trey took me in like it was nothin'. Even A. J. gave me a chance."

I looked at A. J., standing behind the screen door. Did he have any idea the impact he was making on this boy's life?

Dee jutted his chin at the neighboring buildings. "At home, it's—I don't know—like there's this darkness I can't escape. You know what I'm sayin'? The darkness is everywhere. It's…"

"Oppressive." I knew exactly what he meant.

"Yeah, almost like it's fightin' against me. You know?" The dimly lit court couldn't hide the turmoil deepening across his face.

My heart winced. I stared at the single hoop opposite us. The frayed net swayed in a breeze above the paint-chipped pole. The odds against the kids in this neighborhood clung to them as much as traces of the washed-off graffiti still clung to the bricks.

But even if I never fully understood what it'd take to break the chains binding Dee to a life governed by his circumstances, I'd seen hope light up his heart. And I had to believe that hope wouldn't disappoint him. We weren't as different as he might've thought.

"I know what it's like to feel overwhelmed." Way more than I wanted to admit. Memories rushed in. "My dad and I used to sit under the sky until the stars put things back in perspective. He always said it was because nothing could overpower them. Not even the darkest backdrop."

I pointed to the heavens. "See?" Raw vulnerability choked through with a reminder of how much I still needed that light in my own life. "Sometimes it helps to get everything off my chest too. Just face the sky and let it all unload."

Head angled, Dee studied me for a minute and then focused on the stars. "You mean, like, you talk to God?"

"Yeah." I smiled.

He lowered his head and looked at me with the innocence of a child. "Do you think He'll hear me?"

His question cut straight to the one I'd wrestled over and over again. Inhaling, I turned toward the sky. "I think it's pretty hard for us to hear the answer sometimes—a lot of times, honestly. But yeah, I believe He hears us. Even when we don't know what to pray."

As we sat side by side, a quiet moment passed in which no sound was needed. The buildings sheltered us from the wind. Clouds glided by, continually robing and disrobing the bare moon.

"Miss E?" he almost whispered. "What happens when you can't see the stars?"

Starless. I'd felt that way so many times since losing my dad—when storms raged with such intensity that they blocked out all light.

Drawing on the words of wisdom others had given me during times when I'd asked a similar question, I looked at Dee with every fiber of certainty I could muster. "When you can't see the stars, you have to have faith to believe they're still there."

He considered that. After another quiet minute, he nodded at the rundown court. "I'm sorry for messin' up your chance to get money from that rich guy."

"Don't even think about taking the blame for that." I slid my hands into my hoodie pocket. "He's probably just uptight about money 'cause he has to dump half of what he makes into pookie's doggy daycare."

Dee cracked a laugh but then grew pensive again. "I'm not gonna give up on Tito."

He didn't realize the kind of faith he already had, did he? Despite the scabs leaving a reminder of the fight, Tito's damage hadn't scarred his heart.

"Hope the center won't close before then." He hung

his head. "I know you was really countin' on those grant funds."

I stretched my arm around his shoulders. "We'll figure something else out. Courageous, remember? C'mon, say it."

"Aw... Miss E."

My look of persistence left no room for argument.

He tilted his head and rolled his eyes. "I am courageous."

"Now, how 'bout you try that with a little heart this time."

"I am courageous," he roared with a pacifying flair.

I squeezed him and pushed him off the bench. "You got it. Now, here." I grabbed my purse and pulled out the number two pencils I'd meant to give him earlier. "These are for tomorrow. You should get on home. Get some sleep. And don't forget to eat a good breakfast in the morning."

"Thanks, *Mom*." Dee stopped on the other side of the fence, paused like he wanted to say something else, but then kept going.

Once he disappeared from sight, I headed inside. On my way to my desk, I smiled at A. J. "He's a good kid."

He started toward me. "And you're an amazing woman."

"I seem to remember Dee mentioning your name in the mix of influencers."

"And yet you're the one person he singled out to talk to tonight."

With a folder in my hand, I waved off his comment and huffed my unruly bangs from my face. A. J. stopped an inch away, his expression consuming me. I backed into my chair. "Why are you looking at me like that?"

"Because you make it hard not to." He brushed back the hair caught in my lashes. "You don't even realize how beautiful you are."

Beautiful? "A. J., I'm in jeans and a sweatshirt."

"Exactly," he said, unabashed.

I ran my sneaker tip along the crease between the floor's black and white tiles. Why couldn't all lines be that straightforward? I stashed my hands in my pockets, pulled them back out, and tucked my arms over my stomach. My talk with Austin blazed to mind.

"A. J., I—"

"I know."

I looked up toward eyes still holding mine. Honest. Vulnerable.

My cell's ring pulsed between us and hedged A. J. a safe distance away. He must've seen the name on the screen. "I'll be outside," he said while turning.

It took me a minute to find my voice again before answering Riley's call.

"Emma, I've been trying to reach you all day. I have something I need to tell you."

23

TIME

EXTENDED? Whoever said time healed was a liar. Or maybe delusional. Time stole. Always had.

Of course his label had extended Riley's stay in Nashville. If he'd won their hearts the way he had mine, they probably never wanted him to leave. His fans would feel the same way. And I should've been supportive of any direction his career took him, not resenting that it was taking him away from me.

I'd been through all this a dozen times since our call got cut short last night, but my thoughts kept going around in as many circles as it was taking for Trevor and me to find an empty parking spot during the lunch hour.

I raked a hand through the top of my hair and tried not to stare at the person in the car directly beside us. "Jae couldn't have picked a better time for us to meet her here?"

"She doesn't have much flexibility on when she can

tutor." Trevor splayed a hand toward a corner Irish pub. "Besides, what could be better than an afternoon in Portland?"

I could think of a few. Nothing I'd done all night or morning had distracted me enough to forget about Riley's phone call. Memories of being with him in the city weren't bound to help.

Trevor hit the gas pedal, raced the car up two feet, and stomped on the brake again.

I clenched my innocent seat belt. "This traffic is maddening."

Leaving one hand on the steering wheel, Trevor slumped in the driver's seat and cocked his head toward me. "Dangerous driving's my specialty."

"Who are you, James Bond?"

"Em—"

My waving arms intercepted his witty remark. "There's a spot. Go, go, go!"

"Hang on, Suburb Girl. I'm about to show you how we roll in the city."

With the front tires skimming the curb, he swerved onto the narrow side street before I could grab my door handle for leverage. He slammed on the brakes a car-length in front of the open spot. My whole torso flung forward and back.

I glared at him. "Nice."

"Just trying to make sure you get the full Bond experience." He parallel parked the car with ease. "See. Not even a scratch on the bumpers."

"Congratulations." I opened the door.

"Oh, c'mon," he said from over the hood of his Outlander. "You have to admit that was impressive." He strutted toward an adjacent parking meter. "Ha." He flung his hands in the air in a hallelujah motion. "Even the parking meter recognizes talent. It already spotted me fifteen minutes."

Of course it would have leftover time on it. My head circled with exasperation. "Only you have that kind of luck."

"Nothing to do with luck." He filled the overly accommodating parking meter with a handful of quarters and nudged me forward. "C'mon, Jaycee's probably wondering where we are."

A gust of traffic stopped us at the busy intersection. Orange warning signs blocked off the sidewalk to our right, where a jackhammer shrilled into the clamor of engines and car horns.

I elbowed Trevor. "I can see you working on a construction crew like that, except you wouldn't need a hard hat. Your head's inflated enough to take any blow."

"You think that's funny?" He looped his arm around mine. "I'll show you funny." A quick glance in both directions rolled into a sprint across the street with me toted by his side.

I caught hold of the crosswalk sign on the opposite side and swung around it twice before planting my boots on the sidewalk. I launched at him, but his backward jog kept him a stride ahead of each of mine.

Looking past me, he freed my hand from its death grip around his coat. "Um, Em, I think we better keep moving."

The crosswalk light released an incoming stream of travel mugs and briefcases funneling onto our heels. We maneuvered out of the congested pedestrian traffic and into an obstacle course of street vendors and bus stops instead.

Next to one of the stands, a middle-aged businessman embraced a woman who must've come to meet him on his lunch break. He draped his suit jacket over her shoulders and kissed her cheek, then led her to a nearby bench. She sank into his side and snuggled her head beneath his chin the same way I'd seen Mom do with Dad a thousand times.

Austin's spiel screened to memory. Our parents faced the toughest fire imaginable yet still hung on with a love capable of enduring anything. I should've been able to offer that to Riley too. It's exactly what I wanted to give him through all of this. What I'd been trying to give him. But maybe fires weren't the problem at all. Maybe I was.

I tucked one side of my coat over the other and tapped my boot tip against an uprooted chunk of pavement.

Trevor inched beside me. "You didn't take enough aggression out on your seat belt earlier?"

Good thing he was there to distract me. "Keep talking smack, and you're next."

He hopped dead in front of me so I crashed into his

back. Chuckling, he curled an arm around my shoulders. "How about you tell me what's up instead?"

Sometimes, he reminded me so much of Austin. And even a little of Trey, for that matter.

The thought brought Trey's words from the beginning of the term back to mind.

"Just keep learning to love him, and you'll get through this."

Learn to love him. I thought I already had.

A few steps down the sidewalk, I peered back at the couple we'd passed. "Before Riley left, no one could've convinced me I wasn't ready to get married. I mean, yeah, I was scared at first when he'd proposed. But then... I don't know. After spending every day with him over the summer, I guess it got easy to tune out all the doubts. To feel like I really knew how to love him."

"You do."

Did I? A gust of damp wind blew through me with the answer. "My knee-jerk reaction when he first told me he was leaving was fear. Not faith, Trev. Fear." I shook my head. "What does that say about me?"

"That you're human."

A thickheaded one maybe. I knew what he meant, but it was more than that.

"Sorry." I sighed. "I don't know why I'm unloading all of this on you right now. I'm just... frustrated. I thought I was strong enough to give him everything he needs from me. That I was finally whole enough for him. For marriage." But I wasn't. I was still falling short. Still trying to love him from a place of brokenness, as if I hadn't found any healing at all. I bristled against the cold. "Sometimes, I feel like I'm defective or something, you know?"

The voice of accusation coiled around my vocal cords. I gripped my necklace. "How can I expect him to marry me?"

Trevor stared at me. "Em, I think your view of marriage is a little skewed. And don't worry, you're not defective."

I grunted in disagreement.

Big mistake.

He dragged me to the nearest bus stop and approached a stranger wearing a beat-up backpack over a dingy hooded sweatshirt. Clumps of greasy black hair poked out from under his hood above a glazed expression.

Trevor tapped Grease Boy's shoulder. "Excuse me, sir."

The guy removed his earphones and looked us up and down.

"Excuse me," Trevor repeated, completely straight-faced. "Does this girl look defective to you?"

"Oh my word." Mortified, I shoved Trevor behind me. "I'm so sorry. You have to excuse my friend. He's a little disturbed."

I pinched Trevor's leather coat sleeve and lugged him away from the curb. "What's wrong with you? Is it your sole goal in life to embarrass me? And really, haven't you ever heard the expression, 'stranger danger'?"

Trevor's bellowing laugh obliterated any chance he'd taken me seriously. "Okay, A: it's not my *sole* goal in life, but definitely one of the more enjoyable ones. And, B: 'stranger danger?'" He laughed full throttle again. "We're not toddlers."

I wrenched my fingers through his hair and turned his head toward Creepy Guy at the bus stop, whose slimy grin now linked straight to us.

"Um, maybe you're right." Trevor grabbed my hand and hightailed us around the street corner. We backed against the brick building and tried to catch our breaths.

Another wet breeze raced between the buildings. I raised my hood. My hair was getting frizzier by the second.

Trevor peeked around the corner like a clandestine agent.

I laughed. "Good thing you got the whole James Bond persona down."

Ignoring me, he eased back around. "Jack the Ripper just got on the bus. Think we're in the clear."

I flashed him an exaggerated I-told-you-so face.

"Okay, fine. That guy could definitely fit into the broken category. You? Not so much."

"Why is that not comforting?"

"Em, I doubt Riley wants to marry you because he thinks you're perfect. We all carry brokenness into a relationship. You work through it together. You mess up.

You give grace. Repeat." He patted my arm. "Welcome to Marriage 101."

"Thanks, Professor Know-It-All."

Trev puffed out his collar. "Well, I *am* sort of an expert at the giving grace thing."

"Is that right?"

"Have you met my fiancée? Man, the things I have to put up with. And that roommate of hers?" He scrunched his face into a look of hopelessness. "Forget about it."

I slapped his arm with my sleeve. "You just wait till your fiancée and her roommate join forces. Then we'll see who needs grace, buddy."

"Story of my life." He rested his hand on my shoulder, all traces of joking laid aside for however brief a moment. "Look, I know what you're saying. But knowing you should choose faith instead of fear and actually doing it every time?" He shook his head. "Not the same thing. You're gonna blow it sometimes. Get used to it."

"Anyone ever tell you it's a good thing you're not a counseling major?"

Trevor laughed. "I did promise to kick you in the rear when you needed it, remember?"

"Unfortunately." I tried not to smile at the memory.

He tossed his athletic arm across my shoulders again. "Seriously, Em, I know it might feel like you're messing things up, but love covers more than you think. Doesn't make it easy. But the kind you and Riley have?" He nodded. "It's enough."

I stared back at him and grasped onto his belief in us. My cell buzzed in the quiet. I tipped it out of my pocket. *A. J.?* I swiped the screen. "What's up?"

"It's Dee's mom."

My hand found my stomach before my voice found volume. Multiple layers of dread coalesced in seconds. "What happened? Is she okay?"

A. J. released a pained exhale. "They roughed her up pretty good, but she's recovering. Trey's at the house with her now. The police are taking her statement." He exhaled again. "Looks like Tito's warnings aren't over."

Would they ever be?

My boot slid down the wall. *Dee.* No telling what he would do. Words strained against dry swallows. "Is Dee…? He didn't…? Tell me he's okay."

An engine in the background rumbled in place of his response and kicked up my pulse five notches.

"A. J.?"

"He's okay. Just a little shaken up," he said too calmly.

"What aren't you saying?"

A car horn blared in the distance, but I couldn't tell if it was from my end of the line or his.

"He took off after them when he got home and found her."

Another coarse swallow. Hand on my head, I turned away from Trevor and shut my eyes. *If they hurt him, so help me.*

"I went patrolling as soon as Trey told me what happened. I found Dee on West Burnside. He was just sitting there. Kept mumbling in Spanish. Something about Tito's kid brother."

I balled the side of my coat in my fingers. "But you said he's okay, right?"

The car engine cut off. "He's going to be fine. Listen, I just got back to the center. Trey wanted me to wrap up a few things for him."

"Of course. Right." I nodded. "The other kids need you. I'll let you go."

His keys rattled into the sound of a door opening. "Em, I don't want you to worry, okay? I only called 'cause I knew you'd kill me if I didn't."

His warm laugh curled around me and relaxed my shoulders.

"Try to keep your mind off it," he said. "And tell Trev to bring me home an espresso, would ya?"

I turned to Trevor and smiled. "Will do." Lowering my cell, I breathed in A. J.'s reassurance. Dee and his mom were okay. That was what mattered.

Trevor lifted off the wall. His expression showed he caught enough of the conversation to follow what was going on. "It's gonna be all right. All of it. Just give it some time."

I blinked, my lashes the only things not frozen. "What'd you just say?"

He squeezed my arm. "Give it time. Things are going to work out."

Two furled maple leaves circled down the sidewalk.

My thoughts ran after them, the past chasing the present.

He angled in front of me. "What?"

"Sorry. Nothing." I zipped my coat up to my chin. "It's something my dad used to say to me."

Without prying, Trevor pointed behind me to the destination we'd been trying to reach for the last forty-five minutes. "See, the road has a way of getting you where you're going, even when it takes longer than expected."

Jaycee turned from a merchandise shelf in the back of the café when the bell above the door chimed. Trevor's face lit up the way it always did when he looked at her. "And it's worth every stop along the way."

Jaycee waved us down. "It's about time you guys got here."

Trevor hooked an arm around her waist and offered an apologetic kiss hello.

I strolled up behind them and glanced at the menu. If hanging out with two of my closest friends couldn't help keep my mind off things, surely a venti chai would come through for me.

"Jae, how'd you find this shop? You can't even see it from the main street."

A deadpan stare glossed over her eyes, as if she'd stolen a moment to convince herself I'd actually asked that question out loud. "Hello, I have Starbucks radar."

I fake-kicked Trevor ahead of us to keep from joining in his laughter. "The girl's waiting for your order."

The aftermath of a rush we must've just missed dusted the barista's apron. Even her black hat couldn't keep the dislodged tresses of a once-neat ponytail from falling into her eyes.

"Looks like those delays got us here right on time." Trev gave me a quick wink, drummed his fingers on the counter, and perused the overhead menu. "I'll have a grande Pike's Place roast, please."

Jaycee skipped up behind him like a child in a candy store. "I'll have a trenta soy peppermint white chocolate mocha with two pumps and an added shot of vanilla. Can you make that extra hot? And would you mind putting the whip on the side?" Her three-tiered earrings jingled as she turned. "Oh, and a cup of ice water with that, too, please."

Her smile out sparkled the gold Starbucks card she handed the barista, who was still busy marking up the side of the cardboard cup with her long list of demands.

Jaycee's unassuming expression made it downright impossible not to laugh, even with my lips clamped together.

She tucked her wallet inside her purse and her hair behind her ear. "What?"

"How do you spell *high maintenance?*"

The spiky bangs slanting across her forehead had nothing on the pointed look she shot my way. "Not all of us can have simple orders like chai."

Too bad nothing else was as simple.

After ordering my tea, I met them at a table next to a

window. Peppermint-scented vapors rose from Jae's cup like a mentholated diffuser, relaxing me deeper into the seat cushion. With a mixture of cinnamon and cloves sweetening my lips, I eased off my coat and drank in the irreplaceable taste of friendship.

"How was your time with Candice?" I asked.

"You mean before or after she closed her math book in my face?" Jaycee massaged her temples. "The woes of middle school drama."

Trevor tilted his cup at me. "Maybe you can send in Drama Queen, here, as an emissary."

"Hilarious, Trev." I flicked a sugar packet at him.

"I mean, I get the whole social pressure thing," she said, skilled at ignoring our antics. "I just wish she'd believe me when I tell her it's all gonna work out."

The conversation transported me back to the memory Trevor had ignited outside the store a few minutes earlier. I'd rushed into Dad's study after some silly run-in with my middle school friends, convinced my world was coming to an end. Even then, I couldn't comprehend how he could make every worry I had seem to evaporate in front of me.

He'd placed both of his strong, affectionate hands over my bony shoulders and looked at me with the same faith I wanted for myself. *"I know it hurts right now, honey. But God has good things planned for your life—good friendships included. He's always leading us to good, Em. Even when we have to walk through things we don't understand. Sometimes, we just need to give Him a little time."*

Dad had always reminded me I had a choice. Trust or not. Even when it felt like time could cost me everything.

Trevor's distinct laugh drew me back to at least part of Dad's promise—good friendships included. The kind that remained a constant through everything else.

Jaycee craned her cardboard cup back as far as it would go and tapped it dry. Her bottom lip followed the empty cup toward the table. "It's just not right that Starbucks cups have bottoms to them."

I covered my mouth to keep my tea from spilling out. "Agreed," I said once I stopped laughing long enough to swallow. "They should definitely be bottomless."

"You ready to go?" Jaycee rose from the table and looked between the two of us. "Where'd you guys park?"

Trevor and I exchanged an amused glance. "Don't ask."

COST

I LINKED arms with Jaycee as we headed for the door. "I'm riding home with you. My fragile trust in safe driving has been through enough for one day." I glared at Trev.

His scrunched face morphed into a grin the second we stepped outside. "Sure about that?"

A blanket of snowflakes coated us on its way to the ground.

Eyes lighting up, Jaycee held out her hands and squealed. "This is awesome!"

I pitched a brow at her. "Snow in October is awesome?" How about, *wrong*?

Apparently, I was outnumbered.

Trevor moonwalked up the sidewalk. "Sweet. The roads will be perfect for doughnuts." He spun in a circle. "No way you'll have as much fun driving home with Jae."

I bunched the top of my jacket together to block out the snowy wind. "I'll take my chances."

"Your call." Stopping at the corner, he flaunted a devilish grin at Jaycee. "Race you home."

Jaycee put on her game face. "I got this, girl."

Glad one of us did.

The snowfall had covered everything by the time we parked in front of our apartment. I cautiously inched up to the door while Jaycee glided from one foot to the other with the poise of a seasoned ice skater.

Trevor snuck up and grabbed our hands. "Don't even think about it. This is too much fun to miss." We slid back down the walkway into our private winter wonderland.

Jaycee twirled in the grass while the streetlight illuminated misty snowflakes collecting on her gloves. Trevor gave me one good spin before scooping Jaycee up from behind.

"That one's a keeper."

All three of us followed the unexpected sound toward A. J. taking a picture with his phone over by the lamppost.

A second later, a snowball landed smack into his amused smile. One glance between him and Trevor sent Jaycee and I running for cover inside the stairwell before we got caught in the crossfire. Gripping the door handle, we leaned back on our heels to keep the guys from opening it.

As if it were a fair fight. Overpowered, we stumbled

backward into the stairs. The guys swept us up by the waists and hauled us right back outside, where we all tumbled onto the powder-coated ground in fits of laughter and squeals.

Jaycee's arms and legs carved wings into the white canvas. She popped me in the arm when I didn't join her. "Don't be such a grownup."

"Yes, ma'am." Laughing, I casted reservation aside and retreated to the simplicity of childhood. "Snow angels and friendship. The answers to all life's problems."

She wove her gloved fingers through mine. "Don't forget coffee."

As cold as it was, I was half-tempted to want a cup myself. Thankfully, laughter kept us warm instead.

I don't know how long we stayed out there. Minutes melted into translucent icicles stretching from tree branches while snowy white fireflies flitted all around us. It was like someone had drawn us into a painting outside the realm of time. Yet even against such a stunning backdrop, being with my best friends was the artistry I'd remember the most.

The thought stirred a residual ache from Riley's call last night. The compressed snow soaked into me, followed by a whispered reminder of what learning to walk by faith had taught me. I couldn't live without opening my heart. No matter the risk. No matter the cost. I'd never find the fullness of Dad's promise if I surrendered to pain instead of hope. Jaycee and Trevor were right. Love wasn't what was easy. Fear was. And it was far past time for me to lay it down—starting with a phone call I should've made from the very beginning.

I pulled myself up by the backs of my knees and brushed the snow from my hands.

Trevor snagged the edge of my coat. "Where do you think you're going?"

"Sorry, guys." I hobbled to my feet and motioned to the apartment. "I have something I need to take care of."

Inside, I kicked my shoes off at the entryway, grabbed a fleece blanket from the back of the couch, and cuddled it around my shoulders on my way to my room.

I sat at my desk, not bothering to change out of my wet clothes. A thin, colorful object at the base of my desk lamp caught the light and my focus. The laminated leaf from the first time Riley brought me to the clearing in the woods kept its post by my bedside. Unwavering. Steadfast. The same way I should have been loving him.

Holding the leaf in my hands brought a cascade of memories from the woods to life. Months after I'd lived them, they burned with the same intensity. Pulse soaring from the way Riley held my eyes across the field. Stomach fluttering from the electricity that followed his touch. Even then, he'd grounded me in who I was and who I wanted to be. Always.

I tapped Riley's number, twirled the tangible reminder of that certainty between my fingers, and waited for his voice to become more than a memory.

"Emma?" he said above the music in the background.

Whatever jamming session he was in, it was clear he was at the center of it. "Hold on," he hollered again.

I'm trying.

The music tapered until the roar of wind replaced it. He must've stepped outside.

"Okay, sorry, you there?" he asked at a normal decibel this time.

"I'm here."

"Are you okay? I've been calling you since we got cut off last night."

"Yeah, I'm fine. Sorry, I just needed some time to think."

The wind's murmur filled another pause.

"Em, I don't even know what to say. I honestly thought we'd be done recording by now. That I had a chance of coming home early. I've been pushing nonstop so I can get back to you."

Tears mounted. I'd been selfishly resenting his time there. Living in fear it would pull him away. Yet he'd been the one caught in the real fight, torn between two dreams pulling him in opposite directions. And when it came down to it, he was still putting me first.

My lashes creased together. "Do you want to stay?"

The silence ached with the answer I already knew.

"Not more than I want to be with you."

But I never should've made him feel like he had to choose between the two. Love required more than the ease of summertime romance. It required sacrifice. Self-lessness. Putting his heart above my own the way he did for me. If I truly loved him, I couldn't do anything less. Regardless of the risk, that kind of love was the only one worth opening my heart to. And this time, I would choose to trust it.

I held the leaf close and searched for words. "You're exactly where you should be, Riley, and I'm so grateful you're getting to live this dream. Your album is going to be phenomenal, just like your entire career will be. And I get to be your number one fan from back home. That's in the fiancée contract, right?" A tremble shook in my laugh.

"Em, don't—"

"No, it's fine. I mean it. I don't want you to keep worrying about me." I returned the leaf to the empty spot against my desk lamp. "I love you, Riley." Enough to be willing to let him go. Even if he never came back.

25

ILLUSION

Sunlight reflected through the living room window and kissed my skin with enough warmth to tempt me into believing fall hadn't fully surrendered to winter.

Some days it was easier to live under an illusion.

I looped my scarf twice around my neck. "See you later, Jae."

She met me at the door and handed me my gloves. "Be careful."

I peeked out the window again. The semester's nonstop pace left the weeks it stole buried somewhere under the frost. How could we be in November already?

"If your Fiat can handle slick roads, Riley's Civic will be fine." I shoved down thoughts of him staying in Nashville and tucked my hands inside my pockets, wishing I could insulate my heart instead.

Outside, the sight of A. J. and Ashlea at the end of the walkway brought me up short. He rested against his car, ankles crossed. Frozen pieces of his perfectly manicured hair dangled over his forehead.

Ashlea paced in front of him, as though torn between wanting to guard him from an oncoming predator and knowing she needed to release a broken dream.

I felt for her. I felt for all of us. I'd been keeping some distance from A. J., like Austin suggested, but working at the center together made it nearly impossible. Still, I knew he sensed the intentional distance, and it was getting harder and harder to keep him from trying to close it.

I dropped off the stoop onto the salt-covered walkway and headed into the wind and whatever came with it.

Stopped a few feet in front of them, I looked up long enough to extend a non-verbal hello. The fatigue encamped around Ashlea's reddened eyes shot mine right back down.

We each hovered in place with our gazes darting away from the center of our three-person circle. The longer we stood, the farther apart the energy pushed us.

A. J.'s keys jingled against the car. "I thought you might want a ride today."

"Oh, um, actually, Trey said something last week about needing extra vehicles for some sort of cleaning project he's got planned for today. I think he needs us to tote some boxes over to Office Max to use their shredder." And I needed more time and space to refocus.

A look of question tinted his eyes, but he bowed his head in a nod. "I'll meet you there."

Our gazes fluttered clumsily around each other one more time. With an awkward smile, I turned one hundred and eighty degrees and hurried across the street. I didn't look over my shoulder until I reached the top of the stairs leading to the lower level parking lot.

A. J. held Ashlea in a way that honored the delicateness of her heart and broke my own. I'd told A. J. with enough time, brokenness would heal, but what if I was wrong?

Worse, if giving it time meant I could lose love, would it cost me friendship too?

The half-hour drive to the center didn't offer any answers. Parked outside, I inhaled deeply. *The kids. Focus on the kids.* They needed stability.

I entered the office with a smile in place and traces of emotional turbulence hidden. That is, from everyone except Trey. The door hadn't even closed behind me, and his superpower vision had already laser beamed through my mask.

"Everything all right?" he asked.

"Yep." I flew past him to my desk without slowing to make eye contact.

The front door creaked open. Though every kid in the room looked up at A. J., I doubted they understood the look of uncertainty on his face. Unlike Trey apparently did.

He stopped A. J. before he reached my desk, stretched

an arm across his raised shoulders, and steered him in the opposite direction. "I could really use your help today…" Their conversation waned behind the door of the adjacent room.

I slumped in my chair and tilted my head toward the ceiling. Would any of this ever get easier?

A slight tug on my sleeve solicited the attention of a towheaded girl, no more than four, perched at my side. We weren't equipped to take in kids her age, but it was hard to turn them down when they had nowhere else to go.

"Abby." I scooted back my chair. "Now, where did you come from? You're not using that invisibility cloak again, are you?" My animated voice could've passed for my first-grade teacher's.

Lopsided pigtails slapped the sides of her face as she shook her head and sprang on one foot in search of a way into my lap.

In a shirt at least one size too small for her, a pair of stained jeans, and worn canvas sneakers that looked like third-generation hand-me-downs, she giggled with the kind of joy her socioeconomic status couldn't touch.

She tugged on my shirtsleeve and my heartstrings while waving a piece of paper in the air.

I situated her in my lap. "What's this?"

"I drew you a picture."

"Wow." I spread the wrinkled page on my desk. "You drew this all by yourself?"

She'd crayoned an asymmetrical rendition of a girl in

a triangular dress next to a much shorter stick figure with bows in her pigtails and coordinating hot pink shoes.

I squeezed her in my arms. "Is this a picture of you and me?"

She nodded with enough gusto for those adorable pigtails to bop me in the face this time.

I withdrew a box of crayons from my drawer. "How about we finish it together? Which color do you want me to use?"

Her little chubby finger moved from her lip to a bright green crayon on the back row.

"This one?" I pulled it all the way out. "Okay, now you pick one for you."

Her hand darted for the fuchsia crayon, a newly claimed treasure.

"Great choice."

The worries darkening my heart faded behind the vibrant colors filling the piece of paper on my desk. Our picture was now complete with a florescent green sun beaming above two stick figures with fuchsia hair and coordinating dresses.

Nothing compared to the priceless artwork of a four-year-old. Did Dee know at Abby's age what kind of talent he had? Did he ever imagine he'd get to pursue art in college? And where was he? I hadn't seen him today.

Trey stopped inside the doorway and knelt to the floor. "Abby!"

She slid out of my lap and raced to Trey's open arms

with the excitement of a child seeing her daddy come home from an extended absence.

I fanned through some papers for distraction. Sometimes, watching Trey fill the vacant role of a father figure to many of these kids was simply too much.

He shifted Abby onto one hip and planted a fist on the other. "Are you sure you're only four years old? Because I think you look just as tall as your big sister."

Abby beamed, and I couldn't help wondering how Jim Brake—or anyone else—could ever miss the center's impact. With or without a benefactor, we had to keep that mission going.

Trey carried her off into the classroom, where the other kids were busy working on assignments or projects.

He plodded back into the office an hour later.

I leaned on my elbows. "Did they let you escape?"

"I think A. J. has things under control for now." Trey bottomed into his chair and slouched over the pile of bills I'd left on his desk. His glasses drifted to the end of his nose.

I studied his face, worn with exhaustion. "Long day?"

He let out a raspy chuckle. "And the night's still young."

A shared smile led us back into our work. The evening seemed to disappear much faster than the accumulation of papers on my desk. Before I knew it, a stampede of unbridled kids flooded the office on their way to the basketball court or off to the streets.

A. J. maneuvered through a maze of kids half his size and started to close in on another attempt to reach me. "Em, can we talk?"

"Emma," Trey said, already standing in front of my desk. "Would you mind filing these papers in the storage boxes in the basement?"

A. J. reached to intercept the stack, but Trey cut him off. "I could really use a pair of sturdy hands to help me lug these boxes out to my car. Do you mind?"

A. J. looked from me to Trey, obviously catching on to his deliberate interruptions. He shouldered the box Trey had practically thrust into his gut and muttered a tight-lipped, "Sure."

At the top of the staircase, I flipped the light switch on. Off. Then on again. Maybe a jolt in electricity would increase the flicker of light coming from the basement.

Yeah right.

I'd been to the cobwebby dungeon once before—in daylight. This time of night the corners of the rectangular basement drifted out of sight into non-ending shadows.

A musty breeze whirled up the staircase with reminders of the fire that might've happened if Jamal hadn't been brave enough to stand up to Tito. Shaking off the memories, I eased onto the first step. The wooden plank released a drawn-out moan followed by the patter of dirt falling onto boxes underneath it.

I dropped off the last step. The cold slab reached through the soles of my sneakers while something stringy touched my ankles. I jumped away from the stairs toward the center of the room and shivered. Though the damp smell of papers reminded me of an old library, this was the last place I wanted to linger. The sooner I got these papers filed, the sooner I could leave.

By the time I'd finally located the correct storage box, I had enough dust covering my arms to feel like I'd just bathed in insulation.

I reached the top of the stairs in less than four gymnast-worthy strides. Leaning against the back of the door, heart racing, I laughed. *Teaches me to watch scary movies.*

A string of incoming jokes was sure to erupt any second, but Trey wasn't in the office. In fact, no one was. The stillness in the deserted room bled into the eeriness sweeping up my legs through the bottom of the basement door.

Where was everyone?

I wandered outside. The cold, unforgiving wind wasted no time tearing through my body. Before I could turn back for my coat, a flurry of commotion rattling down the walkway from the main street gripped my spine with a wave of unease.

Goose bumps prickled over my arms. My feet didn't want to move. But with my hand grazing the wall for support, one forced step slowly led to another until a scream stopped me in my tracks. Icy breaths scraped down my throat. One. Two. The sound of a second scream thrust me into a sprint to the front of the building without another thought.

A stagnant odor of perspiration hovered over a throng of people standing shoulder to shoulder on the corner. I plowed through the crowd, not caring who or how hard I pushed. Short, shallow breaths fueled the engine of adrenaline pushing me forward.

I broke through the final curtain of people and clasped someone's arm to keep from falling, but it didn't matter. With one look, I lost any shred of stability I had left.

26

STARLESS

MY PULSE THUNDERED in my ears.

"Emma." Stripped of its usual strength, Trey's voice barely reached me. His eyes led mine to someone lying in front of him with a dark pool accumulated by his side.

My chest heaved for air. I couldn't let go of the person's shoulder next to me. I couldn't breathe. Couldn't see. Darkness pressed in.

"Emma," Trey said again. "He's asking for you."

His voice broke through this time. Breath came hard and sharp. I dropped to the ground and took Trey's place compressing my palm over the wound in Dee's stomach.

"It's okay, Dee." I lifted an unsteady hand to his cheek. "Look at me. You're going to be fine. Everything's going to be all right. Just stay with me, okay?" I shucked off my sweater, balled it up, and pressed it into his side to stop the bleeding.

He reached for me, struggling for sound.

I leaned in close enough to hear him.

"Cour-a-geous." Each wheeze expanded a line of blood trailing from the corner of his mouth.

In a moment when the reality of everything he'd fought to overcome crashed to the ground with his fallen body, his eyes didn't retreat to the emptiness they used to carry. They didn't harbor bitterness or fear. They held the one thing that had changed his life.

Unspoken, yet irrevocable, grace.

He squeezed my fingers in a plea for me to understand what he was trying to say.

I cupped my hands around his and smiled through tears I no longer had the willpower to suppress. "Courageous."

A faint smile of relief touched Dee's face just before he looked away. His eyes darkened. And so did my world.

I clung to his lifeless hand. Sound dropped to silence. Sight vanished behind a night that couldn't possibly be real.

"No," I whispered.

On his knees beside me, Trey reached around my waist.

"No," I shouted, pushing him and everyone away. I scraped my arm against the pavement under Dee's back, cradled him in my arms, and rocked in place. *Please, God, not Dee. Not now. Don't do this. Don't take him from me too.*

Distant sirens broke through the shock. I laid Dee back down. We had to save him.

A. J. bounded through the crowd. Out of breath, he fell to his knees beside Trey. "I couldn't find them."

"The police are on their way." Trey set a hand on his back.

I gripped A. J.'s sleeve. "They'll be too late."

A. J. looked at Dee, reality sinking in. Adrenaline trumped all hesitation and kick-started his medical training. He tilted back Dee's head to listen for breath. His eyes shot to mine for the briefest second then back to Dee. He transferred two full breaths and began compressions. "One. Two. Three…"

I held Dee's hand, afraid to let go.

Competing sirens neared. A cop car parted the horde of onlookers from one direction while an ambulance raced from the opposite. Red and white lights thrashed against the darkness. Three men dressed in navy blue jumpers stopped long enough to meet a signal from the officer taping off the scene.

A. J. rose to his feet to meet them. He dragged his sleeve across his forehead and visibly labored to steady his voice. "Victim's a sixteen-year-old male. Gunshot wound to the abdomen. Cardiac arrest. Not responding to CPR."

The tall, lanky paramedic faced the other two. "Bag him."

One wedged a tube down Dee's throat and attached a bag to the end while the one, who seemed to be in charge, lifted Dee's shirt and hooked some kind of monitor pads to his chest. He waved the other medics away. "Clear."

A shock struck the air. Tremors rippled over the concrete and up my body.

One of the younger EMTs checked for a pulse before resuming CPR with his partner.

A police officer prodded us all back from the scene. Shoulder to shoulder, in a crowd of nameless faces, I struggled to keep my balance and see what was happening.

Hazy shapes and muffled noises passed the minutes until the lead paramedic finally lowered a phone from his ear and sat back on his heels. "Time of death, 21:04."

Gravity seized every part of my body. *No.* Trey caught my elbow before I fell.

Time and motion ceased.

A third vehicle arrived. Everything blurred together in meaningless flashes of movement. Nothing came into focus until two men carried Dee's sheet-covered body toward a truck, and the sweater I'd pressed to his side dropped to the ground, sodden.

I launched after them, but Trey held me back by my arms. The doors snapped closed, ripping a piece of life away from me.

"Stop!" My voice raked with fury. I wrestled to reach the truck pulling away from the sectioned-off corner, but it was too late. He was gone.

My knees crashed onto the wet pavement in the middle of the street. Muddy slosh soaked into my jeans as people bumped into me, fleeing a scene I couldn't escape.

Someone's hand brushed the top of my shoulder. A. J. bent down to lift me up. Anger crippled me. I grabbed fistfuls of his shirt until I gained my balance.

"Emma—"

I pushed him away. "Don't." I stumbled to the empty sidewalk and banged my blood-coated fists into the wall. Under a starless sky, I shrieked in torrents to which no response came. When my voice faltered, tears screamed until even they surrendered to the void left behind.

My palms scraped down the wall and fell to my side. "Why?" I whispered. "Why Dee?"

A. J. took me in his arms. I didn't have the energy to resist. I buried my face in his shirt, away from the shadows trapping me inside a moment when all light in my life went out.

The earlier crowd gradually deteriorated. Trey eased me from A. J.'s hold, gestured for him to go on ahead of us, and guided me to Riley's car. "I'll drive you home."

Neither of us made a sound on the ride to school. Despite the inconsolable pain aching in the silence, there were no words to say.

I hardly noticed the car had stopped moving. Trey reached across the seats and unfolded his hand above my lap. "Dee wanted me to give this to you."

He steered my focus down to a folded-up piece of paper. He transferred the note to my hand and curled his fingers around mine. "It wasn't for nothing, Emma. Please know that."

I made it to the front door of my building before being cognizant enough to realize Trey didn't have a way to get home. I turned.

"I called a cab," he said without my needing to ask.

My body moved up the staircase apart from conscious instruction. Detached and emotionless, I stopped inside the doorway, frozen in every way possible.

A. J. must have called Jaycee. Her moment's hesitation dropped with the book in her hand. She jogged across the room and threw her arms around me.

"Not Dee," I said again against her shirt. "How could this happen? How could God *let* this happen?"

She cradled a hand over my head. "We live in a broken world," she whispered. "I think there's so much He never wanted us to go through."

Then what was the point of His plans? Of grace? Did they mean nothing? There was a time when I'd believed they were enough. A time when I'd thought they would safeguard the things that mattered. Laughter. Innocence. Possibilities. Things Dee was supposed to have the chance to live for.

Faith smoldered in a fire of betrayal, but nothing suffocated me more than knowing I was the one who'd taught him to believe it too.

Jaycee shouldered most of my weight while leading me down the hall to the bathroom.

An unrecognizable reflection faced me in the mirror. Nose reddened, lashes matted together, cheeks stained with black smudges streaked down to my chin—a reflection of what hope had cost me.

The shower wall held me up while water hammered onto my neck and back. I dragged a washcloth over my arms in mindless strokes until the sight of the tinted water running off my skin stopped me.

I scraped the washcloth against my hand. One time. Then again. And again. I scrubbed over and over, finally dropping the worn washcloth onto the floor of the tub. It didn't matter if I washed the blood off my hands. Water couldn't remove the stains left inside me.

In my towel at the sink, I watched water drip from my hair down my arms and pool over the counter. Beside streaks of condensation, Jaycee's colored sticky notes begged me not to lose faith in them.

Loved. Unforgotten. Was that what I was supposed to believe? "Then where are You?" My voice trembled. "Tell me where love is in any of this." I banged the counter. "Tell me."

Abandonment flared and brought me right back to the day my father's faith in love hadn't healed him. I tore down the notes, caved to my knees, and ripped the lies apart.

Jaycee flew through the door. One glance at the mess must've been enough. She dropped to the rug and held me in place until I'd drained the rest of my tears into the pile of brokenness surrounding us.

In our bedroom, she tugged my flannel pajama top over my head and combed through my wet hair while I stared blankly at the wrinkled note from Dee lying on my desk.

Jaycee squeezed my shoulders. "I'll be in the kitchen if you need me."

Several minutes after the bedroom door closed, I smoothed out the paper and ran my fingers over the penciled words spaced across the page on every other line.

Miss E,

I can't sleep. I was thinking about what you said on the basketball court—about talking to God. So, I tried it. Probably sounds crazy, but I think he actually heard me. The darkness didn't leave or nothing, but I wasn't afraid anymore.

And that's when it hit me. Maybe God brought you into my life to be like a star for me. You know, like someone to help guide me and teach me about grace. And—I don't know— maybe he wants me to be one for Tito. Show him he can have a second chance too. So, maybe it's cool if I don't get out of this rat hole. Courageous, remember?

Thanks for not giving up on me,

~Dee

Teardrops soaked into the paper over second chances that had been lost. I grabbed my phone, needing Riley more than ever.

"Riley Preston, leave a message."

The beep struck the silence, but I couldn't speak. With Dee's handwritten words clutched to my chest, I didn't know what else to do but wait for numbness to replace the piercing pain of loss.

Logically, several days had to have come and gone, but time blurred as one continuous stretch of night.

Following a knock at the door, Jaycee's voice rang down the hallway. "She still needs some more time."

"Sorry, Jae," A. J. said. "I need to see her."

The front door shut, and our bedroom door flew open. A burst of unwelcome light streamed into the room. At my desk, I squinted away from the glare.

Jaycee hovered in the doorway with her shoulders lifted in apology. "I tried to stop him."

Another flood of light plunged through the open blinds. After working in only the glow from my computer screen, it took a minute for my eyes to adjust.

"Enough." A. J. towered above me.

I glared at him. "Excuse me?"

"You're not doing Dee a favor by camping out in your bedroom, disconnected from life." He waved at the piles of paper strewn across the room. "You think this whole *Beautiful Mind* thing you've got going on is honoring him?"

I came inches from hitting him. "You don't think I'm trying?" I bolted to my feet and grabbed a fistful of papers. "You don't think I've been in here racking my brain for ways to make up for this?"

"You can't."

I choked back tears and the truth. Head down, I turned away. "I know," I whispered. But I had to try.

He caught my hands, touch and voice tenderized. "Don't give the person who did this the satisfaction of taking away more than one life."

The person? "His name's Tito." I wrenched my hands free. "And what does it matter? Game's over. You can't win against people like that. Dee was wrong."

His brow furrowed. "Is that what you think?"

"I watched him die, A. J."

"You also watched him live. With more guts than anyone I know." He drew me close. "Sometimes the most courage comes through surrender."

I raised a brow. "You taking pointers from Trey?"

His mouth slanted. "Maybe I am. It wouldn't hurt you to do the same right about now."

Huffing, I shoved the ratty nest of hair out of my face with my pajama sleeve.

A. J. didn't relent. "If you want to scrap with Tito, fine. I've got your back." He picked a piece of fuzz off my bangs. "But don't give in to hopelessness. Dee wouldn't want you to stop living." He nodded at me the same way Dee had from the sidewalk when he'd urged me not to give up on what we'd started together.

Dee must've known I'd need to stand on the same words I'd made him repeat until they were written on his heart. Must've known I'd need that same courage to look past anger, past sorrow and disillusionment, to see what grace had tried to show me from the beginning.

The rest of the kids at the center mattered as much as he did. I couldn't abandon them. Dee wouldn't let me forget that. And neither would A. J.

A pained smile broke through. The absurdity of the scene set in—my sweaty, tousled blankets holing me up in a fort of grief, A. J.'s friendship buoying me to the surface and rescuing me from myself. Again.

I scrunched my lips to the side. "Thanks."

A. J.'s grin tipped with relief. "What are friends for?" He strode to the door. "A new week's waiting to be lived, Em." Holding on to the trim, he looked over his shoulder with those eyes that never let me back down. "Word of advice, though? You might want to start it off with a shower."

27

SHAKEN

THE REPETITION of going through the motions dragged the end of November into December. I cut back my hours at the center—partly because I had to borrow courage against my bankrupt supply each day I went, partly because I had to make up for the classes I missed after the night we lost Dee. Any time left over, I dedicated to prepping for finals. It was easier that way. Studying kept me distanced from the parts of my life that still felt unhinged.

I sat back in my desk chair. An hour of staring at my economics textbook robbed my eyes of all moisture. I shook out the pins and needles from my calves and headed to the kitchen for a caffeine replenishment.

On the couch, Jaycee had an oversized textbook spread open in her lap and an almost equally giant cup of coffee balanced on the armrest. I was about to suggest she bypass the mug altogether and drink straight out of the coffeepot when I noticed she was on the phone.

She shifted the receiver. "Did the nurse say anything when you called to make the appointment?... Okay, please call me right afterward... I know. Love you too. Bye."

I leaned into the doorframe between the kitchen and living room with my arms tucked into each other, concerned but not wanting to press.

Jaycee must've read the question on my face. "That was my dad. Mom's been sick again. Her doctor wants to rule out possibilities, so she's going in for tests on Monday."

Tests. The word evoked a flood of dark memories from when we'd found out Dad had cancer.

Any number of things could've caused her mom's health concerns. There was no justification for me to assume she had a terminal illness. But the pain of living through loss had confiscated what was left of the small part of me willing to hope life would ever be more than indifferent.

Frayed emotions tied a knot around my voice and triggered another wave of anger. Outside, the beginning of a storm shook the screen against the window, and doubt against my faith. I shut my eyes. *Not her mom too. You hear me? No more pain.* My clenched fingers released my shirt, anger fizzling into an earnest prayer. *Please.*

Jaycee hugged her knees. "I don't know if I can do this."

The whispered admission echoed the vulnerability in my heart when I'd said the same thing to her earlier in the term. Without question, I understood the look of fear in her eyes. But even more so, I understood this was a moment she needed to borrow the faith and confidence of a friend.

"That's what I'm here for, remember?" I sat beside her. "To remind you that you can." I set my fingers over hers. "It's going to be okay, Jae."

When she kept her gaze locked on the whitewashed wall, the fissure of doubt in my chest widened. I swallowed and wrenched it back together. "Waiting can be the most unnerving part. Believe me, I know it's not easy, but try to keep your mind on something else." I squeezed her hand. "We'll cross the bridges as they come."

She nodded, still without making a reply.

I could've been in her shoes. I *had* been in her shoes. And I knew in some seasons, nodding was all we could manage.

I returned one of the reassuring smiles she'd lent me on too many occasions to count and fled to the kitchen before she could see it fall.

The turbulent whirlwind of all that had been going on drove me across the room. I clenched the oven handle and leaned my whole body against it. With my eyes closed, I could almost feel Riley's hands rubbing my arms the way they had in this same spot the morning I'd cooked him breakfast. Warm. Safe. Trustworthy.

I grabbed my cell from the counter and automatically scrolled to his number. Despite all that had changed since that morning, needing him in my life never would.

Each ring drew the sound of his voice nearer and caused the chaos in my heart to settle. It would be okay. Everything was going to be okay. I flipped the burner on under the teakettle, took a deep breath, and headed back to the living room.

Someone answered the line when I reached the edge of the carpet.

"Hello?" a woman asked in a groggy voice.

Had I called the wrong number? I lifted the phone from my ear to check the screen.

"Hello?" she repeated with less patience this time.

"I'm sorry. I'm trying to reach Riley Preston."

The words that came out didn't match the ones racing to answer the questions blaring in my head. I forced them down. Maybe he lost his phone and someone had found it. Or he was in a meeting and left his phone with the receptionist.

"He's... occupied at the moment." A hint of satisfaction tailed another sleep-heavy yawn.

Her voice grated, and I realized then I'd heard it before. In the background of Riley's calls. Always there. *Jess.*

I gripped the top of the nearest chair. "I'll wait."

"Don't bother."

"Excuse me?"

"Considering he's in the shower right now, I doubt he plans on taking your call."

The shower? Apprehension seared. Her words, her sleep-covered voice, her simpering tone… My insides convulsed at the only logical explanation. She'd slept over.

The realization balled into a fist, jabbed me low in the gut, and severed the tattered threads holding me together. I folded in half and dropped the phone. The clatter jutted into the teakettle's high-pitched whistle.

"Em? What's wrong? Who was that?"

Jaycee's voice didn't pull my eyes away from the phone at my feet. *This can't be happening.*

Jaycee pushed her textbook aside. "Emma?"

I couldn't answer her. Couldn't stay there. My legs took over and funneled me down the staircase, through the exit door, and into winter's grip. Every muscle constricted in the cold as icy prongs of bitter air pinched the tips of my ears, but I couldn't go back inside. I didn't know what else to do but keep moving.

Harsh wind tunneled between the buildings and right through me. I hugged my coatless arms to my body. Numbness expanded but not far enough to curtail the pain or block out questions plunging deeper with the cold.

My mind shifted into overdrive, pleading for any other reason Jess would answer Riley's phone while he was in the shower. I ran back her comment. "*I doubt he plans on taking your call."* Because she'd convinced him she belonged in his life instead?

The distance and pressure had stretched us. I knew it had. But we were supposed to be strong enough to make it through this. He promised me we were strong enough.

My own weakness replayed every fight we'd had, every missed call, each day we'd gone without talking. The voice of failure melded into the voice of accusation. I strained to shut them out, strained to hear the whisper of a song fighting against the howl of the wind, but they wouldn't stop. *Please.*

The sound of people ahead of me drew my head up in time to see someone approaching. Fast. He turned and caught my shoulder with his. "Oh, sorry."

I wasn't surprised he hadn't seen me. I felt smaller than the football he'd just caught.

He backed up a few steps and shook his curly hair from his eyes. "You all right?"

No telling what I must've looked like—frayed, distraught. Wind slithered up my back and snaked around my neck. I closed my arms over my sides again and nodded.

"You sure?"

I wasn't sure of anything anymore other than I couldn't keep standing there. I pushed past him without making eye contact with his friend who'd thrown him the pass.

Leaves covered the sidewalk passing under my feet. Some were pasted onto the concrete in the gloss of an earlier rain. Others, brittle and withered, crunched under my shoes. The longer I walked, the more my heart felt trapped somewhere between the two.

The third time I heard the same cluster of girls talking by one of the buildings confirmed I'd been wandering in circles.

"Emma?" Two steps outside his apartment, A. J. met my glance and didn't waste a second jogging over. He stood in front of me with hair flattened from a shower and concern growing on his face. "What are you doing out in this storm?" He drew me close without needing a reply. "You're freezing. I don't know what's going on, but we're getting you inside."

I didn't argue. I followed him until something stopped me at the threshold. Though the bitter air had stung my eyes, I hadn't cried. Not once. But as soon as the shadows I carried clashed with the light streaming in from the comfort of A. J.'s apartment, I came undone.

He held me tight. "Whatever it is, it's going to be okay." He brushed back my hair and rested his cheek over my head. "I've got you."

Thoughts tormented. I couldn't shut them out. Tito. Dee. Jaycee's mom. Jess. The helplessness.

I clasped A. J.'s shirt, too weary to talk. Everything closed in—the hurt, the loss. But most of all, the truth. Falling in love was as easy as falling asleep. Holding on to that love was like trying to hold on to a dream, even when it felt more real than life. Now, I'd lost both.

The look on A. J.'s face burrowed into the pain.

"I'm sorry." I backed up. "I shouldn't be here right now."

He caught me before I could open the door. "Wait."

My fingers slid off the knob. Drawing in a breath, I turned to face him. "I need to go."

"Don't do this. Don't shut me out." He brought his hand to my cheek. "Please, Em. Let me love you."

My shoulder blades pressed into the door. His heart-beat pounded under my palm with the same pace as mine. If he moved another centimeter and brushed my lips with his, we'd erase the lines I'd been pretending we hadn't already blurred.

PIECES

STANDING this close to A. J., I nearly crumbled under the weight of Austin's words. *"It's easy to give away pieces of your heart if you don't guard it."*

Everything we'd walked through had been knitting us together. All this time. Past lines we'd drawn. Past intentions. To a place of vulnerability connected by ties we never should've formed.

My hand trembled over A. J.'s chest. "Please…"

He closed his eyes and rested his forehead to mine. "Emma," he whispered.

"I'm sorry."

His arms slid to his sides.

I didn't wait. Couldn't. I turned.

"Em." He caught the corner of my ring with his finger. Hurt touched his face. He backed away—this time, letting me leave.

Once through the doorway, I didn't hesitate. I ran hard and fast against the wind. At the edge of the creek, I leaned over my thighs in search of breath and everything I was losing.

A borderless cloud dragged the minutes passing deeper into the dark. I didn't know what to pray, what to do. Silence blared until starlight finally pierced through and shimmered over the pavement with the memory of Dad's voice. *"Nothing can overpower them. Not even the darkest backdrop."*

An inner strength lifted me up right as Jaycee approached from the opposite end of the sidewalk. She stopped in front of me, hands on her knees. Puffs of breath collected in the air. "Jeez, girl, you been running a marathon around campus? I've been looking all over for you."

Of course she had. I'd left without saying anything to her. No wonder she was worried.

"Riley asked me to find you." Straightening, Jaycee held out my cell. "Sorry. I couldn't take hearing it ring one more time, so I answered." She pulled her hand back and brandished one of her stern teacher-looks. "If Tramp Girl ever gets on the line again, you better tell me. No way homegirl's hanging up without getting an earful from me next time." She muttered a series of names as she handed over my phone.

I couldn't help grinning. "Thanks for looking out." A peek at the screen showed a string of missed calls. I pocketed the phone, not ready to deal with that.

Jaycee shimmied an envelope out of one pocket and my keys from the other. "Riley also asked me to check if this came in the mail yet."

A sliver of light from the lamppost rested over the return address. Without hesitating, I ripped into it. Riley's handwriting seared into me with a jolt of fresh pain.

Em, I missed you even more than usual today. We recorded "Unveiled." No one else has any idea what I went through when I wrote that song last year. But all I could think about was playing it for you that night on your uncle's deck. Hearing you say you'd marry me made it all worth it.

I wish you were here. In the middle of a run with Jake, the clouds broke and uncovered this amazing view of the sky. I stopped dead in my tracks. Poor Jake. I mean, I knew I was still in Nashville. But for a second, I almost believed I was back on the sports field with you in my arms. I tried calling. Hoped if we looked at the sky at the same time, you wouldn't feel so far away.

I miss you, Em. God, I miss you. I'm counting the days until I get to hold you again. Every day I have to tell myself, 'You're braver than you think you are.' We're almost through this. I love you, Emma Matthews. Always.

Riley

Always. The word shook with the letter in my hands.

Jaycee reached for my arm. I flinched at her touch and backed up, turned.

Someone jogging up the walkway rammed into me.

"Whoa." Trevor's expression morphed from surprise to mischief to concern, all in a matter of seconds.

The look on his face collided with a landmine of already-wired emotions. I rushed past him and fled all the way to the front of my apartment.

I bolted up the flight of stairs. Inside, I snagged Jaycee's keys from the hook beside the door. Logical or not, I couldn't handle driving Riley's Civic right then.

The door to her Fiat shut behind me seconds later. I revved the engine, not knowing where I was going, only that I couldn't stop moving.

Blood pounded in my ears. Highway mile blockers passed one after the other, each post another reminder that I couldn't outrun fear any more than I could outrun time.

The sky darkened. A single raindrop beat onto the windshield, then a second and third. I fumbled around for the wipers just before a solid blanket of water sheeted the glass in an avalanche of sound.

Forced to slow, I glided over to the shoulder. The streaks of rain cascading down the window ignited my own internal downpour. How many more fires did God expect me to walk through? I jerked the gearshift into park and slammed my fist into the wheel. "How many?"

The rain's consistent patter softened to make room for the voice it obeyed. For the first time since I'd gotten in the car, I noticed music coming from the stereo.

There had been plenty of times in my life when a

song had struck me so deeply that I'd felt like it had been written expressly for me. Music had always spoken to me. Had always healed. But not like this.

Note by note, the song on the stereo collected each broken piece of the shattered song inside me. Time stilled. Memories of the way Dad used to place my hand over my heart slowly fused the shards back together. Questions still thundered. Fears still pounded. But right there, in the middle of the hurt, I sensed a father's arms sheltering me from the storm.

Tears streamed into the ending of the song. After a moment longer, I turned the volume down, reached for my phone, and scrolled to a number I hadn't called in weeks.

"'Sup, Fire Starter," Austin said with a laugh so much like our dad's.

The quake of missing him held back any words.

"Em? Everything all right?"

"Yeah, just... needed to hear your voice. How are you?" I picked at a coffee stain in the cup holder.

"Fine. You wanna tell me what—?"

"Things going well at work?"

"Ye-ah." Austin stretched out the word. "But I doubt you called to hear how many key frames I rendered at work today. Why don't you tell me what's really going on?"

No point in hiding it from him. "I miss Dad." So much it hurt. "I need him here, Aust." I needed him here to tell me what I was supposed to do. That everything would be okay.

"I know I'm not him," Austin said. "But I'm here, if you want to talk."

I tucked one foot under my leg in the seat as the piano on the stereo filled the pause between us.

"Does this have something to do with those blurred lines we talked about the other day?"

Of course he'd already know.

"They used to be so clear," I said. "Now, I don't even know which direction I'm moving. I don't know what I feel anymore."

"You can't always trust your feelings, Em. Can't always follow your heart either. Sometimes, you have to *lead* it."

"Said just like Dad."

"Yeah, well, as many times as I heard it, it better have sunk in." His laugh tapered into the quiet. "Guess that's kind of the point though."

"That you're as slow at learning as I am?"

"No one else is *that* slow." He laughed again but turned pensive without missing a beat. "No, honestly, I think we can all be a little slow sometimes. Even Dad. That's probably why he was so intentional about teaching us to trust, especially when it feels like it'd be easier not to."

Trust. Dee believed me when I told him he needed to trust the stars were there even when he couldn't see them. Why couldn't I do the same?

Raindrops bounced in the puddles in front of the headlights' beams. I closed my eyes and listened for any hint of Dad's voice still there to guide me. "It's easier to be brave for someone else."

"Tell me about it." Austin grunted. "And believe me, I wish I could give you an easy answer as much as you do. But this is something you're going to have to answer on your own."

He was more like Dad than he realized. I shifted in my seat. "Love you, Aust."

"You too. And, Em?" An audible assurance filled his pause. "It's going to be okay."

Except he didn't know what I still had to face. "Thanks."

Ending the call brought the tiny voicemail icon on my cell into view. If fire tempered steel, I should've been strong enough by then to take another blow.

The panic in Riley's voice escalated from one unanswered message to the next. "Hey, it's me. When I got on the phone, I heard you and Jaycee in the background, but then the line went dead. Is everything all right? Call me."

"Jess told me what she said. I know how that must've sounded. And trust me, we're gonna have words. But listen, the whole band pulled an all-nighter at the studio. She crashed on the couch beside my phone. I was in the bathroom getting ready when you called. I'd never… Call me, please."

"Em, this is killing me. I know this has been rough on us both, but it hasn't changed my commitment to you. I love you, Emma. Please tell me you haven't lost sight of that."

But I had. Enough to believe he'd cheat on me. I chucked the phone on the seat. Guilt struck. How could I have mistrusted him? Been so quick to jump to conclusions? And Jess… Who did she think she was?

My knuckles whitened around the steering wheel until a glance at my reflection in the rearview mirror drained my anger dry. I had no one to blame but myself.

I picked up my cell again and stared at the dark screen, wishing I could start over with a blank slate. Unmarred.

The phone trembled against my ear.

Riley answered on the first ring. "Emma, thank God." A slow exhale oozed with relief. "Did Jaycee find you? Did she tell you what happened?"

I fiddled with the keys in the ignition. "Yeah."

"So, then you know I—"

"I know. I'm sorry I doubted you."

Another fatigued exhale filtered through the line. "I'm sorry I ever gave you a reason to doubt." A loud clatter sounded in the background, as if he'd knocked something over. "I hate this, Em. I hate what being apart has done to us. What *I've* done to us—"

"Stop." I sat up in my seat. "We *both* made choices. For better or worse."

The silence on both ends of the call waited for words neither of us had.

Riley swallowed. "Does your choice still include me?"

His voice held the same urgency it had the day he flew to Nashville when he'd made me promise to trust in his love. Could we still trust in something so shaken?

Borrowing Austin's assurance, I looked out the windshield toward the road still ahead of us. "Always."

29

EXCHANGE

LAST NIGHT's turmoil gnawed at me all morning. Same as most days at the center since losing Dee, the void of missing him tested my faith. But today felt harder. More strained. When I swiveled in my chair toward the sound of A. J. talking to a group of boys, I understood why.

In place of our usual friendship, a palpable barrier stood between us. A wall resurrected. He wouldn't look at me no matter how hard I willed him to.

Could I blame him? A heart could only take so much pain before closing. I knew that better than anyone. And even though there was no alternative, it killed me to watch his eyes retreat to that distant place they'd hidden behind at the beginning of the semester.

A. J. squatted to the floor and cupped one of the boys' shoulders. His gaze flickered toward me. For one suspended minute, all traces of pretense dissolved. The room tapered until his eyes were the only things filling it. I gripped my desk.

Sheets of paper rustled in a breeze streaming in from the open door. Someone stepped in front of A. J. and obscured him from view.

A woman tilted her head while staring at me. Following a deliberate pause, she closed a folder in her hands and set off in my direction. Her high heels clacked against the tiles with each step drawing her closer.

I shifted in my chair. Something about her face tugged at my heart. The skin around her brown eyes sagged into creases running deeper than they should have for someone her age. Her natural beauty seemed tarnished, as if a dull eraser had left smudge marks over a canvas. I couldn't help staring.

Her heels dragged to a stop a foot away from me. She resituated a weathered shawl that'd drooped to one side and exposed the bare tip of her shoulder. "Miss E?"

"Emma." I held out a hand. "Emma Matthews."

"Of course." Her shoulders relaxed. "I'm sorry. He only ever referred to you as Miss E. I'm Delores Mendierez… Dee's mom."

My legs found the edge of my desk, my thoughts losing balance. What suitable response could I possibly offer a mother who'd lost her son?

Unbidden, a deeper panic set in. Had she come to demand justification of how we could've let this happen? Did she come to cast accusation and blame?

Instead, she met my gaze with honest compassion. No wonder she looked familiar. I might as well have been looking straight into Dee's eyes. The resemblance caused a swift and uncontrollable lump to rise without warning. I looked away before it showed.

"I'm sorry about not having a funeral. The money..." Her voice trailed into a sigh bound by grief. She fumbled with the manila folder again. "I found this in Dee's room." With slight hesitation, she handed it to me. "I think he would've wanted you to have it."

I glanced between her and the folder. My nerves ratcheted. I ran my fingers down the peach cover, the simple action of opening a folder never more difficult.

It hit the ground and disappeared beneath my desk. A single sheet of paper shook in my hands. A sketch. Me on the bench on the basketball court with my guitar. A moment captured in charcoal. Its flawless detail could have passed for a photograph. Centered beneath the picture, an artistically drawn caption defined the memory—*Courageous*.

I traced my finger over Dee's initials penciled in the right corner of the page and fought my tears with every ounce of energy I had. "I don't know what to say." I brought the drawing to my chest. "Thank you. This is incredibly special to me."

"I should be the one thanking you. You gave my boy something I didn't know how to give him myself. Hope."

Despite her smile, her lashes failed to blink back her

own tears. "What you're doing here," she said with a glance around the small room, "is really making a difference. Dee wouldn't have wanted you to stop trying because of what happened to him."

I inhaled, eyes turning glassier by the second. "Your son was very brave, Ms. Mendierez."

She lifted her chin ever so slightly. "No mother could be more proud." She smiled with a level of dignity that surpassed the need for words and returned the way she came.

Still clutching the picture Dee had drawn for me, I watched this woman—battered by a life I couldn't begin to have the endurance to face—hold her head high. As much as I loved Dee, it was only a fraction of what a mother would always carry in her heart for her son. Still, no amount of love was wasted. Dee had taught me that.

I met Trey at his desk. "Listen, I know bills keep coming whether we have money or not. I don't have a single lead lined up for another grant request, and I'm at a loss as to how to make foundations believe in the center. All I know is, it can't close. Not when people like Ms. Mendierez are counting on it. And not when we're still here to do something about it."

I raised my chin the way she had. "From now on, I'm volunteering. Put my paychecks toward other expenses. I know it's not much, but—"

"What about your rent?"

I stood tall. "What about the center's?"

Trey shook his head, a smile peeking through. "You're sweet, kid. Stubborn, but sweet." He squeezed my hand and nudged me toward my desk. "We'll figure something out. Like I said, there's always hope."

Donating my time wouldn't eliminate our financial problems. I knew that. The fight wasn't over yet, but maybe bravery *was* found in surrender. Just not always the way we thought. Same as with love, I couldn't determine the center's fate, only my part in it.

The front door flew open again. A teenage girl swung around the frame. "Miss E. Miss E. You gotta come —quick!"

Trey, A. J., and I exchanged a hesitant glance. All three of us hurried after her to the street corner and through a group of kids mobbing the sidewalk.

A sharp gasp knocked me backward at the curb. One look answered what all the commotion was about.

Trey whipped out his phone.

All sound and motion dissolved. Nothing existed except the sight of the one person who evoked more abhorrence in me than I ever thought possible.

Tito.

He had some nerve showing up here after hiding out from the police. Something inside me snapped. I sprang into the road without bothering to check if any cars were coming.

A. J. lunged after me, but Trey caught him midstream. "Cops are on their way. Give her a minute."

On the opposite side of the street, I shoved Tito against the bricks and held him in place with pieces of his shirt entangled in my fists. My rage evaporated every trace of fear I should've felt.

"Easy, señorita." His gritted teeth glinted an array of gold, white, and silver.

I didn't release my grip on his shirt or back an inch away from his body. My chest heaved a silent threat daring him to utter another word.

"These streets is mine," he said. "Peeps can run with me or pay the consequences."

Adrenaline nearly strangled me.

A tendon on his neck twitched. "I gots a reputation. *Mi familia* wouldn't let Dee just humiliate me like that."

What was he talking about, his *familia*?

A city bus screeched to a stop a block away. Turning toward it, I drew in a ragged breath and fought to regain a hold over my self-control.

"Don't act like you know what it's like to live on the streets, señorita. You don't know nothing of the way we live."

A speck of spittle hit my cheek, but I didn't flinch. I squared my shoulders, refusing to let him intimidate me. He leveled his eyes with mine, and my heart sank over the truth I didn't want to admit. Despite my relationship with the kids in this neighborhood, I'd never experience a firsthand understanding of their lives.

His jaw flexed in and out. An inward battle visibly

clawed through him the way I'd seen it war inside the other kids. "Dee never fought back," he said with audible perplexity. He turned and raised his shoulders, the struggle intensifying.

Silence stood between us.

Slowly, he looked up at me. My hands slid from his shirt, my arms going limp. A well of brokenness I wasn't prepared to see mirrored the torment that'd haunted Dee's eyes when he first came to the center. Shame, confusion, fear.

Tito's jaw twitched again, as though he was giving in to a decision. He kicked off the wall and sounded a shrill whistle through his teeth. On command, a gang of guys rounded the corner. A miniature version of Tito flew to his side—the same kid who was with him that day he'd tailed Mr. Brake's SUV.

Tito dropped his focus from the center to the pavement. "Dee changed."

Competing emotions kept my voice lodged behind my rib cage. "He wanted a second chance."

Tito set his hands over his brother's shoulders and faced me head-on. "Maybe he ain't the only one."

The group surrounding us turned into individual faces. Faces of boys. Boys like Dee.

I backed up. Barely making it across the street, I fell to my knees in the empty spot where life should have been. My pulse raged. Part of me had been so angry. Furious that God would lead me here with a sense of calling if I couldn't prevent Dee from dying or the center's doors from closing. I couldn't see purpose through the pain. Couldn't see how He could work through any of this. Even now, my faith trembled.

A pang drew my focus back to the kids Dee had been brave enough to offer hope to, no matter the cost.

Is this what it took? One life sacrificed for the redemption of all of these?

I faced Trey, unable to move, and silently pleaded for him to intervene.

Responsive as usual, he corralled the regular attendees back to the center while inviting the group of street kids to join them. Police sirens rang in the distance. Trey landed a hand on Tito's shoulder. Expressionless, Tito dipped his head and followed him inside.

He was turning himself in? It didn't make sense. None of this made sense.

A. J. lingered behind. He stood at the corner, one side drawing him toward me, the other pulling him in the opposite direction. I smiled weakly and motioned for him to go on without me. He hesitated a moment longer, then slowly backed around the building.

Alone, I leaned on my thighs and tried to breathe. The longer I sat there, the deeper the coarse sidewalk pressed through my jeans onto my knees with the ache of an unanswered question. Had Dee known this was what it would cost? Had there been no other way?

Flashes of Dee's assurance washed in and stirred a reminder of Jaycee's words. *"We live in a broken world. I think there's so much He never wanted us to go through."*

Including pain? I hadn't wanted to accept that. If God didn't want us to endure such heartache, why wouldn't His love shield us from it? I faced the sky. "Why?" The angered word shook against the wind, begging to be heard.

The trees stilled. The street quieted. But instead of an answer, a question echoed my own—one I'd missed all along.

While I'd been asking Him to spare us from hurt, He'd been asking us to trust Him through it. Even now.

A gentle song in the breeze released the remainder of tears I didn't think I had left to give. My body racked, knowing tears couldn't heal any more than they could wash away the stains left on this sidewalk. It racked even more, knowing the only thing that could was still fighting for me.

Warmth broke through the clouds and flooded that downtown corner. Memories of Dee coalesced with sights of the streets he'd walked. I saw him everywhere I looked; and somehow, I knew. Though the shadow of his death covered the ground, this neighborhood would always reflect the lasting light of his life. And none of it had been wasted. Not my time there, nor his. Not the hope found, nor the sacrifices made. For even in a broken world, what was intended for darkness couldn't overshadow grace.

The very evidence of that awaited me on the other side of the door to the center. I slipped in unnoticed. Dozens of voices rebounded off the walls and competed with the thumping of basketballs out back. A. J.'s eyes flashed from the two youngsters hanging from his arms toward me.

Kids Trey had always hoped but never expected to see come through our doors crowded the room. Many of the newcomers blended in with the others. A few stayed huddled in guarded skepticism.

Some of the older guys lined the perimeter of the room. Every few minutes, they glanced at their leader in search of a signal of instruction. Tito sat in a back corner with Trey with his eyes on his little brother, looking stoic as he waited for the police to arrive.

A CB radio beeped from the front door. Everyone froze. Every conversation halted. Only a single basketball bounce made it through the barrier of immediate silence.

Two police officers entered the hall. The crowd of kids parted on either side of them. Footsteps had never sounded heavier.

Knowing Trey's heart of compassion, I wasn't surprised to see sorrow on his face, but the look on Tito's gave me pause.

Even when the police secured handcuffs around his wrists, he didn't appear intimidated. He didn't hold the same look of arrogance from earlier, or even a mask to hide his fear. As the officers escorted him from the building, he held a look of something far less expected. Something I'd seen before.

Courage.

286 | CRYSTAL WALTON

His departure unleashed a ripple of questions across the stagnant room. Relief swept over some, conflict tore over others. Trey couldn't stop those who wanted to leave. But for those who stayed, his acceptance and encouragement met them in a time when the fatherless needed a father.

Without any measure of surprise, Trey had the place operating in a bustle of activity within the hour. The impact of Tito's arrest hadn't been forgotten, but all I could see around me was the impact of Dee's life.

I clung to that consolation for the remainder of my shift until Trey led me into the corner by the coat rack. "I don't think Tito did it," he said quietly. "I think he's covering for Lucas."

Blinks stood in for my voice. "Lucas?"

Trey set a hand on my arm. "His brother."

The scene from earlier played back Tito's words and almost knocked the wind from me. "*Mi familia.*"

My coat slipped from my hands onto the floor. "The boy?" He couldn't have been more than ten.

Trey nodded, face pained. "Probably thought he was defending his family name." He picked up my coat and draped it around my shoulders. "Tito didn't say as much, but he asked me to take Lucas in and give him whatever Dee found here."

The emotions of it all nearly folded me in half. I gripped his sleeve. "What are you going to do?"

Trey looked from Lucas to a cop coming in from

outside. He sighed as he signaled him over. "What I have to."

He steered me toward the exit. Seeing A. J. standing at the door sent one source of turmoil colliding into another. Despite making it to the end of the day, the anguish in my heart wasn't fully over.

30

FRAGMENTS

A. J. WAITED for me as he usually did. Outside, he took his customary post on my right, hedging me between him and the wall. It could've passed for a normal ending to a normal day. Except that everything had changed.

A. J. strode alongside me but might as well have been a stranger. Each step accentuated the distance re-forming between us.

Around the corner, the city streetlight cast streaks down fractures I wasn't ready to acknowledge. I slipped my hands into my pockets and rocked on my heels, stalling.

We'd circled back to a splintered friendship again. Only now, the weight of things unsaid exposed roots that had gone much deeper than they ever should have.

"You good?" he asked.

His guarded tone drew my gaze up from the side-walk. "Yeah."

The faintest smile reached his eyes. "You should've seen the way you looked pinning Tito to the wall. I don't think you have to worry about anyone messing with you now." He squeezed my bicep. "Yep, definitely intimidating."

We both laughed, but the sound dropped in the air.

A. J. stowed his hands inside his coat pockets and dragged his Nike over a break in the pavement. "You have a lot of self-control, you know. If it were me, Tito would've had a busted jaw before I gave him the chance to say the first word."

"Trust me. It wasn't easy. But something in his eyes reminded me of Dee when he first got here." I breathed out through my mouth. "They're just a bunch of kids trying to cope with hardships the only way they know how." I stared down the wall beside us. "It's hard to stay angry when you know you need grace as much as they do."

A moment passed before A. J.'s stirring breached the stillness. I looked up from the pavement as he edged toward me. His expression burned with something he wanted to say. But when our eyes met, he stopped where he was and turned his head away.

"It's getting late," he said instead. "We should get back to campus."

"Right. Yeah. I'll, um, see you around." My voice came out weaker than I meant it to, quieter. I lingered in place until resignation urged me toward Riley's car, leaving the unspoken trapped with regret.

A huff from behind me drew me back around.

Neck craned, A. J. raked his hands through his hair. "Em, wait."

He caught up to me. I stopped at his touch and braced myself for the confrontation I had no right to avoid.

"I can't do this anymore." He took my hand and pulled me toward him until we were standing inches apart in the middle of the deserted street. "I know I told you last year that I would let you go. And I tried, Em. I swear I tried. But I can't."

His unmasked vulnerability crashed into my own. "A. J.—"

"I can't keep pretending." He set my palm above his heart and tapped his hand over mine. "This is real." He lifted my chin. "This," he said again, touching his thumb to the skin around my eye, "…is real. You can't hide what I see."

"You're one of my closest friends. You know you hold a piece of my heart."

He angled my face toward his. "I want you to look at me and tell me that's all it is." His chest rose and fell in rapid movements under my hand.

My shoulders sank with the weight of knowing that the connection we'd formed through all we'd shared was real… and the very reason we had to let it go.

An ache of regret speared through me.

My lashes lifted toward his. The eyes searching mine

reflected everything racing to my own—the hurt, the tenderness, the loss.

His hand drifted down my back. "Emma."

Swallowing my tears, I hugged him for what had to be the last time. "You asked me to let you love me. Please." I set my chin on his shoulder and faced the stars. "Please, let me do the same for you, even if you don't understand right now."

He held me tight, breath against my skin.

I stepped back. "Goodbye, A. J."

At Riley's car, my fingers burned around the cold door handle.

"I'll wait for you," he said from behind me.

The words we'd exchanged last year branded a mark inside me that would always leave a scar. With my back toward him, I struggled to steady my voice. "Don't."

I sank into the driver's seat. The keys rattled against the ignition until the right one slipped into place. Still without permitting any tears to come, I started down the road I had to take.

A quarter mile passed before I faced the rearview mirror. A. J. hadn't moved. He stood in the middle of the street, watching me drive away.

Neither of us could deny my heart had already fractured. But as we both eyed the fragments left behind, I knew we were waiting for two very separate things. I waited with hope that the pieces would one day fuse back together. A. J. waited with hope that they never would.

31

DAYBREAK

Same as every day that had passed since Riley left, a new morning came as promised. Orange-dusted clouds heralded the sunrise and painted over last night's shadows.

Alongside the creek, early morning dew tipped the grass under my fingertips. Sunshine kissed the back of my neck and expanded into a full embrace across my shoulders. With my eyes closed, memories from the summer warded off the cold December air around me now.

I breathed in the moment a little longer. The stillness. The serenity. The evidence that my father's legacy of love had never stopped guiding my life, not once.

Seated on the grass, I opened my journal.

Dad, this whole time, I've been trying to figure out how to love. So afraid of risking what I'd lose or gain. When, really, you've been trying to show me how to open my heart regardless of either.

I don't know why I expected love to be easy. I don't know why I thought any of this would be. Fear will always oppose faith. Life is always going to test the things you've taught me. Just because we're promised something doesn't mean we won't have to fight for it. I think deep down I always knew that. The hardest part has been learning that sometimes that battle is won through surrender.

If I would've listened to Trey from the beginning, I wouldn't have been spinning my wheels, striving to be strong enough to fight, whole enough to love. Because the truth is, I can't be on my own. I was never meant to be. I've wasted so much time resenting my brokenness instead of trusting God to be able to move through it, even when I can't see how or why.

I hate that it took making a mess of everything for me to learn all this. But I realize now that part of being courageous means choosing which voice I guard my heart from listening to and which one I let lead it. And I can't tell you how grateful I am for all the times your words have been a light in the darkness for me."

"Especially when I'm ridiculously blind," I whispered through a tear-filled smile.

I brushed my fingers down a page my dad would never get to read and released a prayer for all that had been lost. I'd always admired the way he'd never wavered. His assurance, unshaken. It had taken me far longer than it would have taken anyone else to understand love's role in making that assurance my own. But as the sunlight drew my eyes toward the sky and my heart toward a sense of peace, I grabbed hold of the certainty of what I was finally ready to do.

On the other side of our front door, I almost smacked right into Jaycee. She spun in a half circle and lifted two giant coffee mugs in the air, as if an increased height would prevent them from spilling onto the carpet.

Trevor sat on the far end of the couch, flashing a boyish grin that managed to slow down whatever wise-crack was about to escape his lips.

Jaycee glanced at my face and continued walking. "Need a ride to the airport?"

"How'd you know?"

"Wait a sec," Trevor said, unable to contain his sarcasm any longer. "You two have been communicating clairvoyantly for the last three and a half years, and you're asking her how she knew what you were thinking?" He feigned a look of perplexity while strolling toward me.

I sighed. "We'll be fifty years old, and you'll still be amused over that joke, won't you?"

Patronizing as ever, he threw his brawny arm over my shoulders. "Only as long as you keep giving me that same look each time."

I rolled my eyes on principle but couldn't deny how much I loved him, mischievousness and all. I squeezed his side. "I don't know what I'd do without you guys."

"Hey, hey. None of that mushy stuff." He rubbed the

top of my hair. "Listen, give me the details of the flight you need. I have a friend who works at the airport."

Jaycee and I exchanged fleeting glances. "Of course you do," we said at the same time.

The living room lit up with Trevor's laughter. Our synchronization apparently was as amusing to him as his random connections were to us.

But as usual, his networking skills proved to be a lifesaver. Trevor had made all the arrangements by the time my last class ended. His miracle-working friend managed to let me fly standby—on a Friday night, no less.

I hadn't thought about how I'd pay for the flight. Only that I needed to leave tonight.

The energy from rushing all evening succumbed to a level of exhaustion like I'd never known. On board, I tilted my seat back and watched cloud glaciers drifting by the window, taking any chance of falling asleep with them. No position helped. Nothing shut out the thoughts keeping me awake, hour after hour. Would I be too late?

The pilot's voice broke into the silent cabin to announce our descent. My stomach dropped, more from nervous anticipation than from the change in air pressure.

Between my lack of sleep and the gravity of what lay ahead, I was thankful to make it down the ramp without collapsing. I jostled my backpack strap up to the top of my shoulder while the rest of the plane's occupants whirled past me on their way to the luggage carousel.

My single bag felt heavier than it should have. I shuffled in circles. Lights and sounds pulled my focus in every direction until it stopped on the one sign I was looking for. Taxis.

Outside, I slid into the back seat of the nearest cab. A middle-aged man with a slightly cratered face leaned over his shoulder from the driver's seat. I withdrew a wrinkled envelope from my pocket. "Fifteenth and Mason," I read.

A smirk of discolored teeth beamed in the rearview mirror.

At least he seemed to recognize the address.

He turned on the heat. A faint trace of stale cigarettes and some kind of leftover fast food trailed into my seat. Breathing against the window, I watched the murky remnant of an earlier snowfall follow alongside the edge of the road.

The peacefulness of the engine's hum lulled me the longer we drove. I clamped my bag in my lap and gambled with the odds of closing my eyes without falling asleep.

Some gamble. I flinched awake at the creak of glass sliding open.

With his arm across the back of the seat, the driver announced the taxi fare.

I pretended to pass off my gasp as a cough. Fifty bucks? No wonder he'd smiled the moment I gave him the address.

The taxi's rear wheels stirred up a cloud of exhaust before my door shut all the way.

I hadn't exactly expected chivalry from a complete and admittedly questionable stranger, but didn't people have manners? Who left a girl deserted on a street at four in the morning without making sure she reached her destination safely? He'd better at least have had enough integrity to take me to the right address.

I looked around. A lighted neighborhood sign on the corner shined a halo into the darkness. "Thank you," I prayed.

My breathing evened as I followed a lamp-lit sidewalk winding through the complex. Unlike the apartment buildings back home, these one-story condos resembled townhouses, each with an individual front door.

I passed row after row, glancing at the envelope in my hands, until I found the number matching the return address.

Despite the chill blowing off a lake across the street, my body flushed with heat. I stood at the foot of the curb in front of a slender walkway leading to Riley's apartment. A long exhale expanded into the cold air.

One delayed step at a time, I approached a maroon door lit by a porch light. The tremor in my arm weakened the force of my knock. I backed up, waited.

After another three unanswered knocks, I sat on the stoop beside my bag. My jeans clung to the frost-covered concrete. I curled my arms around my boots and pulled my legs in to block the wind and the weariness blustering with it.

Riley was probably at another all-night rehearsal. He had no idea I was coming. Even if he was here, I still didn't know what I was going to say anyway. Why hadn't I thought this through? Should I not have come—?

The answer rose in my spirit the moment I saw someone approaching. Riley stopped short on the sidewalk with Jake flanking his side. He dropped the leash. Jake darted forward, then stopped midway like he was caught in the same suspense grounding the two of us in place.

Riley lowered his royal blue sweatshirt hood, exposing the sheen of a long run left on his forehead and a depth of love that hadn't faded.

Uncertainty dissolved at the sight of the one who still held my heart. I traced every feature until I found his eyes. It made no difference how much time had passed since I'd seen them in person. They still anchored me.

He inched two steps closer at the same time I rose to my feet. Behind him, light crested the treetops as the stars gave way to the sunrise. His gaze swam over my face. "Emma?" He rushed the rest of the distance.

I wanted to stop him. To tell him why I came before I melted under the feeling of his touch, but it was too late. His hands trailed the sides of my cheeks. The sensation collided with memories and sparked life back to my frozen body.

"Em." A mixture of relief and elation swept through his voice.

Before I could convince my lungs to vocalize the faintest sound resembling words, he had me lost beneath his lips and the tenderness of his promise to love me always. Everything outside this moment paled behind feelings I never had, nor ever would, experience with someone else.

His hand warmed my neck as he kept me close. "I'm so sorry for how hard things got. It never stopped. Never slowed down. It was killing me."

His heart beat under my cheek with my song—the one I wanted to fall asleep to every night.

It felt too soon to speak. Too soon to let go.

He lifted me back. "You have no idea how much I've missed you. I wasn't going to make it to January."

My lashes folded. "Aren't you wondering why I showed up now?"

Without the slightest hesitation, Riley's embrace eliminated the need of any question. "It only matters that you're here." He curled me to his side and drew me toward his apartment. "Let's get out of the cold."

He pulled his keys from the lock and pushed open the front door with his foot. Jake bolted straight for his water bowl in the kitchen.

Riley nudged a dog bed out of the entryway and set my bag on a narrow table lining the side wall. He snagged a shirt and jacket up from the couch arm. "Sorry about the mess. I'm not used to having people here."

I took in all four corners of his furnished condo and the world I'd been afraid I didn't belong in. He'd been alone through this more than I had. My stomach clenched over all that I'd gotten wrong and, worse, what I couldn't undo because of it. Remorse cornered me into the couch.

"Whoa." Riley caught my elbow and steadied me. "I think you're a little overdue on sleep."

Not as much as I was overdue giving him every part of me. I didn't want to hold anything back from him. Not anymore. He was worth all I had to give.

The assurance of that took over. I drew his lips to mine, wanting nothing between us. No space. No air. Nothing but right now. This was real. All of it—the desire, the urgency, even the vulnerability.

His body tensed. Five seconds of hesitation surrendered to a longing that had intensified with distance. He dropped the clothes in his hands and backed me against the wall. We couldn't get close enough—both trying to negate what we'd lost, both releasing the pent-up tension of being apart. I gripped his hair, wanting to erase every doubt that had wedged itself between us.

His mouth sloped to the hollow above my collarbone. I balled his shirt in my fingers and lifted on my toes, muscles taut. Everything I felt for him brimmed with tears I couldn't explain or stop.

The stress building over the last several months erupted. "When Tito had me pinned against that wall, all

I could think about was what he could steal from me. From us. Then when I thought you and Jess…"

His lips stalled over my ear.

I ran my hands up the planes of his back, holding on. "I want you to have every part of me." Every fear. Every broken piece. All the love in me. Even if it wasn't enough.

He flexed his palms on the wall on either side of my head and broke away. "Not like this," he said, rapid breaths hard against my skin. "Not like this."

His pulse beat through his fingertips with the same fervency teeming in the way he looked at me. Desire was still there, but an even deeper yearning searched for a way to extinguish fears I hadn't even voiced. He rested his forehead to mine. "I'm not going anywhere," he whispered.

My chin trembled.

"I love you, Em. Nothing's ever going to change that." He kissed me so tenderly, the promise siphoned the venom of regret from an unseen wound. "Your heart's been through enough already. Please let me protect what's left."

My hand slid down his shirt and drifted to my side. Here I was, yearning for a way to give him all my love. And here he was, once again, showing me the right way how.

His selflessness burned with the reason I'd come. It pushed me back outside where the wind could drop my temperature. Riley followed, Jake right behind. An inhale of snow-damp air relaxed my shoulders. But inside or out, I couldn't hide the ache in my heart from him.

"What is it? What's wrong?" His signature certainty shook under a quiver of concern. "You're not still worried about Jess, are you? You didn't come because—"

"I should've trusted you." I looked away. "Should've done so much differently."

He drew me close. His thumb smoothed over my cheek, his lips over my ear. Though his eyes told me he loved me, he whispered it again anyway.

My fingers lost their grip on his sleeve. "When we said goodbye at the airport in August, do you remember what you asked me? You made me promise to trust your love above anything else." I clutched my arms over my body. "I didn't understand then. I knew being apart was going to be hard, but I never expected..." I turned to the lake, fumbling over things I still didn't know how to say.

Riley eased closer. "I'm sorry—"

"Please." I lifted a hand to stop him. "Please don't."

His gaze locked on to the tears filling mine. Perception flickered. He backed up. Jake lunged from the grass and nudged his snout under Riley's hand.

I looked away, breathed deeply, and faced him again. "I had to come. I had to see you. So much has happened."

A glance swept from my face to my hand, as if begging to find my engagement ring still there.

"I told you I wasn't afraid anymore, but that's all I've been since you first told me you were moving. Afraid.

Terrified of what it'd mean for us, for me. I worried I'd lose you to all you'd found here."

My arms came undone. "I thought I was being brave by letting you go. That I was proving I was ready for marriage. But the truth is, there was so much I needed to learn about love. About myself. Life. Things I wouldn't have faced if I'd come instead of staying at Reed."

Every experience I'd walked through this semester— every fire—screened through my mind until the beauty of what I'd learned rose from the ashes. Flames didn't only temper gold. They purified it. As hard as that process was, love wouldn't survive without it. I only prayed I hadn't learned it too late.

Nerves drummed in my chest. I balled my coat cuffs in my hands and closed my eyes. *Please help me through this.*

The clamor in my heart stilled. A soft wind curled around me, and the relentless voice of doubt bowed to the whisper of truth it could never fully silence.

Overwhelmed again by the pursuit of grace, I looked up at the man it was time for me to love with faith instead of only feelings.

I held his eyes and breathed out. "I was so caught up in all that was going on. So worried about the cost of loving something that could break, that I didn't realize I'd begun to turn to other people instead of to you."

Comprehension tore across Riley's face. "Other people. As in A. J. Bowers."

"Riley, I'm sorry. I—"

"I never should've left you." Apprehension stole the stability I'd always found in his eyes. "And I sure as well should've known better than to trust A. J." He backed up, creating a defining distance between us.

I wanted to reach for him, but the question coursing off his shoulders kept me in place. "It wasn't like that. It's my fault for letting him get too close."

He turned and kneaded the base of his neck. The wind rolling off the lake thickened the silence. Head down, he exhaled slowly. "Do you love him?"

Summoning what strength I had left, I moved in front of him. "We went through a lot together. Because of that, I'll always value his friendship, but I'll never love anyone the way I love you."

Riley's eyes, tinged with pain, swept toward mine, and the ghost of a smile slowly broke through. "I've never blamed him for falling in love with you, Em." His brow pinched. He lifted his fingers to my hair and swallowed hard. "It'd be the most excruciating thing I'd ever have to do. But if you choose someone else, I will walk away."

His response didn't hold any traces of anger, no derision, not even a twinge of judgment.

Regret clogged my voice. "I can't reverse the damage I've caused. And I know having a fractured heart is the price of not protecting it." The pain of those consequences streamed down my cheeks. "But even broken, my heart still belongs to you."

I pulled the sides of my coat across my stomach. "I

wanted to be everything you needed, but I've realized I can't. There are going to be times when I mess up and disappoint you. I'm gonna have to ask for forgiveness. We both will. But I'm asking you to walk with me anyway. Through the failures. In spite of weakness. To give all we have, including the brokenness." I breathed in the sunlight and locked on to his eyes again. "I'm asking you to risk trusting a love that's enough, even when I'm not."

Riley didn't look away. He breathed. Frozen. Clouds ushered in and filled the space on that quiet sidewalk. Though doubt tried to wrangle into the silence waiting for his reply, it no longer had a foothold.

Tears landed on the ground at the memory of Dee's voice whispering an assurance I finally understood couldn't be separated from grace any more than love could.

I am courageous.

A Toyota pulled up to the curb. Before it fully stopped, Jess whipped a glare at us from the driver's seat.

We had only seconds left alone. I turned Riley toward me. Surrounded by shadows, I waited for the clouds to yield to the light, and my fears to the words it'd taken me traveling over two thousand miles to figure out how to say.

"Marry me. Tonight."

CONNECT WITH CRYSTAL

When you finish reading a story that grips you, there's nothing better than getting exclusive bonus scenes, behind-the-scenes insider looks, and sneak peeks into upcoming releases.

Join Crystal's list at crystal-walton.com for access to these goodies plus a free book.

FROM THE AUTHOR

Thank you so much for reading *Light Unshaken*. I hope Emma's journey has touched and encouraged you. Like her, your own journey matters—even the parts that may feel broken right now. If this story resonated with you, would you consider leaving a review? Your input just might be what another reader needs to hear. I can't do it without you!

Before you go, connect with me at crystal-walon.com. And join me on Facebook for fun and giveaways.

ABOUT THE AUTHOR

Crystal received her Bachelor of Arts from Messiah College in PA, married her exact opposite in upstate NY, and earned her Master of Arts from Regent University in VA, where she currently resides with her husband and two sons. Crystal writes contemporary clean and inspirational romances fueled by venti green teas. She'd love to connect with you at crystal-walton.com and Facebook.

ACKNOWLEDGMENTS

Dave, thanks for cheering me to press through, letting me cry when I felt I couldn't, and for walking with me through every step of the journey, even the brokenness.

Jessica, queen of brainstorming, thank you for standing in as my surrogate critique partner and for pushing me—and Emma—to live up to our potential.

Erynn, your gifts as an editor continue to amaze me. Thanks for humoring my attempt at converting you into a Team A. J. fan, for not booting me after the story may or may not have made you cry in public, and for cracking me up with your witty comments. I'm blessed to work with you.

Shaela, thank you for sharing your patience, creativity, and talent with me while working on the covers for this series. They are truly stunning and fitting and utterly perfect.

Rachel, the days would be very long without our jokes carrying me through all our plight-worthy moments. Thanks for lending me your mad skills as a proofer.

Jay, thanks for fielding my EMT questions.

Katie, few people can ask you how you're doing and

understand exactly what you mean when you say, "the usual." Thanks for all those Starbucks-date-pick-me-ups. Chapter 23 is just for you.

Nora, thanks for dishing out a healthy dose of tough love when I need it. Your hopefulness is contagious. It carried me through our clairvoyant college days and continues to bless me, year after year.

Amanda, your enthusiasm for this series has been such a huge source of encouragement to my heart. Thanks for your support and friendship. I treasure them both.

Mom, what would I do without my biggest fan? Thank you for loaning me your faith when mine has shaken.

www.ingramcontent.com/pod-product-compliance
Lightning Source LLC
Chambersburg PA
CBHW031118210626
46816CB00016B/1709